"*The Nature of Witches* is a timely, thoughtful tale of the responsibilities we have to our planet and to one another. Griffin's well-developed worldbuilding and complex main character make for a read that will resonate deeply."

—Christine Lynn Herman, author
of the Devouring Gray duology

"*The Nature of Witches* is a love letter to the earth. This lush, atmospheric book charmed me with its magic system, captured my heart with its swoony romance, and stole my breath with its gorgeous words. I want to wallpaper my home with Rachel Griffin's sentences."

—Rachel Lynn Solomon, author
of *Today Tonight Tomorrow*

"I could have stayed lost in the pages and magic of *The Nature of Witches* forever. Griffin's lush prose and evocative imagery adorns and compliments the thoughtfully designed world, and the well-drawn characters triumphantly carry the story from beginning to end. A stunning and timely debut."

—Isabel Ibañez, author of *Woven in Moonlight* and *Written in Starlight*

"Seasonal magic abounds in this addictively thought-provoking tale of love, loss, and self-identity."

—Dawn Kurtagich, award-winning
author of *The Dead House*

The

NATURE

of

WITCHES

The
NATURE
of
WITCHES

RACHEL GRIFFIN

sourcebooks
fire

Published by Sourcebooks Fire, an imprint of Sourcebooks
P.O. Box 4410, Naperville, Illinois 60567-4410
(630) 961-3900
sourcebooks.com

Library of Congress Cataloging-in-Publication Data

Names: Griffin, Rachel M., author.
Title: The nature of witches / Rachel Griffin.
Description: Naperville, Illinois : Sourcebooks Fire, [2021] | Audience: Ages 14. | Audience: Grades 10-12. | Summary: Witches, who for centuries have maintained the climate, are losing their power as the atmosphere becomes more erratic, and all hope for a better future lies with Clara Densmore, an Everwitch whose rare magic is tied to every season.
Identifiers: LCCN 2021000997 (print) | LCCN 2021000998 (ebook)
Subjects: CYAC: Witches--Fiction. | Magic--Fiction. | Weather--Fiction. | Seasons--Fiction. | Love--Fiction. | Environmental protection--Fiction.
Classification: LCC PZ7.1.G75245 Nat 2021 (print) | LCC PZ7.1.G75245 (ebook) | DDC [Fic]--dc23
LC record available at https://lccn.loc.gov/2021000997
LC ebook record available at https://lccn.loc.gov/2021000998

Printed and bound in the United States of America.
LSC 10 9 8 7 6 5 4 3 2 1

For Tyler.
You are my sun.

cardinal flower

summer

one

"Being an Everwitch means two things: you are powerful, and you are dangerous."
                    —*A Season for Everything*

Everything is burning, so many flames it looks as if we set the sky on fire. The sun has long since vanished, hidden behind a haze of smoke and ash, but its magic still rushes through me.

The fire has been raging for six days. It started with the smallest spark and became all-consuming in the span of a breath, flames spreading chaotic and fast, as if they were being chased.

Starting the fire was easy. But putting it out is something else entirely.

It's our last wildfire training of the season, and it's more intense than all the other training sessions combined. The fire is larger. The flames are higher. And the earth is drier.

But wildfires are a threat we now have to deal with, so we must learn. There are more than one hundred witches from all over the world here on campus to take this training.

The other witches help. The springs provide fuel, growing acres and acres of pines to sustain the fire. The winters pull moisture from the trees, and the autumns stand along the perimeter of the training field, ensuring the fire doesn't spread beyond it.

We have to learn, but that doesn't mean we're going to burn down our entire campus in the process.

The rest is up to the summers, and we have one job: make it rain.

It's not easy. The winters pulled so much water from the ground that it feels more like sawdust than dirt.

My eyes sting, and a layer of ash clings to the sweat on my face. My head is tipped back, hands outstretched, energy flowing through my veins. Summer magic is a constant rush, strong and powerful, and I push it toward the forest, where water soaks the earth and a lazy stream moves through the trees. The power of the witches around me follows, and I send it deeper into the woods.

It weaves around trees and skims the forest floor until it finds a particularly wet stretch of earth. Goose bumps rise along my skin as the heat of my magic collides with the cold moisture. There's enough water here to coax from the ground and into the clouds, enough to vanquish the fire and clear the air of smoke.

This is the first time I've been involved in a group training session since I was on this same field last year, practicing with my best friend. Since the magic inside me rushed toward her in a flash of light, as bright as the fire in front of me. Since she screamed so loudly the sound still echoes in my ears.

I try to push the memory away, but my whole body trembles with it.

"Keep your focus, Clara." Mr. Hart's voice is steady and sure, coming from behind me. "You can do this."

I take a deep breath and refocus. My eyes are closed, but it isn't enough to erase the red and orange of the fire, a dull glow I'll continue to see long after the flames are out.

"Now," Mr. Hart says.

The rest of the summers release their magic to me, weaving it into my own. I tense under the weight of it. Our combined power is far stronger than individual streams flitting around the forest, the way a tapestry is stronger than the individual threads within it.

But it's so heavy.

Most witches could never support the weight of it. Only a witch tied to all four seasons can control that much magic. Evers are rare, though, and our teachers didn't have one in their generation—I'm the first in over a hundred years—so this is a learning process for us all. But it doesn't feel right, holding the magic of so many witches.

It never does.

"Deep breaths, Clara," Mr. Hart says. "You've got this."

My hands shake. It's so hot, heat from the fire mixing with heat from the sun. The magic around me hangs heavy on my own, and I focus all my energy on pulling moisture from the ground.

Finally, a small cloud forms above the trees.

"That's it. Nice and easy," Mr. Hart says.

The cloud gets bigger, darker. Magic swells inside me, ready to be released, and the sheer power of it makes me dizzy. It's a terrible feeling, like I'm on the brink of losing control.

I've lost control twice before. The terror that haunts my dreams is enough to ensure it will never happen again.

Sweat beads on my skin, and I have to work hard for each shallow breath, as if I'm breathing atop Mount Everest instead of in a field in Pennsylvania.

I temper the flow and give myself three good breaths. Just three.

Then I start again.

Ash falls from the sky instead of rain, flames leaping toward the heavens as if they're taunting me.

I find my thread of magic hovering above the forest floor. I let enough energy flow from my fingertips to keep it going, but no more than that.

"Rain," I whisper.

Water rises from the ground and cools. Tiny droplets form, and all I have to do is combine them until they're too heavy to stay in the air.

That's it. I can do this.

I pull the cloud away from the trees, closer and closer to the flames until it hovers above the heart of the fire.

Power moves all around me like a cyclone, and I send it spiraling into the air, toward the droplets that are so close to being rain.

More magic surges inside me, desperate to get out, stealing my breath. There's a deep well of it, but I'm terrified of letting go, terrified of what could happen if I do. I send out a small stream of magic that does nothing to ease the pressure building inside me, and I force the rest back down.

It isn't enough.

The rain cloud flickers, threatening to undo all the progress I've made. It needs more energy.

"Stop fighting it," Mr. Hart says behind me. "Just let it happen. You're in control."

But he's wrong. Letting go would be like breaking a dam and hoping the water knows where to go. I know better than that. I know the devastation my power can cause.

There are so many sets of eyes on me, on the rain cloud churning above the fire. I split my focus between controlling the flow of my own magic and commanding everyone else's, but it doesn't feel right.

I can't do it anymore.

I won't.

The thread of magic collapses, energy thrashing every which way like a loose fire hose.

A collective groan moves through the witches around me. My arms fall to my sides, and my legs buckle beneath me, the pressure no longer holding me up. I sink to the ground, and heavy exhaustion replaces everything else. I could sleep right here, on the sawdust earth, surrounded by witches and fire.

I close my eyes as Mr. Hart's steady voice begins directing the other witches.

"Okay, everyone in the northeast corner, you're with Emily.

Northwest, Josh. Southeast, Lee, and southwest, Grace. Let's get this fire out." Mr. Hart keeps his tone even, but after working with him for over a year, I know he's disappointed.

After several minutes, four strong threads of magic are restored, and the cloud above the fire gets larger and darker. Emily, Josh, Lee, and Grace make upward motions with their hands, and all the water they've extracted from the ground rises into the atmosphere, going up, up, up.

They clap in unison, and the droplets of water combine, too heavy to remain in the air.

I look up. When the first raindrop lands on my cheek, a sick feeling moves through my body. It took four of our strongest witches to do what should have been natural for me. Easy, even.

Another raindrop falls.

And another.

Then the sky opens up.

Cheers rise all around me, the sound mixing with that of the rain. People clap each other on the back and hug. Josh pulls me up from the ground and wraps his arms around my waist, twirling me through the air as if I didn't just fail in front of the entire school.

My hair is soaked, and my clothes cling to my skin. Josh sets me down and high-fives the other witches around him.

"We did it," he says, wrapping his arm around my shoulder and kissing my temple.

But a training exercise is nothing compared to the unrestrained wildfires burning through California. We're going to graduate this year, and then it'll be up to us to fight the real fires. And they're getting worse.

Witches have controlled the atmosphere for hundreds of years, keeping everything steady and calm. We've always succeeded. We've always been strong enough.

But the shaders—those without magic—were swept away by the possibilities of a world protected by it, of a world where every square inch could be used for gain. They began to push the limits of our power and our atmosphere. At first, we went along with it, caught up in their excitement. Then their excitement turned to greed, and they refused to slow down, ignoring our warnings and charging ahead, behaving as if magic were infinite. As if this planet were infinite. Now they've overplayed their hand.

We've tried to adapt and handle the shifting atmosphere on our own, but we can't keep up; it's as if we're blowing out candles when the whole house is on fire. When we realized that what the world needed was rest, we pleaded with the shaders and pleaded for our home. But we were outnumbered. The shaders couldn't see past their desire for more, developing land that humans were never meant to touch, requiring control in areas that were only ever meant to be wild.

There isn't enough magic to support it all.

And now the atmosphere is collapsing around us.

Three years ago, we didn't train this hard for wildfires. They spread and caused damage, but the witches were always able to put them out before they became devastating. Now there aren't enough of us to manage all the ways the Earth is pushing back. I think about the acres of land that burned this year in California and Canada, Australia and South Africa, and it's so clear. It's so painfully clear.

We aren't strong enough anymore, and the administration is relying on me to make a difference, to make *the* difference.

But they really shouldn't.

By the time graduation comes, I won't be able to make any difference at all.

two

"*Just remember: the choices you make today will be felt by who you have yet to become.*"

—*A Season for Everything*

I stay in the field for a long time. The ground is covered in ash, with scattered embers sending trails of smoke toward the clouds. It's hard to believe our Summer Ball was just three nights ago, a thin tent set up in this very field to honor the end of the season.

The sun has dipped below the horizon, and everything is quiet.

These are the last moments of summer. The equinox is tonight, and witches will flood the gardens to welcome autumn's arrival. The summers will mourn the end of their season, and the autumns will celebrate.

I hear footsteps behind me and turn to see Mr. Hart walking over the charred remains of the field. The springs will be out here in full force tomorrow, and the grass will grow back in a matter of days. In a week, there will be no traces of the wildfire left.

Mr. Hart sets down a blanket and sits on top, watching the plumes of smoke with me. After several minutes he says, "What happened out there today?"

"I'm not strong enough." I don't look at him.

"It isn't a matter of strength, Clara. For as long as I've been in charge of your education, you've held yourself back." I open my mouth to object, but he holds his hand up, silencing me. "I've been doing this a long time. Most of my students have to fight to get their magic *out*. I know what that looks like. But you're constantly fighting *against* it, trying to keep it in. Why?"

I stare at the barren field in front of me.

"You know why," I whisper. He wasn't here when my best friend died, when my magic sought her out and killed her in one instant, one single breath. But he's heard the stories. And yet, he has never shied away from me. When he was brought in to take over my education, he never worried that he might share Nikki's fate.

He moved toward me when everyone else moved away.

"There's too much of it," I say. "I'm not in control."

"And you'll never be in control if you don't let me teach you. Do you really want to live in fear of who you are for the rest of your life? Control doesn't come from avoiding the power you have, Clara; it comes from mastering it. Imagine the good you could do if you were to dedicate yourself to that."

"How can I dedicate myself to something that has taken so much from me?" I ask.

Mr. Hart keeps his eyes straight ahead. He shoves his wire-framed glasses up his nose, and moonlight reflects off his frizzy white hair.

"At some point, you have to stop punishing yourself for the things you can't change. Learning to use your magic does not mean you accept the loss it has caused. You have to stop equating the two."

"You say that like it's easy."

"It's not. It's probably the hardest thing you'll ever do."

Tears burn my eyes, and I look down. I've never cried in front of Mr. Hart, and I don't want to start now.

"Then why do it?"

"Because you deserve some peace."

But he's wrong. I don't deserve peace.

I know Mr. Hart is getting pressure from the administration. But he never pushes me to go further than I'm comfortable with. He meets me where I am. But I should be the most powerful witch alive by now, and the school is starting to lose patience, with him and me.

"Besides, aren't you tired?"

"Tired?" I ask.

"It takes a lot of energy to fight your magic, so much more than it would take to use it."

"Can't you just tell everyone my magic doesn't work?"

"No one would buy that. It's there, Clara, whether you want it to be or not. We need you."

I'm silent. The school pushes me as if I'm the answer, as if I can single-handedly restore stability in the atmosphere. But if that were true, if I were supposed to use all the power within me, it would never target the people I love. It wouldn't come with a death sentence.

It has taken so much, *too* much, and I hate my magic because of it.

"Look at me." Mr. Hart faces me, and I meet his eyes. "What did I tell you when we started working together?"

"You'll never lie to me. You'll tell it like it is."

He nods. "This is how it is."

We're quiet for a long time. Darkness has all but enveloped the field, and stars shine brightly overhead. A breeze picks up in the distance, blowing the remaining smoke out toward the trees.

"Yes, I'm tired," I finally say, my voice nothing more than a whisper. "I'm so tired."

For the first time, Mr. Hart sees me cry.

It's late by the time I get to my small cabin in the woods. Its shingles are weathered and old, but the two small windows are clear as crystal. They're the only way light gets into the small space, and I clean them almost obsessively. The cabin was built for the groundskeeper fifty years ago, but he married and moved off campus, and it sat empty for years.

Until I moved in. I dusted the cobwebs from the cracked white ceiling and scrubbed the walls until the dust was gone and the warm wooden planks were bright. But no matter how much I clean, I've never been able to get rid of the musty smell. I'm used to it by now.

Sometimes I wonder if I'll ever stop aching when I pass the dorms where everyone else lives. I was living in Summer House when Nikki died, and the administration forced me to move to the little cabin beyond the gardens.

At first I was devastated. Moving out of the dorm where Nikki had lived felt like losing her again. But I understood why I couldn't be there anymore.

When someone dies because you love them too fiercely, you turn off the part of yourself that knows how to love. Then you move to a cabin away from other people and make sure it never happens again.

I push the door open, and the floor creaks when I walk inside. Josh is waiting for me, sitting in my desk chair. Equinox is next to him, shoving his black head into Josh's side, purring.

"What are you doing here?"

"It's my last night. I want to spend it with you." He scratches Nox's head. "And you, Nox," he adds. His accent gets heavy when he's tired. Tomorrow, he'll fly back to his campus in the English countryside, and we won't see each other again.

He got here three weeks ago for the wildfire training. He didn't heed the warnings about me because he's arrogant, and I didn't stop him because there was no risk of me loving him.

Maybe years ago there would have been, but not anymore.

Besides, tonight is the equinox, and when summer turns to autumn, any affection I have for Josh will fade. It's a consequence of being an Everwitch—being tied to all four seasons means I change with them.

Tomorrow morning, my feelings for Josh will disappear, just in time for him to fly home to London.

But right now it's still summer, and what I want more than anything is the false comfort of his warm body next to mine.

"Then stay," I say.

I take Josh's hand, and he follows me the three steps to the bed. He tugs me close to him, brushes his lips against my neck.

Until this moment, I didn't realize how much I needed this, needed him. I close my eyes and let go of the heaviness of the day. It will be waiting for me in the morning, but for now, all I want is to shut off my brain, shut off the worries and expectations and crushing guilt that rule my waking thoughts.

I pull Josh onto the bed, and his weight on top of me replaces everything else. For one more night, I can pretend I'm not so lonely that it has practically hollowed me out.

For one more night, I can pretend I remember what it feels like to love someone. To be loved in return.

So I do. I pretend.

We fill the darkness with heavy breaths and tangled limbs and swollen lips, and by the time the moon reaches its highest point in the sky, Josh is asleep beside me.

The autumnal equinox is in seven minutes.

In seven minutes and one second, the reality of my life will come crashing down on me. My magic will morph to align with autumn, and I will be a more distant version of myself.

Suddenly, I'm furious, searing-hot rage coursing through me. It isn't enough that I'm dangerous, that my magic seeks out those closest to me. I'm also forced to change with the seasons and watch versions of myself drift away like leaves trapped in a current.

My skin gets hot, and my breaths come shallow and quick. I try my best to calm down, but something inside me is breaking. I'm so sick of losing things.

Of losing myself.

The sun will pull me to autumn the way the moon pulls the tide.

My chest is tight. There's an ache so deep, so strong within me I'm sure it's radiating out my back and into Josh's stomach.

Four more minutes.

My body hurts from trying to stay still, perfectly still, so Josh doesn't see how torn up I am. He shifts behind me and tightens his arm, pulling me close to his chest.

The room is silent except for his slow, even breathing, and I try to match my breaths to his.

Thirty seconds.

I scoot back into Josh, getting as close as possible, no space left between us.

This time, I'm going to fight. I will hold on to Josh and refuse to let go. The equinox will pass, and I'll stay right here. I'll *want* to stay right here.

I grasp Josh's arm, and he sleepily murmurs my name, nuzzles his face into my hair.

A shiver runs up my spine, and I cling to him with both hands, refusing to let go.

Three.

I won't let go.

Two.

I won't.

One.

chicory

autumn

three

"*The first day of autumn is notable because the air turns to blades, imperceptible points and edges that remove any trace of summer. The seasons are jealous like that, unwilling to share the spotlight.*"

—*A Season for Everything*

I let go of Josh's arm. My palms are hot and sweaty from gripping him so tightly. My breathing returns to normal, and the anger inside me fades to defeat.

I lost. Again.

I don't know why I try, why I keep doing this to myself. It is always the same.

And yet, I wonder what it would be like to go to sleep knowing with absolute certainty that I'd feel the same way about the person lying next to me in the morning. But as soon as I think it, I bury the thought.

I'll never wake up knowing anything with absolute certainty, least of all how I feel.

We're too close, Josh and I. I roll out of bed and open the window as far as it will go. The autumn air is sharp, and a cloudless night stretches out beyond the glass.

Josh stirs, and I slip into my sweats and put the teakettle on. I watch Josh sleep, still and calm. When the kettle whistles, he wakes up.

His presence isn't as strong now. As the Earth's position to the sun changes and we get further from summer, Josh's magic will weaken. And when summer arrives once more, his power will reach full strength for three extraordinary months.

But as of today, he's dimming, and I can see it in his face.

I won't look any weaker, though, because I'm not. My magic never falters. It never fades. It just changes.

"Happy equinox." A hint of sadness softens his tone.

"Happy equinox. Tea?"

He nods, and I grab two mugs from the corner of the counter. Josh stands and gets dressed before sitting back down on the edge of the bed.

I can hear all the witches outside, welcoming autumn even though it's the middle of the night. Josh watches me, his blue eyes following along as I make the tea.

I hand him a mug and sit on the chair beside the bed. Steam rises and swirls in the air between us.

"Hey, today's your birthday, right?"

"It is," I say. "How'd you know that?"

"Mr. Hart mentioned it." He holds his mug up to me. "Happy birthday, Clara."

"Thanks." I give him a small smile, but I can't meet his eyes.

Witches are born on the solstice or equinox, but no one knows what ties an Everwitch to all four seasons. I was born on the autumnal equinox and should be a regular autumn witch. Instead, something happened when I was born that turned me into this: someone who can barely look at the person she's with because her feelings for him vanished in an instant.

"You weren't exaggerating when you said you'd be different," Josh says. His tone isn't aggressive or mean, but it still feels like an insult. "Your demeanor, the way you hold yourself... You seem so closed off."

I don't say anything.

"What does it feel like?" he asks.

The question catches me off guard. "What does what feel like?"

"The change. Shifting from summer to autumn. All of it."

No one has ever asked me about it before, not like this. Once it's obvious I'm no longer interested, no one wants to stick around, and I don't blame them. But Josh sounds genuinely curious.

"It's jarring at first, like I was thrown from a hot tub into the ocean. Even though I know it's coming, it's hard to prepare for. My magic changes instantly; autumn magic isn't as intense as summer, so everything slows down a bit. And I guess I slow down too. Whatever passion I had in the summer just seems to fade away." I take a sip of tea and shift in my seat.

"Like me?" he asks.

"Exactly."

He flinches and looks into his mug.

"I'm sorry, Josh." My tone is gentle even though I'm screaming inside. I hate apologizing for who I am.

Or maybe I just hate who I am.

I'm not sure.

"Don't worry about it," he says. "After all, you did warn me." His voice is casual and even, but when he smiles, he looks sad.

The sounds of laughter and singing float in through the open window. "Trust me, it's better than the alternative." As soon as I say the words, I wish I could take them back. He's leaving tomorrow; he doesn't need to know the parts of me I want to keep hidden.

"What do you mean?"

"You don't want me to care about you." I look out my window, but it isn't the night sky I see. It's Nikki. It's my parents. I squeeze my eyes shut and force the images away.

Josh blows on his tea, even though it's cool by now. "Your friend, right?" I guess everyone knows the rumors, even someone who got here three weeks ago.

I nod but say nothing. Nox jumps on my lap and looks at me, as if to ensure my affection for him hasn't changed. I kiss him on his head, and he purrs.

"Anyway, you're leaving tomorrow, so you don't need to worry about it." I let my voice lift, try to clear the air of the tension that has filled the room.

"For what it's worth, I've had a great time these past few weeks. It was worth the fifty quid."

"I'm sorry?"

"I bet a few of the guys that you'd still be into me after the equinox." Josh laughs, but he sounds self-conscious. "Can't win them all."

A gross feeling starts in my stomach, and I drink some tea to calm it. "You made a bet about me?"

Josh meets my eyes, and his expression softens, as if he's just now understanding how awful that sounded. "That came out wrong," he says. "I just meant I had a great time with you. I really did."

He reaches for my hand, but I pull away. "So great a time that you went to your friends and put money on it."

"It was a stupid bet, that's all. I'm really sorry, especially because I meant what I said." Josh looks at the floor, and I don't have the energy to stay upset.

I'm embarrassed enough as it is. But more embarrassing than the bet is the fact that he hurt my feelings. And I don't want him knowing that.

"I had a good time with you too," I finally say. "At least fifty quid worth." The words sting on the way out, but Josh smiles.

"At least," he agrees.

And just like I do at the end of every summer, I vow never to have another fling. Summer is the season I crave touch, crave the closeness of another person, and I've given into it for the past three years because it doesn't matter. My feelings don't last, so whoever I'm with is safe.

But over time, the fact that I change has started to feel like a curse, and I don't want to do it anymore. Don't want to see my own insecurities reflected in the eyes of whomever I'm with.

And sitting here now in autumn, seeing the disappointment on Josh's face and forcing an apology from my lips, I know it wasn't worth it.

I take Josh's empty mug and stand just in time to see a flash of brilliant green light move across an otherwise black sky.

I stare out the window, and Josh comes and stands next to me.

It happens again.

"Did you see that?" I ask him.

"I saw it." An edge creeps into his voice that wasn't there before.

Then a deep-red light glides across the sky like a satin streamer in a gymnastics routine, impossible to miss.

I drop the mugs. They hit the floor and shatter.

I sprint out of the cabin with Josh right behind me.

The instability in the atmosphere stings my skin as soon as we're outside, thousands of tiny shocks burning my arms and causing the hairs to stand on end. The light show continues overhead as we run toward the gardens. Colors dance across the night sky in waves of green and blue, spirals of purple and yellow, as if the Sun herself is finger painting on the upper atmosphere.

The aurora borealis lights up our campus, drenching us in amazing color. But we aren't in Alaska or Norway or Iceland. We're in northern Pennsylvania, nestled up against the Poconos.

The aurora borealis is the last thing we want to see.

Students were already in the garden to celebrate the equinox, but anxious whispers and nervous silence have replaced the laughter and cheering from earlier. Cups of cider and cinnamon tea lie abandoned on the cobblestone paths, and everyone has their heads tilted toward the sky. Josh stands next to me, his usual loose stance replaced with a straight spine and clenched fists.

"Have you ever seen this before?" His eyes are wide, and there's wonder in his voice. Wonder and fear.

"No."

A band of neon green arches across the sky, pulsing upward into shades of red and pink. Someone behind me gasps, and a shiver runs up my spine.

For the past twenty years, witches have been stationed at both poles to help direct the sun's charged particles. We're immune to the radiation the particles carry, but if they were to get through the atmosphere, the rate of radiation poisoning in the shaders would soar.

The shaders insist that magic is our area of expertise and that they don't want to get involved, don't want to be in our way. That's what they don't understand—they *are* in our way, a huge barricade so wide we can't get around them, their indifference so toxic it's destroying the only home we have. Magic is a stopgap, a stabilizer. It isn't a solution. We need the shaders' help, but no one wants to hear they're part of the problem—that they *are* the problem now.

We're doing all that we can do, but the rest is up to them.

"What the hell is happening?" Josh keeps his eyes on the lights above us, and I'm not sure if he wants an answer or not.

"There aren't enough witches to temper all the places the shaders have developed. Magic was never meant to be used this extensively—the Earth needs untamed territories, free from humans and free from control." I keep my head tilted toward the sky. "Now it's fighting back, and we can't handle it all."

Another burst of solar wind hits the atmosphere, and violet light glides across the sky, momentarily illuminating the garden where we're standing.

"We should be strong enough to stabilize things," Paige says from beside me. I didn't see her walk over, but I'm not surprised she's here.

"What do you mean?" Josh asks her.

Paige looks him up and down. She frowns before turning her eyes to me. "Haven't you heard? Our generation has been blessed with an Everwitch."

"Don't do this, Paige." Heat rises up my neck. I glare at her, but she isn't fazed.

"Do what? Don't you think he has a right to know that you're willingly putting us all at risk by not using the power you have? It's no coincidence that the first Ever in over a hundred years was born now, when we need her so badly. Only we got one who doesn't want anything to do with magic." Paige practically spits the words out.

That's the problem with letting someone see your insides: they still know your secrets long after the relationship ends. They still know exactly what to say to hurt you.

"She has her reasons." It's sweet of Josh to stand up for me, but it won't do any good.

"I know her reasons a hell of a lot better than you do." Paige's tone is so biting that Josh closes his mouth and swallows the words he was about to say. Paige looks at me. "The game has changed, and if a few people have to die in order for you to help, it's worth it." She says it like a true winter, but the smallest hint of sadness softens her words.

"I'm not sure Nikki would agree with you." My voice is so quiet only Paige can hear, and I watch as the words slap her in the face. She recoils slightly and swallows hard.

I want to take it back as soon as I say it. Nikki's death hit Paige as hard as it hit me. The three of us had been inseparable, Nikki's passion and spontaneity a perfect contrast to Paige's candor and precision, both of their steadiness a perfect balance for me.

When Paige and I started dating, Nikki was never weird about it. Paige and I spent hours planning how we'd tell her, agonizing over every word. When we finally told her, she burst out laughing and shrieked, "You both look terrified!"

She was laughing so hard she started choking, tears streaming down her face, and soon I was laughing with her. It was the kind of laughter that was so unbridled, so utterly ridiculous, that even Paige couldn't keep a straight face. And that was that. We never brought it up again, and Nikki never let herself feel like the third wheel because she never was.

I blink the memory away and look at Paige. "I will not let you or anyone else tell me what I should be doing with my life."

Paige's eyes turn from angry to sad. She shakes her head. "What a waste," she says.

Solar wind strikes the nitrogen atoms sixty miles up, bathing Paige's back in a vibrant blue glow as she walks away.

What a waste.

I try to shake it off, but her words echo in my mind the way dripping water echoes in a cave.

"Are you okay?" Josh asks me.

"I'm fine," I say, even though I'm not.

"Okay, everyone, back to your rooms." Mr. Donovan's voice carries across the garden, and I'm able to pick out his tall frame in the crowd.

Students walk back to their houses, but I feel stuck, the colors in the sky illuminating my guilt and fear, judging my choices the way Paige does.

"Get some sleep, Clara," Mr. Donovan says. He runs a hand through his thick brown hair and winces as another flash of light steals the darkness. He's young, probably in his midthirties, but worry creases the skin around his eyes.

"Is there anything we can do to help?" I ask.

Mr. Donovan shakes his head. "We're too far south; it's up to the witches stationed at the pole. There's nothing we can do from here."

I try to ignore the apprehension in his voice, but it stays with me as Josh and I walk back to my cabin. Josh packs his things and leaves his phone number and mailing address so I can contact him if I want to.

"Just in case," he says, even though we both know I won't reach out.

After he leaves, I stand at my window and stare outside. I pick up Nox and scratch his head, pull him close to my chest.

If I devote my life to this the way Paige and Mr. Hart and the administration want, I'll be giving in. I'll be saying it's okay that people have died and will die for my magic.

But I'm not okay with any of it.

Which is why in eleven months, as the rest of the witches flee from the total solar eclipse that's coming, I will stay outside and stand in the shadow of the moon. I will lose my connection to the sun and be stripped of my magic. And no one will die because of my power ever again.

I've been planning this as long as I've known it was coming. Total solar eclipses are rare, and to have one occur where I live during my lifetime is an opportunity I refuse to waste.

There are only two ways for a witch to lose their magic: to be in the path of totality during a solar eclipse, or to be depleted. Most witches die from depletion, though, and other witches usually step in if they see it happening, which makes it a suboptimal plan.

I've heard that being stripped is absolute agony, pain unlike any other. But it won't be as painful as burying my parents was. Or burying my best friend.

I'll survive it, and then I'll start over.

Maybe I'll go to a shader school and make real friends. Learn about things I'm interested in, no longer forced to practice a magic that takes and takes and takes.

I don't know what I'll choose to do, but that's the point: I'll have a choice.

CHAPTER

four

"The calm before the storm is a myth. It's simply the moment in time when you're most certain nothing will happen."

—*A Season for Everything*

I still see the colors of the aurora even though it happened weeks ago. Greens and blues and violets flash across the lids of my eyes the way lightning flashes through clouds.

It was all over social media, the shaders posting picture after picture. They thought it was beautiful, a wonder of nature, instead of an indication that the atmosphere is becoming erratic. The shaders trust us, but a consequence of that trust is their complacency. It hasn't occurred to them that something might be wrong.

And as hard as it is to admit, we need their trust.

We've told them things are getting harder for us, but they reply the same way every time: "We know you'll figure it out. You always do." And we have always figured it out. When they wanted to expand, to industrialize the most unforgiving places on Earth, we warned them against it, said there was only so much magic to go around. But they didn't listen, certain we were being overly cautious, and when the terrain we told them was inhospitable turned out to be just that, we stepped in so no one would die. We figured it out.

But these events, the wildfires and the aurora, they're like drops in a bucket. We see the bucket filling, we watch it closely, and we try to control the rising water as best we can. But at some point, it's going to spill over, and we won't be able to stop it.

We've lived peacefully with the shaders for so long, protected them for so long, that they thought we were giving them a brilliant show with the aurora. But we can't keep protecting them at the cost of our home. We won't. And if they want to survive, they'll have to make the same choice.

Assembly let out ten minutes ago, a tense, strained hour of announcements that was hard to get through. The aurora has covered our campus in a fog of anxiety that's difficult to see past. Everyone, even the faculty, is stressed.

I'm sweating beneath my assembly robe, the satin resting heavily on my shoulders. The dark navy makes my red hair stand out more than normal, and I pull several strays from the material. Orange, crimson, emerald, and sky-blue silk line the shawl around my neck and weigh me down with crushing expectation.

Mine is the only striped shawl the Eastern School of Solar Magic has ever issued.

I take my time walking to the farm. Rays of sunlight reach

through the trees and reflect off the old brick buildings and pathways, drenching the stone in bright-yellow light the color of daffodils.

A group of autumns is in the orchard harvesting apples. They talk among themselves, dropping their apples into burlap sacks that hang from their shoulders. Part of me wants to join them, to give in to the pull and harvest alongside them. But it's too risky.

Magic is deeply personal, intertwining itself with all the emotions of its wielder. And because mine is so fierce, so powerful, my training isn't enough of an outlet for it. It builds and builds and builds, and when the pressure is too great, it searches for another means of escape, gravitating toward the people I'm closest to because it recognizes the emotional connection I have with them. It's the same connection it has to me.

But none of those people can handle the force of it. Either they don't have magic at all, like my parents, or their magic isn't nearly strong enough to contend with it, like Nikki.

Either way, it kills them.

That's why I can never get too close to anyone, can never develop emotions strong enough for my magic to sense.

Realizing you love someone is like noticing you have a sunburn—you don't know exactly when it happened, just that you were too exposed for too long.

So I minimize my exposure.

To everyone.

When the farm comes into view, I slow my steps. Ms. Suntile is waiting next to Mr. Hart, along with a man I've never seen before.

It takes all my energy not to turn around and go back the way I came. Ms. Suntile has been the head of school since I enrolled here twelve years ago, when I was five. The last thing I want is her watching over my training as if she can scare me into doing better.

Rows of green stalks stretch out before me, all the way to the woods that border the farm. The soil is soft and loose, and the sun drenches the wheat field to my right, making it look golden. Mountains rise in the distance, and for a moment I let the peacefulness wash over me.

I walk onto the field and drop my bag to the ground in between rows of celery. I take off my striped shawl and robe and place them on top of my bag. My pale skin is flushed, pink splotches running up my arms. My T-shirt is damp with sweat.

"Ms. Suntile wants to watch our lesson today," Mr. Hart says. I can tell by his tone that he isn't thrilled about it either. "Mr. Burrows is from the Western School of Solar Magic, and he'll be watching as well."

Mr. Burrows nods in my direction but doesn't extend his hand or otherwise greet me.

"We were disappointed with your performance during the wildfire training." Ms. Suntile looks at me like I'm a problem to be solved instead of a person. Her bun is so tight that it pulls at her dark-brown skin. Ribbons of gray weave through her black hair. Her eyes are tired, outlined with wrinkles, but they sparkle more today than they did in summer. She's as thankful to be back in her season as the rest of the autumns.

"I did my best."

"We both know that's a lie, Ms. Densmore. If you had done your best, you would have been able to hold the summers' magic and extinguish the fire yourself."

"It didn't feel right," I start to explain, but Mr. Hart jumps in.

"Why don't we start our training for today?" He gives me an apologetic look and motions me over to where he's standing. "We're going to work on getting more of your power out in a controlled environment so you can feel more comfortable—"

"No," Ms. Suntile says, holding up her hand. "I want you to ripen the celery, using my magic, Mr. Hart's, and your own."

I look from Mr. Hart to Ms. Suntile. They're both autumns, but I don't know if I can do it. "I've never worked with anyone as experienced as you. I've only ever tried it with other students."

"You aren't being pushed enough, Ms. Densmore. This is the only way to learn." Mr. Burrows nods along with her words, and it makes me inexplicably angry.

Mr. Hart clenches his jaw and looks away, as if he's trying to decide if he wants to argue with Ms. Suntile in front of me. He chooses not to.

"Okay, Clara, you heard her. We'll warn you before combining our power with yours. Do you have any questions?"

"No."

I turn my back to them and get started. Bunches of celery line the soil in front of me, and if left alone, they would be ready to harvest in a month.

I'm relieved to be back in the calm that comes with autumn. Summer magic is big and bold, taking advantage of the heavy dose of sunlight. It feels like a flood, one I'm constantly worried I'll drown in.

But in autumn, magic is slower. I send out a small pulse of energy, a test to make sure I know what the crop needs. That's how it works in autumn: I ask a question, and the world answers.

Magic swells inside me, and I release it into the soil. It crawls through the dirt and picks up water as it goes, then wraps around the celery in tight circles. I do it over and over until the thread is full of the cool, calming weight of water.

I'm just about to release it to the crop when a heavy pulse of energy collides with my own.

"I'm not ready yet," I say, trying to keep my focus.

"You won't always be ready. You have to learn to work with the environment around you." Ms. Suntile's voice is sharp. "Autumn magic is transitional—use it to your advantage."

"You can do this, Clara." I calm at the sound of Mr. Hart's voice and refocus my energy.

In one swift motion, I turn away from the water and focus on the sunlight, a quick change in magic that's only possible in autumn. I punch through the fog and pull sunlight from the sky in controlled streaks that illuminate the stream until it's glowing. This time I'm ready when Ms. Suntile sends her magic to me, but something's off. Instead of trying to weave hers in with my own, it feels like she's trying to wrap hers around mine and crush it.

It's too heavy.

"Combine it with the water," Ms. Suntile says. I steal a glance at her, and she squeezes her outstretched hand. Her power closes around mine, threatening to undo it.

Sunlight pulses in the stream of magic, responding to Ms. Suntile's force.

She isn't releasing herself to me; she's *fighting* me. And that's when I realize what she's doing. She knows I'm not using all my power, and she's trying to force me to free the rest of it.

"We're here," Mr. Hart says. "You're safe. We won't let anything happen."

I desperately hold on to my magic. Ms. Suntile squeezes again, and I groan under the pressure. It hurts, a physical pain that follows the stream from the sun into my body, like she's squeezing each individual organ with hands made of fire.

I try to find the water I wrapped around the crops, but I can't get back to it.

Ms. Suntile clenches her hand, and I cry out from the pain. Sunlight surges into my body and burns beneath my skin. I lose the thread and collapse to the ground.

"Enough!" Mr. Hart shouts.

"Why are you doing this?" I look up at Ms. Suntile, who is standing over me.

"Because things are worse than you can possibly imagine. Do you know how many witches died of depletion trying to deal with the aurora?"

I shake my head.

"Four. Four witches in one night. Before this, the most witches we've ever lost to depletion was thirteen in an entire *year.*" She levels her stare at me. "You're more powerful than you realize, but if you can't learn, you're useless to us. We'll try again tomorrow."

Ms. Suntile walks away from the farm without looking back, but her words stay with me, a cruel echo of what Paige said during the aurora.

I wish it didn't hurt.

I wish I didn't wonder if she's right.

Mr. Burrows remains still, watching me, saying nothing. He cups his jaw with his hand as he studies me. Then he shakes his head and follows Ms. Suntile.

Mr. Hart kneels on the ground next to me. "That was unfair of her to say, and I'm sorry you had to hear it. Are you okay?"

I don't answer his question. "Is she telling me the truth? Can I actually make that big of a difference?"

Mr. Hart is quiet for a few moments. "Yes," he finally says. "She's telling the truth."

"How bad is it?"

"Bad," Mr. Hart says. "We're losing witches to depletion at a startling rate. If it keeps up, there won't be enough of us to manage the basics, let alone the anomalies we're facing." He pauses and straightens his glasses. "For now, try to forget about that and listen to me. I know you wish you were like the rest of us and didn't have to deal with all the expectations that come with being an Ever, but change is what makes you powerful. Don't be afraid to claim that power."

Mr. Hart helps me to my feet and walks to his bag. He pulls

out an object wrapped in brown paper. "I have something for you," he says, handing me the package. It feels like a book.

"What is it?" As soon as I ask the question, there's a change in the air above me. Goose bumps rise along my skin, and I shiver.

"It's something I've worked for years to get you," he says. His eyes sparkle with excitement, but I barely hear him. He doesn't feel it yet.

I want to open the gift, but something isn't right. My hand hovers over the brown paper. I close my eyes and listen. Feel the gradients and shifts. The warm air. The cold air.

Now I'm sure of it. Everyone needs to get inside.

"Clara? What is it?"

"Something's happening," I say.

"What do you mean?"

I look toward the sky. "We need to get inside."

Mr. Hart tilts his head up.

I sense it before I see it: a change in atmosphere. Pressure. The fog burns away, revealing clouds so dark they suck up the daylight. Wind picks up in the distance, violent gusts that none of us summoned.

"You're right," he says.

Then we hear it: five short, loud rings screaming from the speakers.

One long ring: class is over.

Two short rings: class is about to start.

Five short rings: emergency.

"Get to the assembly hall," Mr. Hart says. The sky is getting darker by the second. It churns above us, the clouds like waves in a roaring sea.

I shove the unopened package into my bag and sling it over my shoulder. "What about you?"

"I'm right behind you. Now, go!" Mr. Hart's voice is full of alarm.

A storm is coming.

A storm we had no hand in making, one we're totally unprepared for.

And it's big.

five

"You're a witch, for Sun's sake. You should have a cat."
—*A Season for Everything*

The assembly hall is loud, people calling to one another, frantic voices and chaos.

I've been at Eastern for twelve years, and this is the first time I've ever heard the emergency system go off outside of scheduled drills for earthquake or fire. The room is dark, the large glass windows showing the ominous sky.

"Everyone in the basement, now!" Mr. Donovan shouts from the back of the room. Students flood down the staircase as the sirens blare. The wind is building outside. Ms. Suntile and Mrs. Temperly, our guidance counselor, talk in low, hushed voices, but I'm able to pick up bits of what they're saying.

They're wondering what we're all wondering: What are the witches in charge of this region doing?

The storm is so unexpected that the staff has no time to coordinate with the other witches in the area. It would be too dangerous for them to try and help; too much conflicting energy directed at one storm cell can make things worse. If any faculty member tries to step in, they could lose their job.

But it doesn't matter. None of them is strong enough to stop a storm of this magnitude on their own.

We have to trust the witches in charge of this region. But looking out the windows at the darkening sky, it's hard to trust.

I'm rushing down the stairs to the basement when I freeze. Dread moves through my body like lava from a volcano, hot and slow and heavy. Nox is outside, exploring this massive campus.

I drop my bag and turn, running back up the stairs, pushing and fighting against the flow of bodies. Someone behind me calls my name, but I don't stop.

I run out of the assembly hall and toward the trees.

"Nox!" I yell, frantically scanning the ground. "Nox!" I shout again, running farther away from the assembly hall.

A huge crack sounds in the sky, and rain pours from the clouds. Large, thick drops drench me in seconds. I wipe the water from my face and rush into the trees.

"Nox!" I'm deep in the woods now, searching for any sign of him. *Keep running, keep looking.* My ankle rolls off a large root, and I crash into the dirt, a jolt of pain shooting up my leg. I ignore it and force myself back up.

A second thunderstorm follows closely behind the first, making it difficult to see. It's so dark.

I have to find Nox. My ankle throbs, and when I put weight on it, I almost fall back down.

The entire sky flashes as lightning tears through the clouds.

One.

Two.

Boom!

The thunder is so loud it reverberates in my chest. Settles in my stomach.

Then I see him, I finally see him, in the arms of someone I don't know.

I rush toward them and grab Nox. He's shaking, and his fur is soaked, but he's here. He's safe.

"He was hiding next to the shed when I locked up," the guy says. "Is he yours?"

I nod. Nox's rescuer is Asian, tall and lean with golden-bronze skin and thick black hair that's soaked through with rain. His long-sleeved thermal shirt clings to his skin, and his hands are caked with dirt.

"Thank you." My face is shoved into Nox's fur, muffling my words. "I'm Clara, and this is Equinox," I say above the rain. "Nox for short."

"Sang," he returns.

The rain beats down on us. Another flash of lightning illuminates the dark clouds.

A loud crack tears the sky open. I jump back in time to see lightning strike a nearby tree. The ground shakes.

"We have to get out of here," Sang yells.

We rush toward the assembly hall. I clutch Nox to my chest and run through the wind and rain and searing pain in my ankle.

But when Sang and I round the corner, something in the distance catches my eye. I squint through the water pouring down my face and see three boys standing in the field. Their hands are tense and held open in front of them. A horrible feeling settles in my chest.

"What's wrong?" Sang shouts over the wind.

I point to the students in the field. "We can't leave them."

Sang looks back toward the assembly hall and then up at the sky. Another bolt of lightning rips through the clouds, and thunder claps a second later. The sky stirs. It won't be long before the two thunderstorms join together and a tornado hits our campus.

"Shit," Sang says, but he runs toward the field.

"What are you doing?" I yell when we reach the boys. All three are freshman in intermediate weather control, but they aren't strong enough to stop this.

None of them answers me. Their arms are tense, their faces strained. And every single one of them is about to be depleted.

I can feel it. When there's too much energy in one weather system, you create an unending feedback loop with the sun, using more and more magic trying to stop a storm that's only getting stronger. You can never get on top of it. If you stay stuck in the loop for too long, your magic burns out, almost like a short circuit.

I hand Nox to Sang and jump in front of the boys.

"You're all being depleted!" I yell. "If you don't stop, you'll be stripped."

But they're too caught up in what they're doing; they don't even hear me. I grab one boy by the shoulders and shake. He looks dazed, but he stops pouring energy into the storm.

"Stop your friends before they're both depleted," I yell.

He grabs the other boys by the arms and pulls. They stumble forward, and it's enough to break their concentration and dissipate the energy.

"Kevin, right?" I ask, looking at the first boy.

He nods. "We just—we thought we could help," he says. He looks like he might cry.

All of us are drenched, and the wind whips around us, unrelenting.

"It's too strong," I say. "There's nothing you can do, especially since you aren't autumns."

But then I understand: they're springs, and that's why they want to help. They're best at dealing with tornadoes, because most tornadoes happen in spring. But they're too weak now, too far outside their season to do much.

It's up to the autumns, but tornadoes are difficult for them.

"We have to go. *Now*," Sang says. Nox squirms in his arms.

But something is keeping me planted here. I don't want to move.

"Clara," Sang says.

I'm no longer certain I should run away. The storm is calling to me, reaching for me as if it wants to be held. The boys would've been depleted—too much energy, and not enough magic. But I'm stronger than they are, and if the storm calls and I answer, if I work *with* it, maybe I can stop this.

Ms. Suntile and Paige and Mr. Hart all believe I'm powerful, believe I can make a difference. I've never let myself think that way, because this isn't the life I want for myself. But right now, as the sky churns and darkens above me, I wonder if they're right.

Sang sees me gazing at the sky, head tilted in consideration.

"Clara, the storm is too powerful. Even if it's your season, this is too much for any one of us."

"She's an Everwitch," one of the boys says. I wait for some kind of reaction from Sang—wide eyes or hurried words or infinite questions. But his only reaction is the faintest pull of his lips, as if he wants to smile.

It's irresponsible of me to try to intervene without first talking to the witches in charge of this area, but there's no time for that. I wait for Sang to say as much, but instead, he just looks at me.

"It's your call," he says. "What do you want to do?"

I know it's dangerous. I know I could get in a lot of trouble. But the storm beckons to me, reaches for me.

"I want to try."

I grab Nox from Sang and hand him to Kevin. "Please keep him safe. Get to the assembly hall, and I'll do everything I can out here. And don't tell anyone you saw us." Kevin holds Nox close to his chest, and the boys rush off the field.

Another strike of lightning brightens the sky. My clothes are soaked through, and my ankle is throbbing, sending shots of pain up my leg.

"You should get out of here," I yell to Sang.

"It's too risky," he says. "You need someone here in case things get out of hand. I'll watch and make sure you're never at risk of depletion."

If I get stuck in the same feedback loop as the boys, feeding magic into a storm I have no hope of stopping, I could be depleted and stripped. And I'm not ready for that. Not yet.

I nod and tilt my head upward. Lightning splits the sky in two, followed by a deafening thunderclap when the air crashes back together.

"Where the hell are you?" I whisper to the witches who are supposed to be handling this. But all I get in response is another bolt of lightning.

CHAPTER

SIX

"The tornado does not care where it touches down, only that it does."

—*A Season for Everything*

Two thunderstorms hang above me, absorbing the daylight, casting darkness over campus. Rain pelts down, and I wipe my eyes. I raise my hands, and my body responds, energy coursing through me like a river rushing toward the ocean.

The first cumulonimbus cloud shifts and settles directly over me. The thunderstorm in the distance rages on, getting closer.

I close my eyes and focus on the storm right above me. Wind tears through my hair, wet strands of red slapping across my face. Blood rushes in my ears, mixing with the sound of the moving air. I sense every part of the thunderstorm. The updrafts and downdrafts. The hail forming high above us. The rain and the electricity.

The downdraft is what I want.

I single it out and push with all my strength. My muscles

burn, and my arms shake. But the cloud responds. I keep my left hand outstretched, guiding the downward air toward the ground, and move my right hand in circles, faster and faster.

All at once, the air understands what I'm asking of it and dives toward the earth.

"It's working!" Sang yells from behind me.

With all my might, I pull my magic away from the downward air and throw it toward the upward current. I hold my hands steady, making a slow, constant motion that keeps the air from rising.

And when the air can no longer rise, the cloud fades.

The second thunderstorm lurches toward me, trying to grab hold of the cloud I'm working on, but it's too late.

The rain turns light, only a drizzle, and very slowly, the thunderstorm vanishes from bottom to top.

The second storm cannot meet it, cannot dance with it, cannot form a tornado.

I breathe out, long and heavy. I'm exhausted, every inch of me begging to sleep, to rest my weary muscles. My ankle is so swollen that the edge of my shoe cuts into my skin.

But the first storm is gone.

The remaining thunderstorm gets angry. It's heavier, darker, and pelts us with hailstones.

"Clara?"

I turn to Sang, but he isn't looking at me. He's looking into the distance, beyond the remaining storm. He points, and my eyes follow his finger.

I see it at the same time the thunderstorm senses it. The storm turns away from us and reaches for a new storm behind it.

A storm I hadn't noticed.

I shoot my arms out in front of me, try to pull the thunderstorm back, away from the other. But I can't. It's too large. Too severe. And it wants nothing to do with me.

I keep trying.

I pull and shake and pull some more. The storm gives a little, drifts back toward me, and I relax my hold for one second.

It's a second too long, and the storm drives forward with renewed force. I can't pull it back.

Maybe if I'd let Eastern train me the way Ms. Suntile wants to, let them push my power to the limit, I'd have the strength to fight this storm. But I don't know how to use all the magic inside me, and I'm terrified of letting it loose and causing more damage.

And now I'm paying for it. Our entire campus is.

I'm not strong enough.

Sang sucks in a sharp breath as we watch the two storms meet.

Their collision causes instability in the atmosphere. I feel it in the tightness of my chest, in the twisting of my stomach. My magic begs for release, but the storm is too powerful.

Then a change happens. The winds begin to move in a different direction.

They get faster.

A horizontal spinning motion takes over, and the rising updraft crashes into the spinning air, tilting it.

It tilts.

And tilts.

And tilts.

Until it is vertical.

A funnel forms and stretches toward the earth. I should be scared, should run and seek shelter, but I'm stuck to the ground beneath me.

Amazed.

The tornado touches down, a tall, dark, violent tunnel of wind that roars in the distance.

I reach for the cloud above it, try to form a connection, try to break it up. I'm shocked when the cloud responds, a tangible weight in my hands, inviting me in.

"We have to go!" Sang yells.

The tornado barrels toward us, but the cloud is letting me control it, and I have to try.

I'm dripping wet. My muscles are so tense I'm sure they'll snap from the bones they cling to. But the cloud wavers, the edges fading into sky the way day fades to night. It's so close to dissipating, so close to taking the tornado with it.

But a sudden surge in updraft is too much for me, and I can no longer hold on to it.

The cloud strengthens, its edges sharpen, and its tornado heads straight for us.

I reach for it again, begging it to stop, but it drives on. In one final push, I throw as much magic as I can at it, trying to send it away from us. It lurches backward, out toward the farm, giving us just enough time to find cover.

But we stay put, mesmerized by the spinning column of air. The tornado hangs back for one second, two, three. Then it charges toward us.

"Run!" Sang yells.

But I don't want to run. I'm amazed by the force, the absolute power of the wind rushing toward me. I want to touch it.

I'm not scared anymore. I'm exhausted and have nothing left to give, nothing left to try and stop what's right in front of me, and for a single moment, I understand the tornado.

All it wants is to touch the earth.

"Clara, now!" Sang grabs my arm, and the moment is broken.

A tall pine tree lurches sideways, crashes to the ground.

We will die if we don't run.

I turn toward the assembly hall, but the tornado is blocking our path. Spring House is in the distance, the closest building to us, and we sprint toward it. My ankle screams. It takes all my energy to keep running, to stay upright.

The tornado chases us as we burst through the front doors of Spring House. The first floor is a greenhouse, tall glass windows encircling the room, the only thing shielding us from the storm. We get as far away from the windows as possible and hit the floor.

We're out of time.

The tornado slams into the building.

Windows shake, then blow out, sending glass shards sailing toward us. I cover my head, vaguely aware that I'm bleeding. Plants fly across the room, flowers in every color swirling in the air as if they have wings. I look up through the broken glass ceiling.

I want to see the storm.

Warm blood trickles down my forehead. Sang presses his hand against the cut.

"You're okay," he says, his tone calm and even, as if we're taking a stroll on the beach, as if a violent cyclone isn't reaching for us.

Blood seeps through Sang's fingers, crawls down my face, and drips onto my chest. Clay pots shatter on the floor around us, mounds of dirt fall on the cement ground, and debris flies through the room.

The tornado sounds like a freight train. We're in the worst of it. I see the narrow base out of the corner of my eye, see how it twists and turns and picks things up before tossing them aside.

"Look out!" I yell as an arbor is torn from its base and crashes down.

Sang keeps the pressure on my forehead firm and tucks my head into his chest, covering me.

The corner of the arbor falls on him, but he remains steady.

More glass clatters to the floor, and a rock sails over our heads before hitting the wall behind us. Branches slam into the side of the building. The entire room shakes when a massive tree plummets to the earth.

Hanging plants swing wildly back and forth. A large table full of sprouts collapses when a tree trunk rams through a broken window and slams into it.

Then nothing else falls.

Nothing else breaks.

The howling gets fainter, and silence fills the room. The darkness retreats from the sky, and tentative sunlight streams through thin clouds.

It's over.

seven

"Autumn is the Earth just before it falls asleep."
—*A Season for Everything*

I push myself up. Sang and I are both quiet. The floor is covered with dirt and broken clay. Sunlight reaches through the fractured windows and reflects off shards of glass. I wipe my forehead, and the back of my hand comes away red. The same color as Sang's palm.

"We need to get that cleaned up," he says, looking at the gash. He finds a yarrow plant and grabs a handful of leaves on our way out. A deep-blue bruise is forming around his right eye.

My ankle throbs, and I bite my lip, forcing myself to walk. The campus is in disarray. There are toppled trees and cracked cement, hanging gutters and shrubs torn up by the roots. A large pine rests against the top of Avery Hall, the roof caved in beneath it.

But the campus survived. It's still here.

It needs a lot of cleanup and a lot of repairs, but it will be okay.

Students slowly emerge from the assembly hall across campus. I want to find Nox, make sure he's safe, but I can barely walk. I limp toward my cabin in a trance, taking in the odd contrast between the debris-covered walkways and the pure sunshine warming my skin.

Sang stops and wipes my forehead with the hem of his shirt. "We'll never make it to Autumn House at this rate."

"I'm going as fast as I can," I say dryly. "And I don't live in the dorms. I live in a small cabin behind Autumn House, just beyond the tree line."

"Well, we'll never make it there either." Sang crouches in front of me. He reaches over his shoulder and pats his back. "Hop on."

"Absolutely not." Sang looks back at me, and I hope my expression reflects the mortification I feel at his suggestion.

"I'm serious. Hop on."

"I don't even know you. You're not going to give me a piggyback ride across campus."

"I don't see why not," he says. "Besides, we just survived a tornado together. That's got to count for something."

I exhale, weighing my options. Sang gives me an expectant look.

"Fine, but this is ridiculous."

"Yet much more efficient," he says.

I wrap my arms around his neck and crawl onto his back. He loops my legs through his arms, being especially careful of my ankle, and weaves his way through campus.

"Are you new here?" I ask, keeping my grip on him tight.

"Sort of. I'm an advanced studies student in botany."

That explains a lot. His kind demeanor, his patience. He's a spring.

"I just graduated from Western and jumped at the opportunity to study somewhere that experiences the full range of the seasons. I'll be doing an independent study here for a year or two with my mentor." Western School of Solar Magic is our sister school in California. Witches graduate at eighteen, so he's just a year ahead of me.

I don't say anything more and try not to focus on the embarrassment I feel at being on the back of someone I just met.

When I see my cabin, I push myself off Sang and hop the rest of the way. He doesn't say anything and instead shoves the door open. I sit down on the edge of my bed.

"You need to get those cuts cleaned up. I'll be right back."

"You don't have to do that," I call after him, but he's already out the door.

There's a large crack in my window, and the roof is covered in branches and pine needles, but otherwise the cabin is exactly as I left it. Several minutes go by before Sang knocks on the door and pokes his head back in.

"You have a visitor," he says.

Nox bounds into the cabin and launches himself onto the bed. He's shaking, and his black fur stands on end. He looks both happy to see me and angry, as though this is somehow my fault.

I guess in a way, it is.

"Where did you find him?"

"Kevin was on his way here looking for you. He said there's an all-school debrief at seven tonight."

I take Nox's bowl to the sink and fill it with water. I scratch his head and thank the Sun he's safe.

Sang is carrying towels, a big bowl of ice, plastic bags, and a bottle of hydrogen peroxide. He sets everything down on the bed next to the bundle of yarrow leaves.

"No," I say. "I just want to rest for a while."

"You're covered in cuts, and some are pretty deep. You don't want them to get infected."

I sigh. "Let me change first."

"I'll be right outside." Sang gives Nox a quick pet and steps out the door, closing it behind him.

I peel off my shirt and wince when the fabric moves over my forehead. It comes away bloody, and I put it in the hamper before throwing on my Eastern sweats and a clean T-shirt.

"Okay," I say, opening the door. "I'm done."

"Sit," he says, motioning to the bed. I do as I'm told, too tired to argue. Sang pulls over my desk chair and faces me. The cabin feels small with another person in it, the wooden walls and low ceiling making it seem tighter than it is. The floor creaks when Sang leans toward me. He opens the bottle of hydrogen peroxide and pours some on a towel.

"I can do it myself," I say.

"You can't see all your cuts."

"I'll stand in front of the mirror."

"On your ankle the size of a tree trunk?"

I sigh. He's right. I don't want to stand up. He must sense my defeat because he asks, "Ready?"

I nod. He places the towel on my forehead, and I cringe as it bubbles and stings.

"You okay?"

"Great." I keep my eyes closed. Sang goes over the gash on my forehead several times, then moves to the cuts below my collarbone.

"So, why do you live here instead of one of the houses?"

I'm not ready for the question, and I take in a sharp breath. Sang must think I'm reacting to the stinging, though, and he mouths an apology.

"I used to live in the houses." Sang waits for me to elaborate, but I don't say anything else. I'm thankful when he doesn't push.

"All done," he says, setting the towel down. "Do you have a coffee mug somewhere?"

I point to my desk. "You can take the pens out of it."

Sang takes the pile of yarrow to the desk and dumps a small amount of water over the green leaves, then grinds them down with the bottom of the mug. Then he scoops the grounds inside and adds more water until it gets thick. It smells fresh and spicy, masking the mustiness of the cabin.

The edge of Sang's hand is stained with green and pink and brown, and I want to ask what it's from, but I stay quiet.

"Head back," he says. I tilt my chin to the ceiling, and he applies the yarrow paste to the gash on my forehead, then puts a bandage over the top. "That'll help stop the bleeding," he says.

"Thank you."

"Now, let's get that leg propped up."

"Why are you being so nice to me? You don't even know me." The words come out laced with annoyance, but I genuinely want to know.

"Because I'm a decent human being who just watched you try to save this school from a tornado?"

I don't respond. I raise my legs onto the bed, and Sang moves a pillow under my ankle. He pulls my pant leg up and winces.

"That's one hell of a bruise," he says.

He puts some ice in a plastic bag, then sets it on my ankle. "You may want to put some crushed lavender on there for the swelling."

"Thanks."

Sang starts cleaning up his supplies, but I stop him. "Not so fast," I say.

"What?"

"I'm not the only one who got hurt." I don't know why I say it, but he was nice enough to help me. I should do the same. "Sit," I say, motioning to the chair.

"I'm fine," he says. "Arbors fall on me all the time."

"Is that so?"

Sang nods. "I hardly notice when it happens."

"Your eye is swelling shut," I point out.

He sits.

I dump a bunch of ice into the remaining plastic bag and wrap it in a towel. I hand it to him, and he puts it against his swollen eye.

"Are you okay?" he asks me.

"I'm fine." I know he's asking about the storm, but I haven't had time to think about it. Process what it means.

"You were so close," Sang says, shaking his head. "The storm bent to you, almost like it *wanted* you to control it."

"And what good did it do? I wasn't strong enough."

"What you did out there was extraordinary," Sang says.

"It doesn't matter. Getting close didn't do a damn thing," I say.

I jump when there's a frantic knock on my door. I nod at Sang, and he opens it.

"Oh, I'm so happy to see you both," Mrs. Temperly says, her words so fast I can barely decipher them. She clutches her chest, and I notice my messenger bag hanging from her shoulder. She drops it on the ground and pulls out her cell phone.

"They're okay," she says to whoever is on the other end of the line. "Yes, they're both here. Will do."

There haven't been this many people in my cabin since I moved here, and it feels wrong, like the tiny room knows I'm supposed to be isolating myself. If Mrs. Temperly, Sang, and I were to stand side by side and stretch out our arms, we would span the entire cabin.

I ask Sang to open the windows.

Mrs. Temperly ends the call and puts on her best guidance counselor look. Her bright-blond bun is messy on top of her head, and some of her pink lipstick has migrated down to her chin.

"You were both unaccounted for in the basement. Where

were you?" Her pale skin is flushed, and she fans herself with a stack of papers she takes from my desk.

I'm too tired to lie. "I tried to dissipate the storm."

Mrs. Temperly covers her mouth with her hand.

"What happened?" she asks as her eyes find the gash on my forehead and my swollen ankle.

"It obviously didn't work, and we had to take cover in Spring House. I rolled my ankle, and I was cut by some glass when the windows blew out."

"And you?" she asks, turning to Sang.

"An arbor fell on me."

"Apparently, it happens all the time," I say.

Sang tries to keep a straight face, but the corners of his mouth pull up, giving him away. A dimple appears on either side of his mouth, and he clears his throat.

"Clara, we should get you to the nurse for that ankle," says Mrs. Temperly. "You'll need to go to the hospital if it's broken."

I nod.

"Sang, if you're feeling up to it, would you check in with Mr. Donovan in the gymnasium? He wants to do a preliminary survey of the damage before the debrief."

"Sure thing," he says.

I want to thank him. For staying to make sure I wasn't depleted. For holding his hand to my forehead. For blocking me from the arbor.

But more than anything, I want to thank him for letting me make my own decision. Letting me decide if I wanted to try to stop the storm or not.

"It was nice meeting you, Clara," he says, and I have to laugh. What a ridiculous thing to say after being chased by a tornado together.

He leaves before I have a chance to respond.

Mrs. Temperly looks frazzled and exhausted. She fans her face with the papers once more, then sets them back on my desk. "Neither of you should have been out there in the first place. What were you thinking?"

"I had to try."

Mrs. Temperly sighs, but her eyes soften. "I'm going to call Mr. Donovan and see if we can get a cart out here to take you to the nurse's office."

"Thank you." I pause before asking the question that's lodged in my mind. Part of me wants to know, and the other part is terrified. I swallow hard. I'm going to find out eventually, so I ask.

"Mrs. Temperly? Have there been any reports on the storm yet? Do we know if it moved beyond our campus?"

Mrs. Temperly sits down in my desk chair and looks at me. Her gaze drops to the floor, and for a moment I think she might cry. She's a summer, so that wouldn't be out of character, but it still causes my insides to tighten into knots.

"The tornado only traveled four miles beyond campus."

I sink back in my bed, and relief washes over me. But Mrs. Temperly continues.

"There are two reported fatalities so far. Neither from Eastern. At least one witch was depleted during the storm." She pauses and looks at me, sending a shiver down my spine. "But Mr. Hart hasn't checked in with us yet. He's the only person on campus who is unaccounted for."

"What do you mean he's unaccounted for? I saw him right before the storm, and he said he was on his way to the assembly hall."

"I'm sure he'll check in. He probably got caught up trying to secure some part of the farm. You know how he is. For now, let's get that ankle taken care of."

My breath stops when she mentions the farm. That's where I pushed the tornado to give Sang and me time to run. If Mr. Hart was on the farm, I sent it right to him.

Mrs. Temperly must notice the look on my face because she pats my shoulder and says, "It's still early, and the campus is a bit chaotic. Give him some time."

I nod, and Mrs. Temperly goes outside to find a cart. But uneasiness spreads through my body and stirs in my stomach.

I'm taken to the nurse's office. My ankle is wrapped, and I'm sent back to my cabin.

Mr. Hart never checks in.

eight

"The only thing harder than gaining control is giving it up."

—*A Season for Everything*

Mr. Hart was looking for Nox when the tornado touched down. It turns out he did go to the assembly hall, and someone told him they saw me running out, looking for my cat. Mr. Hart was on the farm, and when I pushed the tornado back, it swept across the field and picked up a plow. The airborne plow struck Mr. Hart, crushing his skull on impact.

He wasn't out there for Nox though. He was out there for me. Mr. Hart had always been uncomfortable with how isolated I am, even though he understood the necessity. He probably thought I wouldn't be able to cope if Nox died.

What he didn't factor in was how I'd cope if *he* died.

But he probably mapped the trajectory of the tornado and knew it was headed away from the farm. He thought he was safe where he was, and had I not tried to intervene, he would still be alive.

When I first found out, I was sure my heart would never beat again, would never be able to pump with the thick layer of grief and guilt clinging to it. But I'm still here, destined to live with all the absences I've created.

I think of the wrapped gift sitting on my bedside table, the gift I can't bring myself to open. He was so excited to give it to me, and I don't think I can handle never getting the chance to say thank you. I've been in a fog ever since I found out about his death, and at the worst moments, it feels as if I might never emerge from it. Maybe I won't.

"Clara, they're ready for you now," Ms. Beverly says.

I grab my crutches and slowly make my way into Ms. Suntile's office. She is sitting behind her desk with Sang and Mr. Burrows, the man who was at my last training session with Mr. Hart. I feel sick to my stomach. I give Sang a questioning glance, but he doesn't meet my gaze. The bruise around his eye has gotten darker, and I remember how steadily he held my forehead after I was cut, how he didn't shy away from the blood.

"Have a seat, Ms. Densmore," Ms. Suntile says, banishing the memory. "This is Allen Burrows, whom you met briefly, and you already know our advanced botany student, Sang Park. They both come to us from the Western School of Solar Magic."

Knots form in my stomach when I remember Sang telling me he's here to study under his mentor. I haven't forgotten the way Mr. Burrows didn't introduce himself to me, the way he studied me after I failed to hold Ms. Suntile's magic. The way he looked at Mr. Hart with disrespect and impatience.

I wipe my palms on my jeans and try to stay calm.

"We understand that you tried to intervene during the tornado," Mr. Burrows says. His short brown hair is parted down the side and kept in place with gel, and he wears thick black glasses that stand out against his fair skin. He's middle-aged, and his chin is tilted up slightly, making it seem as if he's talking down to me.

"I thought I could help," I say. I look to Sang for reassurance, but he keeps his eyes on the desk between us.

Mr. Burrows nods. "That's precisely the problem. You should have been able to."

That's not the answer I was expecting. "I'm sorry?"

"You should have been able to dissipate that tornado. We're concerned that an Everwitch who has been training at a highly regarded school for solar magic was unable to stop an F2 tornado." Mr. Burrows looks at me as though he's annoyed.

"I tried—"

"I'd like to finish, Ms. Densmore. This is more an implication of your training than it is of you."

Ms. Suntile shifts in her chair.

"The point is that you should have been able to prevent that tornado from forming. It never should have gotten to the farm. It never should have moved beyond campus. No one should have died from this."

His words collide with my guilt, and I can't breathe. *No one should have died from this.*

Mr. Hart should not have died from this.

"How do you know what I should be capable of?"

Mr. Burrows looks at me over the top of his glasses. "Because we trained Alice Hall."

I jump at the sound of her name, and everything inside me stills. "Alice Hall, the last Everwitch?" I say the words slowly, carefully, as if they're sacred.

"Of course."

I've wanted to know more about Alice Hall since I first heard her name, since I first learned there was an Ever who lived before me. But Alice is an enigma, more legend than fact at this point. I wish that wasn't the case. I don't think I'd feel as alone if I knew more about her. "I don't understand. She was alive in the late eighteen hundreds."

"It's true that a poor job was done of documenting her—*your*—kind of magic, which is regrettable. But her training was cataloged, and since we had the most contact with the last Ever, Ms. Suntile felt it made sense to involve us in your training going forward. And she's right to do so; we know more about this solely because we've done it before."

Anger flares inside me, heating my center and rising up my chest and neck. Even before Mr. Hart died, Ms. Suntile was going to replace him, pull him away from my training. My hands squeeze into fists, and I say a silent prayer to the Sun that he didn't know. The room feels tight, as if it's filled with something heavier than air. I stay silent.

"We will not be reporting your involvement with the tornado, nor will it go on your record. I will be replacing Mr. Hart as primary overseer of your education. If, at the end of the school year, I'm satisfied with the progress you've made, we'll forget this ever happened."

"I don't want to forget this ever happened. Mr. Hart died because of me—I forced the tornado in his direction. It would have never hit the farm otherwise. You *should* report me." My voice is pleading, begging him to turn me in.

Begging for someone to sentence me to a life without magic.

Please, forbid me from using it. Label me as a danger. Force me to get stripped.

I don't want it. I've never wanted it.

I remind myself that all I have to do is make it to the eclipse this summer, and then I can be rid of my magic for good.

"It was an accident, and we don't report our students for accidents. Punishing you wouldn't do any of us any good. What we need from you is progress. We need you to get stronger."

"Mr. Hart was an incredible teacher," I say. "It wasn't his fault I didn't progress. I held myself back." It takes everything I have to keep my voice from breaking.

"Understood. But holding yourself back isn't an option anymore, and I hope you fully dedicate yourself to this going forward. The tornado you saw is nothing."

Mr. Burrows waits as if he's giving someone else the opportunity to speak, but no one does. "Sang will be working with you on day-to-day training. He'll be following a plan laid out by Ms. Suntile and myself and will update me on your progress regularly."

"Why Sang?" The question is out of my mouth before I think

better of it. He looks at me, and I look back. The person who helped me during the tornado has been replaced by the person sitting next to Mr. Burrows, across the large desk from me, and I realize he isn't on my side—he's on theirs.

"Because Alice trained most successfully with her peers. Sang was at the top of his class at Western, which makes him the obvious choice. I've been mentoring him for several years and trust him implicitly. Your school counselor seems to think working with someone your own age will make you more comfortable and thus likelier to progress the way Alice did. If that turns out not to be the case, I'll take over and train you full-time."

The trust I had in Sang disintegrates more and more each time he avoids my gaze, each time he nods along with what Mr. Burrows is saying. But I'd rather train with Sang than Mr. Burrows. I don't know how he doesn't suffocate beneath the weight of his own ego.

"I understand," I say.

Mr. Burrows takes off his glasses and rubs his temples. "I know you were close to Mr. Hart, and I'm sorry about what happened. We all are. If you excel the way we know you can, he won't have died for nothing."

I'm silent, horrified that he would use Mr. Hart's death to motivate me.

"Have they told you the risks?" I stare at Sang, practically spitting the words. I'm not sure what makes me say it. I'm angry and hurt and miss Mr. Hart so much my chest throbs.

"He knows the risks," Mr. Burrows says.

"Can he not speak for himself?"

Mr. Burrows nods at Sang. I cross my arms and wait.

He clears his throat. "When your magic gets out of control, it only targets those you have an emotional connection to. It was the same for Alice. We don't know each other; there's no history between us. I'm not at risk." Sang says the words as if he's memorized them, stiff and unconvincing.

I swallow hard. Images of Mom and Dad, of Nikki, threaten to overwhelm me. I was so young when my magic went after my parents, but it's only been a year since Ms. Suntile pulled me away from Nikki's broken body.

The day is still so clear in my mind. I'd failed a basic drill in weather control in front of the whole class. Mr. Mendez looked disappointed, and people whispered about how I must be the only useless Everwitch in history.

Nikki stood up for me in front of everyone, said that one day they'd all have to eat their words. And when everyone went to dinner, Nikki insisted we go back to the control field, just the two of us, to practice. To replace the events from earlier.

So we did. We repeated the same drill, and I did it flawlessly. We laughed and danced beneath the setting sun, letting our magic roam around with no objective. It was a perfect evening. Until it wasn't.

I force the memory away and take a steadying breath.

"Satisfied, Ms. Densmore?" Mr. Burrows looks at me expectantly, and it takes me a few seconds to come back to the present. I nod.

I'll do everything I can to succeed in my training so I don't get stuck with him.

"Neither of you will be even half the teacher Mr. Hart was." The words sound childish and immature, but I don't care. I want to stand up for him somehow, let him know that all I want is to train with him again. Tell him I'll try harder. I'll get better.

"He sounds like an incredible person," Sang says.

"Ms. Densmore, here's the truth," Mr. Burrows says, ignoring Sang's words. I've never hated anyone as much as I hate this man. "Witches are being depleted at a rate we've never seen before. The atmosphere is getting more erratic as the number of witches goes down, and the shaders are only just starting to take responsibility for the damage they've done. Whether you like it or not, you have a kind of power the world needs. It isn't about me or Mr. Hart or the accidents you've had in the past. It's about learning to harness the power you've been given. If you can learn to control your magic at its full strength, you'll be unstoppable."

"What does that mean? You don't even know enough about my magic to tell me what I should be capable of."

"It's a learning process for us all, Ms. Densmore. We're trying our best," Ms. Suntile says.

"That's why we're changing your training. We won't be giving you exercises tailored to each season; we won't be asking you to weave other witches' magic in with your own." I wince at the not-so-subtle reminder of the wildfire training as Mr. Burrows continues. "Every session from now on will be dedicated to learning to control your own magic. You must get stronger so that when it comes time to add others' magic to your own again, you'll be able to handle it."

"I don't want to hurt anyone." I curse myself when the words shake in my mouth, sounding so much weaker than I intend.

"We're doing everything we can to ensure that won't happen. You'll be in a controlled environment with someone you don't have any connection to; your magic won't gravitate toward him at all. Nobody will get hurt."

Flashes of light fill my mind. It was the same both times. Only the screams were different.

I feel like the walls of this office are closing in on me, threatening to crush me at any moment. I need some air, some distance from all this. Everything is spinning. I stand and grab my crutches.

I pause at the door. "I'll do everything I can to strengthen my magic, and I'll work harder than I ever have. But if it doesn't work, I'll get myself stripped before I let another person die because of me."

Ms. Suntile's eyes widen, and Mr. Burrows opens his mouth to speak, but I cut him off.

"I swear it."

nine

"Words are power. Use them."

—A Season for Everything

I swear it.

The words spilled from my mouth before I had time to consider their weight. I've shown them my hand, the one thing I always kept to myself. Most witches consider being stripped a fate worse than death.

It was one thing when I told only myself that I'd do it, that I'd run toward the solar eclipse while everyone else ran away. But now the administration knows, too, and the secret I've kept hidden for so long is out in the open.

Being stripped of one's magic leaves a constant physical ache in every inch of the body. At least, that's what they say. And even though the pain dulls over time, you become a walking memory, an echo of the power you once had—power you're still drawn to but cannot access no matter how hard you try. You spend the rest of your life longing for something you can never get back.

But I already live that way, longing for things I can never get back. I've been waiting for the solar eclipse for years, counting down the days until I'm free. I'm not afraid of being stripped. I don't think it will feel like pain.

I think it will feel like relief.

It's been almost a month since the tornado, and I'm still committed to the words I spoke.

My ankle has finally healed enough for me to start training again. Ms. Suntile has been hovering like an anxious parent, impatient for me to be rid of my crutches so I can start working with Sang. I've been going to all my regular classes, but I haven't done any hands-on magic since the storm.

I sit on the edge of my bed and hold the unopened gift from Mr. Hart. My fingers trace the brown paper, and I hug it to my chest. Today is my first session with Sang, but I'd give anything to be meeting with Mr. Hart instead.

I take in a breath and tear the paper off. It falls to the floor, and Nox bats at it.

Inside is a bound book with the title *The Unpublished Memoir of Alice Hall*. My breath catches. I open the front cover, and a note from Mr. Hart falls out.

Dear Clara,

It took me years to get this. The Hall family is famously private and has never shared the manuscript with anyone.

*They were kind enough to meet with
me on my last trip to California, and
when I told them I was training you,
they agreed to let me make a copy of
the manuscript. I had it bound and
printed by a local press, but other than
the handwritten copy the Hall family
has, this is the only version in existence.
One of the conditions under which they
let me have this is that only you can see
it; I haven't even read it myself. I hope
it gives you some comfort, knowing you
aren't alone.*

With admiration,
Mr. Hart

I've known that Alice Hall wrote a memoir ever since one of
her distant relatives went to publishers, trying to get bids on it.
The attempt to publish it was ultimately unsuccessful, as the rest
of the Hall family stepped in, but it's been public knowledge since
then. I knew Mr. Hart had tried to get them to share a copy with
me, and I can't believe he finally succeeded.

My eyes burn with tears, and I hug the book close to my body.

All he wanted was for me to love my magic, to give myself
over to it, and my chest tightens with the knowledge that I'm
disappointing him. But I hate my magic more now than ever

before. If the eclipse were tomorrow, I'd stand beneath it without a second thought and let it drain me of my magic until every last drop was gone.

Nothing left.

Nox jumps up on my bed, and I scratch his head as I flip to the first page of Alice's memoir. She weaves together words that could have been taken straight from my own heart, and I'm caught completely off guard. It's like reading a transcript of my thoughts, and it makes me feel exposed. Vulnerable.

Being an Ever feels like my body is made of heavy gears instead of organs. Each change in season makes the gears grind and move, winding my insides tighter and tighter. By the time the gears settle in their new positions and relief floods me, the season changes again, and I change with it. I ache for consistency and routine. Normalcy and quiet.

I ache to be understood.

My entire life, I've been asked why I change so much, and it has created a certainty within me that something went very wrong when I was born. That certainty has become a permanent pang in the pit of my stomach that I cannot soothe. I'd give anything to feel whole and normal and right, just for a single day.

Alice thrived. Eventually. She dedicated her life to her magic and loved it deeply. She felt powerful and truly herself when the world around her bent to her commands.

But she also isolated herself. I shudder when I read that she accidentally killed three witches and two shaders, then turned to extreme isolation to keep others safe. She chose magic over all else, and an intense loneliness settles inside me, knowing I don't have the same love for magic that Alice did. I feel broken in some critical way.

I have loved magic more deeply, more wholly than I could ever hope to love another person, and magic has loved me back. The sacrifice is great, but the bounty is greater.

Reading those words makes me angry, but more than that, it makes me feel alone. How could she love something that took so much from her? I want to understand, but maybe I never will.

I'm so lost in my reading that I don't realize how late it is until Nox runs out through his door and I check my phone. I pull myself away from Alice's book and quickly get dressed before rushing outside. I sprint the entire way to the control field, and Sang is there waiting when I arrive. I've only seen him in passing since the meeting where I learned I'd be training with him. His eyebrows rise when he sees me.

"I almost thought you weren't going to show up."

"I'm sorry," I say, out of breath. "I got caught up in some reading and didn't notice the time."

"No worries," he says. "It looks like you're all healed up." He sounds hesitant and unsure.

I'm about to say the same to him, but then I remember that he's reporting to Ms. Suntile and Mr. Burrows, and I no longer want to respond. It's hard to remember the witch who rescued Nox and ran from a tornado with me when all I can see is the witch whose job it is to take notes and talk about me behind my back.

I feel an invisible barrier rise between us, tall and strong and impassable.

Sang kneels next to his bag and pulls out a piece of paper with the Eastern School of Solar Magic letterhead on top.

"Is that the lesson plan?"

"Yeah." He stands, and his tone is short. Distracted.

"Don't sound so excited."

Sang puts the paper back in his bag and sighs. "I'm sorry, it's just—" He pauses and meets my gaze. "I moved twenty-five hundred miles across the country, away from my family, to study botany. I was supposed to go to Korea with my parents and spend an entire month there visiting family, and I gave that up because Mr. Burrows insisted this was such a great opportunity. But instead of doing my research, I'm helping you train. He didn't tell me this would be part of the deal." He motions around the control field.

It makes me feel better, in a way, knowing he doesn't want to be here any more than I do. He pushes his hand through his hair and gives me an apologetic look. "I'm sorry, I know this isn't your fault. I shouldn't take it out on you."

"I didn't realize they'd pulled you away from your research. I'm sorry."

He shakes his head. "I didn't ask to get involved. I didn't even know about it until Mr. Burrows and Ms. Suntile called me into the office twenty minutes before you showed up."

"That makes two of us. You'd think Mr. Burrows would have mentioned something to you *before* you gave up your trip and moved all the way out here."

"He didn't know Mr. Hart was going to die," Sang says.

But he did know he'd be taking over my education. He knew his focus would be on me instead of Sang.

I think back to how Mr. Burrows was at my last session with Mr. Hart, and it's so clear that Ms. Suntile brought him out here to take over my training. She always meant for Mr. Burrows to replace Mr. Hart—his death just made it easier.

The ache in my chest returns.

Sang looks at the paper peeking out of his bag. "I know he seems a little rough around the edges, but he's brilliant. And even though my time here isn't going exactly as I thought, I'm glad I get to keep learning from him. You'll get to know him, and you'll see it too."

"He seems like a total jerk," I say.

Sang's jaw clenches, tiny muscles pulsing beneath his skin. He's angry. "Maybe we should just get started."

I drop my bag to the ground. "Sure." The word comes out sour, and I catch Sang shaking his head out of the corner of my eye. I silently scold myself, then soften my tone and ask, "What's on the agenda?"

"A drill that's repeatable in every season. It's going to become our home base while we're training together—by the end of the year, you will have done it so many times, you'll never want to do it again. Today, we'll use it to establish your baseline. Mr. Burrows needs to know your starting point so he can properly gauge the progress you make."

Even the mention of his name puts me on edge; it'll be impossible for me to get stronger if I'm constantly worried about Mr. Burrows looming over me, about having to train with him full-time if I don't improve.

"Let's make a deal: you try not to mention your mentor's name unless it's totally necessary, and I'll try not to respond with unwelcome comments about what a jackass he is. Fair?" I'm trying to make a joke, but it comes out harsh. *Too far, Clara*, I reprimand myself, but Sang doesn't shake his head or tighten his jaw. Instead, the corner of his mouth tugs up just slightly, and he swallows—he's trying not to laugh.

"Fair," he agrees.

"So, how are we going to establish my baseline?"

"We're going to work with the wind, since that's something every season is comfortable with. See that tree line?" He points to the end of the field, where acres of evergreens and towering pines stretch out toward the mountains beyond. "It's a calm day. We're going to see how far through the trees you can send a gust of wind. Then we'll mark that tree and have our baseline. Pretty simple."

"That's the drill? Sounds easy enough."

"That's the point. The best way for you to learn to control your magic is by making it approachable and routine. A habit. The theory is that eventually, by performing the same drill over and over without the distraction of anyone else, it will become second nature to you, and you'll no longer tense up when you do it. You'll grow comfortable with what it feels like to channel your own power, and once that happens, you can start working with other witches again. But you have to learn to control your own magic before you can learn to control that of others. Make sense?"

I hate the way he's talking to me as if he knows me, as if he knows the hurt my magic has caused. He doesn't know anything. He's just repeating what Mr. Burrows has told him, and it makes me want to leave and refuse to train with him. Refuse to train with anyone.

Just nine more months, I remind myself.

When I don't say anything, Sang keeps going. "We'll do a few practice runs, then we'll do the real test to set your baseline. Sound good?"

I nod.

"Okay, ready when you are," he says.

It's a simple task, but I'm nervous and can't pinpoint why. My heart beats faster, and I wipe my palms on my jeans before getting started. I close my eyes and raise my hands in front of me, but I put them back down when I realize they're shaking.

"I'm sorry," I say, embarrassed. "I haven't done any magic since the tornado."

"No worries. Just take your time." The tension between us seems to have faded, and Sang's voice is even and kind. The way he was the first day I met him.

I take several deep breaths and start again. This time, my hands remain steady as I call my magic to the surface.

Autumn magic builds on an undercurrent of thankfulness and sorrow, a symphony of contrasting emotions that's easy to get lost in.

Thankfulness for the harvest and the fruits of the earth.

Sorrow because death is on the horizon. The days are getting shorter, the skies turning gray, the plants growing dormant.

Soon I forget that Sang's eyes are on me, and I get lost in the magic, in the way it feels to summon the wind from nothing, the way the cool air dances across my neck and face. The way my power comes easier when there's nothing at stake. I build the wind up, stronger and stronger, and on Sang's mark, I send it into the trees.

I open my eyes and watch as the wind enters the woods, dying out after just a few rows of evergreens.

I must look disappointed, because Sang says, "That was just a practice run. Let's try it again."

I nod. But this time, when I raise my hands and get started, something feels different. A calming sensation drifts over me, slowing my heart and steadying my breath. It makes me want to give in to the power inside me, makes me feel like I can. Like it's safe. My eyes snap open, and I look at Sang.

"What are you doing?" I ask, my tone more accusatory than I intend.

"Sorry, I should have warned you," he says. "Mr. Bur—" He cuts himself off and starts again. "Spring magic is calm, as you obviously know. And for whatever reason, I can isolate that characteristic and project it outward. It's the same as feeling another witch's magic when they're working right next to you. Mine just happens to feel calm." He shrugs.

"It's so strong," I say. "I've felt other witches' underlying emotions while I was practicing with them, but it's always fleeting and subtle. It's amazing that you can control it that way."

"I wish I could take credit for it, but it isn't something I had to learn to control. It's always come naturally to me."

"Amazing," I say, more to myself than to Sang.

But something about it doesn't sit right with me. It can't be just a coincidence that Sang has a type of magic that calms me down as I'm using my own.

Then it hits me: Mr. Burrows didn't bring Sang here to study botany. He brought him here to help me with my magic, hoping that his calming effect would take away my fear of losing control.

"Is something wrong?" Sang asks.

Part of me wants to tell him he was duped, but I don't want him to leave, stranding me to train alone with Mr. Burrows.

I swallow hard. "No, sorry. I was just surprised. Let's try again."

I feel Sang's current of magic instantly, calming the anger that's brewing inside me. I take a long, deep breath and release the tension in my shoulders. I straighten my back and raise my hands.

Autumn magic rises up inside me, its melancholic song pouring from my fingers and into the space in front of me, building up the wind as it goes. My hair blows out behind me, and my jacket flaps in the current, getting stronger and stronger as more magic builds.

My instinct is to push it down, force it to stay put, but there is no one here for it to gravitate toward. No one here for it to hurt.

The thought relieves me and makes me so lonely it's hard to breathe.

The wind lessens around me, but then I'm met with more of Sang's calming magic. It helps me refocus, and this time, when the wind builds to its highest point, I send it barreling toward the trees.

It makes it farther than the first time, and Sang nods in approval.

"You know, I won't always have a witch around who can calm me whenever I need it," I say dryly.

"You won't need it," he says. "The point is that you'll learn what the full extent of your magic feels like in a controlled, *calm* environment. You'll get used to it. You'll learn to control it. And then it won't scare you anymore."

"Memorize that from the Everwitch 101 pitch they gave you?"

Sang shakes his head and looks at me with such earnestness that I have to look away. "Not everyone is out to get you, you know."

I sigh. "I'm sorry. I don't mean to be a jerk."

"I know you've had a rough few months. But as long as we're doing this together, we may as well make the best of it. I'll give it my all if you do."

"Okay," I say. "Deal."

"Let's get your baseline set and call it a day."

I go through the same routine as before, Sang's calm blanketing me, and this time, when I send the wind into the woods, Sang tosses a large red ribbon into the current. We watch as it blows through the trees, past the rows where my previous attempts stopped, until it finally slows and the ribbon catches on a branch.

"I should be able to obliterate this entire forest," I say as we walk to find the ribbon. "I'm so used to pushing my magic down, I'm not even sure I know how to let it go. I don't think I could lose control even if I wanted to."

"You'll get there." He says it as if it's obvious, the surest thing in the whole world.

When we get to the tree where the ribbon is caught, Sang takes out a large roll of bright-red tape and wraps it around the trunk several times.

"Congratulations," he says. "You've set your baseline."

"It's not much," I say, embarrassed by how far I have to go. "But I guess it's something."

"It's something," Sang agrees.

We walk back to the control field and gather our things.

"Hey," he says, pausing. "I can't imagine how hard it must have been, coming to train with me today instead of Mr. Hart."

I look at him. His dark-brown eyes have rings of gold in the centers, as if the Sun herself wanted to live in his gaze. I didn't notice it before, but now that the bruise around his eye is gone, it's all I can see.

"It was hard," I say. "But I didn't really have a choice." I remember what he said about his research and soften my tone. "I guess neither of us did."

Sang shrugs. "I came out here to study botany, and instead I'm running from tornadoes and getting black eyes. What can you do?" He slips on his sweatshirt and slings his bag over his shoulder.

"The black eye wasn't so bad. It made you look pretty badass."

"I don't think the word *badass* has ever been used to describe me before."

I drop my mouth open and give him my best shocked face. "But you're a botanist who loves to study!"

"I know," Sang agrees. "It's baffling." He zips his sweatshirt and follows me off the field.

"I'll see you Tuesday," I say, walking off toward my small cabin. I'm anxious to get back to Alice's book, but something makes me stop and turn. "Hey, Sang?"

"Yeah?"

"I'm sorry you got stuck with this. With me. I hope you get to make up your trip soon."

"I'm sure I will. And I'm sorry you got stuck with me too." The way he says it makes me sad, like the sorrow that flows from autumn magic.

"There are worse people to be stuck with," I say.

"I'm flattered, truly." I can't help but laugh, and he flashes me a smile. "See you Tuesday," he says.

Instead of leaving as well, I stay where I am, watching Sang as he walks off the field. It's only when I can no longer see him that I finally walk away.

CHAPTER

ten

"If spring is a whispered promise that everything can be made new, autumn is a brilliant sacrifice born of love. Because if the autumn did not love the spring, it would not fall to winter just so the spring could rise."
—*A Season for Everything*

Finals week at Eastern is unlike finals week anywhere else. There's a heaviness that settles on the shoulders of those whose season is nearing its end and a lightness in those whose season is about to begin. The autumns move around campus like zombies, slow and unkempt and easily agitated. They're mourning the loss of their season, their perfect position to the sun, the most important part of themselves, and it won't be back in its entirety for nine months.

Even I feel it. Right now, I believe autumn is the best season. I don't want it to end.

But on the first day of winter, I'll forget all about autumn, the way warmth makes you forget what it's like to be cold.

Our last final was this afternoon, and now it's time for our season-end celebration before the new quarter starts. Gravel crunches underneath my heels as I walk down the path to the library. The remaining leaves dance in the breeze before finally falling to the earth, and the wind blows my burnt-orange dress against my legs, the long silk skirt billowing out behind me.

The dress code for the Harvest Ball is formal, and seeing everyone dressed up after a quarter of jeans and sweaters is always satisfying.

I didn't want to come tonight. So much noise, so many people, and the breathtaking loneliness of being alone in a crowded room.

But it's important to honor the season.

The Harvest Ball doesn't start until late in the evening, when the sky is perfectly black. It always happens on the full moon. The moonlight casts a blue glow on the path, interrupted every few minutes by a passing cloud. Mounds of fallen leaves have been swept to the sides, covering the dark earth with beds of color. The library is lit up in the distance, music and voices carrying out into the cold night air.

I walk up the cement steps, through the front doors of the old building. The stone that covers the outside of the library makes up the inside walls as well. Large windows stretch all the way up to the third story. Shelves of books line the walls, and the smell of old paper hangs in the air. All of the tables and desks have been moved out of the center of the room, where a dance floor is set up and a live quartet plays for the students and faculty.

Hundreds of candles, fake but beautiful, line the bookshelves and railings, the perimeter of the floor and the tops of the cocktail tables. Flower arrangements in deep oranges and rich greens fill dozens of vases. Ivy wraps around the staircase railings, and dark-purple orchids decorate the hot-cider stations. Burgundy linens and silver goblets adorn the tables.

The ball is gorgeous every year, but this year I'm especially taken with it.

The Harvest Ball is our way of thanking autumn for its many gifts, thanking the Sun for taking us with her for another season. This was a particularly brutal season, but we still show thanks.

On a gold stand in the corner of the room is a picture of Mr. Hart. Ivy drapes over the top of the frame, and candlelight flickers off the canvas. I miss him and wish he could see that I'm trying, even when all I want to do is give up. Mr. Hart's belief in me is the only thing that keeps me showing up to my training sessions with Sang. We've only been training together a few weeks, always working on the same drill, but we're finding our rhythm. And I'm giving it my all. I owe at least that much to Mr. Hart.

"Thank you for the book," I whisper.

I'm so sorry. Those are the words I can't get out, so instead I play them over and over in my head.

I'm so sorry.

So sorry.

I look at his picture for a long time and turn away only when it becomes hard to breathe.

I walk the perimeter of the library. A large table full of harvested fruits lines the side of the room. Bowls of apples and pears, figs and persimmons sit on a bed of dried leaves. Twinkle lights weave through the arrangement.

It occurs to me that in years past, a botanist has done our floral arrangements, and I turn to look for Sang in the crowd. But he's already walking toward me, and before he has a chance to speak, I say, "You didn't do the floral arrangements, did you?"

"That depends. Do you like them?"

"I love them. The ivy down the stairs, the orchids, the fruit. It's all gorgeous."

"Thanks," he says, following my eyes around the room. "But the flowers do all the work." He smiles, momentarily lost in thought, then looks at me. "I want to show you something."

I follow Sang to a nearby cocktail table. He pulls an arrangement closer to us, and the gold in his eyes seems to shimmer as he looks at the flowers. The edge of his hand is smudged with faint yellow paint.

"See this flower?" He points to a bright-orange one with big petals and white stripes down the middle. I nod. "This is called a sleeping orange. Nobody uses it in arrangements because the bud stays closed and the stem has all these microthorns on it." He pulls the flower out a little, and I look closely at the stem.

"See how it looks like there's fuzz on it? Those are tiny thorns—hundreds of them—so this poor flower is forgotten about, cast aside as unfit. But if you soak the flower in water and honey the night before, the thorns break down just enough to feel soft. Touch it."

I reach my hand out and touch the stem with my finger. Sure enough, the tiny thorns are soft.

"And only then does the flower bloom."

"Incredible," I say.

"They really are. And while most people aren't willing to put in the work to get the payoff, I can't imagine a better use of my time. Why are we expected to show our most vulnerable selves to the world, anyway?"

Sang strokes one of the petals, then pushes the flower back into the arrangement.

His honesty mystifies me, and I study him like he's a subject I don't understand. He practically is.

Sang's cheeks turn a deep shade of red. He coughs, and an awkward laugh comes out. "Sorry," he says. "I'm not sure why I said all of that."

I look at the orange flower and wonder what it would feel like to trust someone so much that I'd let them see my hidden parts. I used to have that with Paige and Nikki, the kind of trust that never felt like work. The kind that was as natural as sunlight in summer. Sometimes I don't think I'm capable of it anymore. And even if I were, it wouldn't be safe. My magic would always know.

It's too hot in here, and I look away from Sang. My eyes find Paige's in the crowd of people, and she looks from me to Sang and back again. I can't be in here anymore—too many people, too many memories, too many questions.

"I need some fresh air," I say.

Cold hits me when I exit the library, and the moon illuminates the bench where I sit. Ever since Nikki died, I've perfected the art of never opening up, never letting anyone in. But something about Sang makes it harder for me. I'm not used to his kind of openness, and I don't like it. I don't trust it.

Someone sits down next to me, and I try to come up with an excuse to ditch Sang again, but when I turn my head, it isn't him sitting next to me. It's Paige.

Her light-blue eyes catch mine, her long blond hair reflecting the moonlight.

She is the one person who knows everything about me, all my back alleys and dark closets where no one else has ever looked.

And I know hers.

She was my summer fling last year, but calling it a fling isn't fair to what we had. We were best friends first. She somehow climbed over all my walls and broke into my heart. When spring gave way to summer, our friendship caught on fire.

Then Nikki died, and I ended things right away. I couldn't risk it, couldn't risk her.

I'm still not sure if I got out in time or if she's still at risk. Paige's name weighs heavy on my shoulders. She was so angry, so hurt when I ended things that she pushed me out of her life entirely, slamming the door on everything we had—not only with each other, but with Nikki as well. I know it was for the best, but losing my relationship with Paige felt like losing Nikki again too.

It's been over a year, and I miss her. She's sitting right next to me, and I still miss her. But our friendship got mixed up with our romance.

I loved Paige as a friend, a fierce, loyal love that lasted season after season. So maybe she was never safe, romance or not. Maybe my magic would have found her regardless. I pray the Sun doesn't recognize her anymore, doesn't feel the pull between us.

It takes Paige a while to speak, and I wonder if she's thinking about all our loose ends the same way I am.

"I've seen you out there training with Sang," she says. "You're getting better."

"I'm behind."

"You'll catch up."

I look at her, but she's focusing on a point in the distance. Things have been over between us for a long time, but she lingers, the way a hearth stays warm long after the last flame dies out.

I don't tell her that. I don't tell her that when I can't sleep, I still play the games that used to keep her, Nikki, and me up until the morning. I don't tell her that the rush of magic that took Nikki would have taken her, too, had she not been sick that day. I don't tell her how I've never been more thankful for someone being sick in my entire life.

I think about the upcoming eclipse, about how I'll never have to worry about this ever again. I can train now, gain control of my magic enough to tide me over, and then leave all of this behind. The hope of never hurting another person swells in my chest, beats in time with my heart.

Paige opens her mouth to speak again, but Sang comes out, erasing the moment.

"Want to get in one last session before the solstice?" he asks.

I don't hesitate. I don't remind him I'm in a dress and he's in a suit. I don't tell him I'm tired.

Instead, I glance at Paige, think about our tie that's still too strong. Too dangerous.

I stand up, grab my purse, and say, "Yes."

eleven

"Autumn is its own kind of magic; it reminds us of the beauty in letting go."

— *A Season for Everything*

The control field is still, silent. Stars shine overhead, and the full moon provides just enough light for us to see what we're doing. My heels punch through the dirt, so I take them off and toss them aside.

"One of the best things about training at night," Sang says, his voice soft and low, "is that no one can see you."

He's right. The darkness wraps me up like my very own security blanket, protecting me from the curiosity and judgment that follows me in daylight.

It's freeing.

"And you can't see the trees," he adds. "Let's keep working on the same drill, but tonight, focus on how it feels. Forget about the results; forget about how far you throw the wind and how much progress you're making. Forget about being perfectly in control. Just focus on what it feels like to have that kind of power inside you."

Something about the way he says it creates an ache deep inside my core. I push it down, ignore it.

"We're witches," he says. "Let's enjoy it."

I know he doesn't mean anything by it, but the comment feels so flippant, given why we're here in the first place. I swallow. "Easy for you to say. How can I enjoy something that causes so much pain?"

"For starters, you can stop feeling sorry for yourself." He says it so simply, as if stating that the stars shine brightest after a good rain or that winter follows autumn.

"Excuse me?"

He lets out a breath and shakes his head, frustrated. "You're so caught up in the bad that you refuse to acknowledge the good."

"People *die* because of me."

"No, they die because of magic you never asked for. Your friend who died—she was a summer, right?"

"Nikki," I say.

"Nikki. Did she love being a summer?"

"There wasn't anything she loved more." The words catch in my throat, but I force them out.

"And she loved it even though she spent nine months out of every year longing for summer to come. Even though the moment the equinox arrived, she could feel herself getting weaker. Even though for seventy-five percent of her life, she didn't feel truly herself."

"That's different."

"Of course it is. But my point is that she still loved her magic—we *all* do, even though it comes with real pain. Pain that you will never have to experience because you're an Ever. Your magic comes with its own kind of pain, and you can acknowledge it, hate it, wish it didn't have to be that way, and still live your life. Still be happy."

His eyes reflect the moonlight. There's something about the way he talks about hard things that makes them easier to approach, and I feel the tension rush out of me. I don't want to fight anymore. But the best manipulators are disarming. I think about Sang and his calming magic, Sang sitting on the other side of that desk with Ms. Suntile and Mr. Burrows, Sang respecting a person who seems so horrible, and it suddenly makes so much sense that they chose him. He *is* disarming.

And I refuse to fall for it.

I clear my throat. "You make a better botanist than armchair psychologist. Let's train."

Sang tips his head down as if he's embarrassed. But he recovers fast, nods, and says, "Let's train."

I get to work. The wind comes easily, responding to me as if it's been waiting all night for us to stand on this field.

I know Sang is working beside me, his calming magic always close, but tonight it's an undercurrent. An afterthought. What I feel the most is raw power rising inside me, tumbling around, excited to spill into the night.

As Sang and I work side by side, me summoning the wind

and him letting magic flow from his fingers solely to make me feel safe, the tension between us eases, floats away into the night.

We don't have to be best friends. I don't have to like him, and he doesn't have to like me, but I think we're starting to understand each other. And that's something.

I keep building the current in front of me, and soon I'm lost in it. My mind stops worrying, and my shoulders relax. For the briefest moment, I'm not scared. I'm not fighting against it. Slowly, I ask for more magic, release my hold on it and let it rush into the wind, making it stronger. Faster. I keep at it until I'm certain it's the strongest current I've created since Sang and I started working together.

I send one more surge of magic into the wind, then push it out into the woods.

I keep my eyes closed and tilt my head back, reveling in the sound of the current moving through the oaks and pines, listening as they bend and sway.

Then it stops, and the world is quiet again.

I open my eyes and look toward Sang, thinking we're done for the night. Without a word, he turns to the forest beyond the field, raises his hands, and closes his eyes. The branches begin moving, a soft rustling at first, then a loud whooshing sound as the treetops sway from side to side.

He calls for more wind, and it answers, leaving the trees and rolling onto the field.

Let's enjoy it. Sang's words echo in my head.

"Wait," I say.

Sang pauses.

Magic rolls from my fingertips and into the woods. I imagine the fallen leaves on the ground and raise my hands. The air gets heavy as all the leaves rise from the forest floor and pause, waiting for my command. I pull them toward the field and open my eyes.

A wall of countless leaves rushes through the air and then comes to a stop. Sang looks at them and raises his hands.

"Ready?" he asks.

I nod, and he sends his tower of wind barreling into the leaves. I take control of the wind and circle my hands, around and around and around, faster and faster. Then I pull it toward me.

Orange, yellow, green, and red dance in the air, swirling together as the massive tower of wind glides toward me. The cyclone gets faster and sends the leaves chasing after one another in dizzying circles. I pull my hands apart to create a large eye in the center of it.

The wind parts, allowing me inside.

With one large motion, I send the wind spiraling around me. The leaves swirl in a tower, and I stay in the center of the storm. My orange dress slaps against my legs, and the wind howls in my ears and rips through my hair, sending strands of red in every direction. The sound is so loud it drowns out everything else. I spread my arms wide, feel the wind tearing through my fingers, watch the leaves as they whip around me.

And I laugh. I actually laugh.

I sense Sang working on something new, and my magic pauses, forgetting the leafnado and waiting.

A heavy layer of fog descends on the field. In one even motion, I push the cyclone away and pull the fog from Sang, revealing him and hiding me.

I move between the two, going back and forth between the fog and the cyclone, pushing them away and pulling them back.

"Amazing," Sang says under his breath.

The other seasons can't move their magic around like that; it takes a ton of energy to pull their power from one thing and focus it on another. But autumn magic is transitional. It flows from one thing to the next, sensing the environment and changing to meet its needs. In some ways, it can feel unsteady, changing so rapidly.

But it's also an incredible advantage the other seasons don't have. It's one of the reasons I was able to get as close to dissipating the tornado as I did—I wasted no time moving my magic from one thunderstorm to the next.

"Come here," I say, and Sang walks toward me. I step in front of him so we're facing each other, just inches apart. I push the layer of fog up into the darkness until it vanishes. Then I grab hold of the leafnado and send it spiraling around us.

All my energy flows into the cyclone, leaves everywhere, the sound drowning out everything else. It rotates around us with incredible speed, Sang's tie flapping wildly along with my hair. He reaches out his hand, touching the tunnel of wind around us.

It's too dark to see him clearly, but I feel how near he is to me. How quiet and still he is. His warm breath reaches my skin, unhurried and even. I'm thankful there isn't enough light for him to see the way he's transforming before me, the way my eyes soften and my jaw relaxes as he changes from someone I resented to someone I want to share this moment with.

I let my fingers stretch to the wind and feel the air rush through them.

My heartbeat is slow. Steady. Oddly content in the eye of the storm.

Then I clap my hands together, and the wind vanishes.

For one breath, the leaves hang in the air, frozen in the memory of the wind, before they finally float to the ground.

Silence.

Sang looks at me, his hair windswept, his tie hanging loosely around his neck. His top button is undone, and he has abandoned his suit jacket on the grass. He looks so perfectly unkempt it makes me blush.

"You were made for this," he says.

And for a single second, I think maybe he's right.

queen anne's lace

winter

twelve

"Women are discouraged from being direct and saying what we think. That's why I love winter: it taught me to stand up for myself when the rest of the world was happy to walk over me."

—*A Season for Everything*

There is a distinct bite in the air when I wake up. The steady flow of autumn magic has been replaced with the deliberate, aggressive pulse of winter. Even the magic itself is colder, a constant shiver running under my skin. I'll be used to it by tomorrow, but today I'll be unable to warm up.

I get out of bed and open the window. I stick my arm into the air and close my eyes, reading the temperature.

I dress appropriately, then head to class with Nox following after me. A thick, low layer of clouds hovers over the school. My breath appears in front of me with each exhale.

Winter is the most hated season by the nonwinter witches. The autumns, springs, and summers tend to stay inside and huddle around fires. They wear too many layers and drink copious amounts of cider and spiced tea.

But I like winter. Winter is the truest of the seasons. It's what remains after everything else is stripped away. The leaves fall. The colors fade. The branches get brittle. And if you can love the earth, understand it when all the beauty is gone and see it for what it is, that's magic.

Winters are more straightforward than anyone else. We don't soften ourselves with indirectness or white lies or fake niceties. What you see is what you get.

And winter is good to those who respect it.

When I get to the control field, several people look my way. It's my first group class since Mr. Hart died. Ms. Suntile thought it would be good for me to start working with other witches again, but I won't be trying to hold their magic. My primary training will still be with Sang, learning to control my own magic. Ms. Suntile doesn't want me to forget what it feels like to work in proximity to other witches, though, so here I am.

I put my bag down and stand at the edge of the group. The field is larger than the one Sang and I train on, forty acres of flat earth on which to practice our magic. The grass is green and short, kept immaculate by our springs. The far edge of the field is lined with trees, eastern hemlocks and bare oaks and soaring pines stretching all the way to the Poconos. When I was younger, the field felt impossibly large, and it was only as I got older that it started to feel suffocating instead.

Mr. Donovan gives me a welcoming smile, then walks several

yards away from the group and demonstrates a near-perfect thunderstorm. Looming clouds. Flashing lightning. Clapping air.

It's perfectly confined, maybe three hundred feet above his head and only ten feet or so in diameter.

Thunderstorms aren't common in winter, so we aren't as good with them. We have to fight for the level of precision Mr. Donovan demonstrates. He's a spring, and thunderstorms come much more easily to him. He looks calm and focused, hands out in front of him, no sign of strain or stress.

It's amazing to think about how something that will come so naturally to me next season will be a struggle today. But winter has its own set of skills, and once the temperature drops more, we'll get to put them to use.

Mr. Donovan crosses his palms in front of him, then lowers his hands.

The storm vanishes.

We erupt in applause.

"I forgot how much I like teaching winter sessions. You're much more impressed with me than the springs are," Mr. Donovan says, and we laugh.

"I know thunderstorms don't come as naturally to you, but after the tornado last season, Ms. Suntile wants everyone refreshed on the basics. Thunderstorms are most common in spring and summer, but they can happen at any time, and we want you prepared. You probably know more than you think; remember that every time you deal with hail, you're dealing with a thunderstorm. We're aiming for acceptable, not perfect, so don't stress out over it.

We'll have two thunderstorm classes before moving on to winter magic. Got it?"

We all nod.

"Good. Paige and Clara, you're partners. Then Thomas and Lee, and Jessica and Jay. Remember, you're working *together*. You are not trying to overpower each other. The weather doesn't tolerate egos, and neither do I, so let's keep it friendly, okay? Now, spread out and get to work."

I walk to the southeast corner of the field. Paige follows. Her eyes bore into my back, burning holes in my jacket.

I stop when we get far enough out and turn to face her.

"Let's see what all those hours with the botanist have done," she says, joining me so we're standing no more than a foot apart.

It's obvious why I fell in love with her. She is poised, confident, and self-assured. She's brilliant, and she knows it. And she's beautiful, even more so now that we're in her season. Her eyes are clear and sharp, and her long hair is pulled back in a ponytail.

The look on Paige's face when I broke up with her left a permanent scar on my heart. I hurt her, a tragic kind of hurt because I did it even though we loved each other, and it still echoes between us. Paige walked out of my room that day before I could articulate everything I had to say. I should have run after her and tried to explain. But I didn't, because it was better that way.

But the look on her face, her always-composed face, broke something inside me that I don't think has healed. Maybe it never will.

"What?" Paige asks, impatience lacing her tone. I look away.

"Nothing. Let's get started."

I raise my hands between us, and Paige does the same. Magic rushes out of me, and I pull away, surprised by the force of it.

Paige raises an eyebrow. "Welcome back, Winter."

I roll my eyes and start again. This time I'm ready, and the burst isn't so surprising. I send it into the air above me, and soon a cumulonimbus cloud hangs overhead.

"Let's light her up," Paige says. We hold our hands up in front of us, palms facing one another, and an electrical charge crackles and pops in the space between us.

But something doesn't feel right.

This isn't the normal aggression of winter magic. It's building too fast, too much energy too soon. We haven't produced a single lightning bolt yet, but there's enough electricity between us to set the trees on fire.

It's the tension. The anger. The hurt and the memories. The air between us is thick with secret moments and open wounds.

That's when I realize what's happening.

"Paige, stop," I say, jumping back. My hands are almost down to my sides, expelling my half of the energy, when Paige grabs my wrists and pulls me back in.

"I'm not failing this assignment because of you." Her grip on me is tight, and I try to move out of her grasp, but she's too strong. The energy flowing from me is building, my skin buzzing with power, my fingertips aching to produce light. I close my eyes and focus, doing everything I can to lessen it.

"Let me go," I say, yanking my hands away.

"No."

There's isn't much time left. We'll set the whole field on fire before Paige lets go.

"Why are you doing this?" Anger burns my eyes and sharpens my tone.

"You don't get to call all the shots, Clara. This is my assignment, too, and we're going to finish it." Her grip tightens.

She's being impulsive. Reckless. Maybe that's what pain does.

I squeeze my eyes shut. There is so much magic building off of Paige's energy, off all the emotions and things left unsaid.

"Stop holding back on me," Paige says. "I know you can do better than this." She's trying to provoke me, but her voice is strained. She feels the tension too.

I take a breath. Imagine the way her long hair fell over her shoulder when she laughed. She never laughed in public, not like that. But when it was just the two of us, she laughed with her entire body.

On my exhale, I shove away from her as hard as I can.

I break free of her hands, and she tumbles back, losing control of her magic. It reaches for my own, and panic seizes me as my magic rushes out to meet it.

I struggle against the force of it, but my magic recognizes her instantly.

I see the flashes of light that erupted when my parents died. When Nikki died. And all I can think is, *Not Paige too.*

I run at her and tackle her to the ground, rolling her out of the way as magic releases into the air with incredible precision.

But I'm not fast enough, and lightning strikes the space we fall through, catching me in the side before finding the gold chain around Paige's neck. It follows the metal all the way around before vanishing.

Paige shakes beneath me. I scramble off her and stay by her side.

There's a burn under her necklace, and she stares at me, eyes wide. Then she looks away, and her chest turns red, the way it always does when she's embarrassed.

And suddenly, I'm stuck in a memory. The first time I noticed that blush, we were in my room in Summer House, studying for a history exam. We were sprawled out on my bed, books open, highlighters and pens lost in the sheets, when Paige said she'd never kissed anyone.

It came out of the blue, unprompted. And it was surprising. Paige was always confident, sure of herself, and the vulnerability in her voice made my throat tighten. It wasn't anything to be embarrassed about. Paige had never been in a relationship because she'd never thought anyone was good enough for her. I wished I was more like that.

But sitting on my bed, her hair cascading past her shoulders, she trusted me enough to punch through her hard exterior and hand me a part of the softness she kept hidden. Red splotches formed on her pale skin until her chest matched the color of my hair.

"Will you kiss me?" she asked.

My first thought was how brave it was to ask. I didn't know if I'd ever been that brave. I wanted to emulate her.

My second thought was how badly I wanted to.

When our lips touched for the first time, I knew there was no going back.

And for the next two months, there wasn't.

Mr. Donovan rushes over, but I'm frozen in place, trapped between the memory of Paige's lips on mine and the image of her body on the ground. I'm shaking beside her, terrified of what just happened. Terrified of how much worse it could have been.

"You're okay," I whisper. Without thinking, I take her hand.

She looks down at it, up at me, and back to her hand.

I let go.

Then her head lolls back, and she's out.

CHAPTER

thirteen

"It never occurred to me that change was undesirable until someone who prided themselves on consistency told me it was."

—*A Season for Everything*

Paige is lying on a narrow bed in the nurse's office. She has a mild burn on her neck from the lightning heating up her necklace. Ironically, the pendant on her necklace is a little gold lightning bolt that Nikki gave her years ago.

I have a matching one. Nikki was buried in hers.

I'm in a chair beside Paige, a similar burn on my left side where the lightning passed over me. I can't stop seeing images of my parents and Nikki, can't stop thinking about how easily Paige could've joined them.

I'm a danger to those around me, and I can never forget it, not even for a moment.

The nurse comes in and gives us each some topical cream for our burns, but there's nothing more to do. It was a minor incident; the electricity never touched her body and barely skimmed my own. We got lucky. But seeing her shake on the ground reminded me how little control I have over my own power, and it fills my stomach with a sick, twisted feeling.

"Don't do that," Paige says. Even in that narrow bed with grass stuck in her hair, she looks strong.

"Do what?"

"Spiral into self-pity like that."

Defensiveness rises in my chest, and I force it back down. Even after so long, Paige still knows me. It's comforting in a way, realizing there's a part of myself that isn't just a curiosity kept hidden in a tiny cabin beneath the trees. That part of me survived Nikki's death and continues on. But it's also painfully sad.

"You have no idea what it's like being so out of control."

"Yes, I do." Her voice is strained, and I know she isn't talking about magic. She keeps her eyes fixed on the wall in front of her. "And your 'woe is me, I'm so powerful' garbage is getting old."

I shake my head and look at the ceiling, the wall, anywhere but her face. "So is your insistence that you know how I'm feeling better than I do. You don't have a clue." My voice rises, and my skin gets hot.

"And whose fault is that?" She sits up in bed and glares at me. Her voice is loud and laced with anger. I don't say anything, and she lies back down.

We used to be everything to each other, and now we can barely be in the same room. It takes my breath away, the loss of it all.

I avoid her eyes, and she avoids mine. A silence louder than our worst yelling match takes over the room, and I jump when the door opens.

Ms. Suntile walks in, followed by Mr. Donovan and Mr. Burrows.

"Girls," she says, looking at us over her glasses, "I trust you're feeling better?"

"Yes, thank you," Paige says.

"Yes," I echo.

Mr. Donovan pulls up three chairs, and they all sit. I press my palms into my knees, trying to stay calm. I have no idea what kind of trouble I'll get in for this.

Mr. Donovan has a clipboard and a pen, ready to take notes.

Ms. Suntile looks from me to Paige and back again. "I don't have all day."

"It wasn't Clara's fault," Paige says. I stare at her. "Something didn't feel right as soon as we started, and Clara tried to pull away, but I wouldn't let go of her. I didn't want to fail the assignment."

"That was incredibly reckless of you, Ms. Lexington."

"I know," Paige says. She doesn't sound sorry or defeated, and her tone never falters. She is even, always.

"You should never have been paired together, given your history," Ms. Suntile says, more to Mr. Donovan than to us. He shifts in his seat. My cheeks flame, and I look down.

Mr. Burrows looks at me. "Until you gain more control over your magic, we'll be removing you from group classes again and focusing on your one-on-one sessions instead."

I sit up straighter and look at Ms. Suntile and Mr. Donovan for help. "I'd rather pull back on the private sessions and do more group work. I'll never be comfortable in groups if I don't practice with them."

Mr. Burrows shakes his head. "Today is a clear indicator that you shouldn't be training in normal classes, especially given how long you've been in school with these people. There's too much history. You'll continue to train with Sang, and we'll reevaluate as the year goes on. As soon as you develop enough command over your magic, we'll get you training with other witches again. But for now, your focus must remain on learning to control your own power."

Neither Ms. Suntile nor Mr. Donovan argues, and I slump back in my chair. I know why the school favors private training, private housing, private *everything* for me. And I appreciate it most of the time; these measures help ensure that the people around me stay safe. But I can't shake the feeling that sometimes Ms. Suntile keeps me isolated just because she can.

"I want you both to take the rest of the day off and see how you're feeling in the morning. If you need another day to rest, you may have it." Ms. Suntile turns to look at me. "I'll let Mr. Park know you won't be training with him today." She stands. "Get some rest tonight, both of you."

Ms. Suntile pushes through the door, leaving a gust of cold air in her wake. Mr. Burrows follows without another word, but Mr. Donovan hesitates.

"I owe you both an apology. Ms. Suntile is right—I should

have put more care into who I paired you with. This falls on me, not you." He stands. "Get some rest."

We both nod, and Mr. Donovan leaves. Paige clears her throat. "I'm tired."

"I'll go," I say. "Do you want me to wait outside and help you back to Winter House?"

"No."

I slowly ease out of my chair and head to the door. "Paige," I start, but then I pause, my courage faltering. There is a chasm between us, so deep and so wide that whatever I say will tumble into the depths, never making it to the other side. "I'm glad you're okay."

She doesn't say anything, instead staring off to a place I can't see. I leave and shut the door behind me.

After a fitful night of tossing and turning, dreaming of Nikki and Paige and lightning, I'm even more thankful Ms. Suntile gave me the option to take another day off. I'm in my cabin reading Alice's memoir when there's a knock at the door.

"Come in," I say over my shoulder. I'm curled up on my bed with Nox, and I pull my sweater tighter around my body. The cabin windows are thin and old, and cold air seeps through the weathered seals and into the room.

My mind is frantic with what I did to Paige, with the way it's so easy for me to lose control. I've read the same paragraph over and over again. I shut the book and place it on my bedside table, where it has stayed ever since I received it.

Sang tentatively pokes his head in.

"Did Ms. Suntile not tell you our session was canceled for today?"

"No, she did," Sang's voice trails off, and he looks embarrassed. "I just wanted to make sure you're okay."

"I'm fine," I say. "Paige took the brunt of it."

Sang closes the door behind him and sits down. Nox jumps off the bed and wraps around his legs, purring.

Traitor.

"That must have been terrifying."

I don't understand why he's here. I lean back on my pillow and stare at the ceiling, trying to forget all the pain my magic has caused.

I'm about to ask Sang to leave when he says, "I hurt someone once."

I sit up straighter and look at him. "You did?"

He nods. "I was eight. My parents had set up a planter box for me in the backyard, and I was growing all kinds of things. One day I was working on *Abrus precatorius*—you know, crab's eye?— and thought the seeds were so cool. It had taken me less than an hour to grow, and I was so proud of myself." He pauses. "It was before I knew certain plants are poisonous to shaders."

His voice is quiet, and his eyes shine with the memory. I swallow hard. Ingestion of a single seed can be fatal, and I'm scared for him to continue.

"When my mom called me in for dinner, I sprinkled some seeds on her salad. I couldn't wait for her to try them, to tell her I'd grown them especially for her. But when she bit into the first one, the shell was so hard it hurt her tooth. She swallowed it and ate around the rest. She would have died had she eaten them all."

I exhale, loud and heavy. Nox jumps into Sang's lap, and he pets him as he continues.

"She got really ill. Vomiting and pain, so weak she could hardly stand. My dad saw the seeds on her plate. He looked them up and realized they were toxic. He called poison control, and my mom was rushed to the hospital. She was ultimately fine, but I've never forgotten it."

"I'm sorry you had to go through that."

Sang shakes his head. "It's so vivid still, all these years later. Even now, my heart is pounding just talking about it. For a few hours, I was sure I'd killed my mom. I still have dreams about it."

"I still have dreams about my parents and Nikki. And now, Mr. Hart." The words rush out before I can stop them. I wish I could take them back.

Sang looks at me.

"Sorry, I didn't mean to turn the conversation to me." My fingers grip the blanket over my legs, and I look away. "I just meant—" But I cut myself off. I'm not sure I want to tell him what I meant.

"What?" He looks so genuine, so interested in what I'm going to say. His eyes still shine from his story about his mom, and he's scratching Nox's head, not noticing or caring that his white sweatshirt is covered in black hairs. Watching him with

Nox, the way he's so comfortable in this small space, awakens something inside me.

I swallow hard and look away.

Trusting Sang with my messiest wounds when I don't trust him with anything else would be foolish.

I need him to go.

"I just meant that I know what it's like to dream about moments you'd give anything to forget."

Sang nods, but he looks down, and his shoulders slump. He knows there's something I'm not saying. He clears his throat and stands.

"Well, I'm glad you're doing okay. I'll see you tomorrow?"

I nod. Sang walks to the door and looks back at me. For a second, I think he might ask me a question, but then he shakes his head slightly and leaves.

Nox stands at the door, watching the space Sang occupied just moments earlier.

Guilt pricks at me, but I push it down. I don't owe him my secrets just because he shared his.

I don't owe him anything at all.

fourteen

*"I don't know if I like myself equally in each season.
I value different qualities at different times, but don't
we all?"*

—*A Season for Everything*

The next morning, I beat Sang to the control field. Winter is
slowly taking over campus, bare branches and mornings touched
by frost. The days are getting shorter, and the plants are preparing
for the long season ahead.

Nighttime reigns in winter. There are fewer daylight hours,
and the sun hangs lower in the sky. The atmosphere scatters the
sunlight, making it less intense.

Winters are special in that way: we need the least amount
of energy from the sun in order to produce magic. Summers are
almost useless in winter because they require such an incredible
amount of sunlight. But not us.

It's a clear day. The grass sparkles with frost, and the forest
beyond the field is quiet and still.

A quote from Alice's memoir is swirling in my head, words I haven't been able to forget since the accident with Paige: *If people I care about are going to die because of me, I'm going to make damn certain my magic is worth something.*

She wrote it in anger after losing one of her closest friends when she was nineteen. Something snapped in her, and she decided the only way to move forward was to immerse herself in the thing she feared.

I've tried everything—holding my magic back, isolating myself, keeping my guard up at all times. Everything except leaning into my magic. Seeing Paige on the ground highlighted something I think I've known all along: what I've been doing isn't working.

There are two seasons left before the solar eclipse, and if I'm going to make it until then without hurting anyone else, I need a new strategy.

When Sang walks onto the field, I'm ready to use my magic.

All of it.

"Hey," he says, dropping his bag on the ground. A wool scarf is wrapped around his neck, and the tips of his ears are pink. He looks so comfortable, so cozy, like a mug of hot chocolate or my favorite blanket. The perfect person to curl up with beside a fire.

I clear my throat.

"How are you feeling today?" he asks.

"I couldn't sleep last night. I kept thinking about how Paige could have been hurt so much worse, about how lucky we got. I don't ever want that to happen again." I pause, look out across the field toward the trees I've been trying so hard to reach in our drills. "Before Mr. Hart died, he told me I'll only ever gain full control over my magic if I master it. I want to let it all out and hold nothing back. I need to know what I'm actually capable of."

"I thought that's what we've been doing. Have you been holding back this whole time?"

"Not on purpose. But I think I've been holding back for so long that I don't know how *not* to do it. I don't know what it feels like to use all my magic because I never let myself get close. And I'll never learn to control it if I don't even know what it feels like."

Sang nods. "That makes a lot of sense." He looks around the field. The mountains in the distance are capped in white, as if their peaks have been dipped in frosting.

"Would you walk me through it? How it feels for you when you use all of your magic?"

He looks surprised, but he nods. "Sure, of course."

"I'd like that."

His eyes land on mine, and for one, two, three seconds, neither of us looks away.

I force my eyes to the ground and take a deep breath. There was nothing in that look.

Sang reaches his hand out to me, and I step back. "You'll feel it more if you take my hand," he says.

Hesitantly, I step forward. When I put my hand in his, he laces his fingers through mine. For a moment, I'm frozen, staring at our intertwined fingers. His skin is rough, indicative of all the hours he spends in the dirt, and blue smudges stain the edge of his hand. My heart races. I force myself to focus on our drill, because that's all this is: training.

"Okay?" Sang asks me.

I nod and swallow hard. "I'm ready when you are."

He closes his eyes, and I do the same. I instantly feel it when he calls his magic to the surface, the calm I'm so used to by now drifting through the air, moving up my arm, settling in my core.

I breathe deep.

Wind starts to build around us, Sang's scarf dancing in the current, brushing against my skin.

My heart slows.

"There's a moment," Sang says, his voice even, "when your magic waits for you to make a choice. It pulls you along like the current of a river, your back in the water, eyes closed, arms stretched out, palms toward the sky. The current gets faster and stronger as it rushes toward a waterfall. And there's a moment when the river stills, gives you control, and asks, 'Are we going back the way we came, swimming against the current? Or are we falling over the edge, trusting the water below to catch us?'"

My eyes stay closed. I nod along with his words, understanding exactly what he's saying; the image is so vivid I can almost feel it. His calm, the absolute control he has over the power inside him, hangs in the space between us. It hovers in the air like a mist of perfume.

"How do you make yourself fall over the edge?" I ask, my voice so quiet I'm not sure he hears me.

"You inhale all your fear, all your worries, all your hesitation," he says, breathing in so deeply I can hear it despite the wind. The calming magic that flows from him pauses at the top of his breath, waiting for his answer.

I take in a deep breath with him.

"On your exhale, you let it all go—all the fear, all the tension you're carrying in your body—until all that's left is you and your magic. You surrender to the current and drop over the waterfall, knowing you're safe. It's so much harder to swim against the current, to try to go back. Falling is the only way forward."

Sang exhales, and I do the same. His entire body relaxes as magic rushes through him, pours into the air, wraps itself around me.

The column of wind he's summoned takes off for the trees. I open my eyes and watch. It doesn't go far, only into the first few rows, but we're in winter; come spring, Sang will be able to drop a windstorm over this entire field if he wants to. The trees sway side to side, and then the wind dies out and they rest, motionless.

My fingers are still laced with Sang's. I pull my hand back, ignoring the way the cold air invades the space previously kept warm by his skin on mine.

Ignoring the way I want his warmth back.

"Your turn," he says, bringing me back to the field.

I look at the evergreens in the distance and keep the image in my mind when I close my eyes. I take a deep breath and exhale slowly.

I can do this. It's just a little wind.

Magic rises up inside me, and instead of focusing on holding it back, I focus on the task. I picture the evergreens swaying in a breeze. I imagine myself floating down the river, water at my back and sky above me.

I picture myself in total control.

The wind gets stronger and stronger around me, then pauses. My magic waits. I'm at the waterfall.

I inhale, and as my chest rises, I acknowledge my fear. I see it. There's so much of it, so much pain. I see my parents lying motionless on the ground, Nikki as she slams into a tree, Mr. Hart as he's hit by a plow, Paige as she's struck by lightning. It's an insurmountable barrier I can't get through, and my hands begin to shake as my magic retreats.

I can't hold on to it.

"There is no one here to hurt. It's just you, me, and this field."

I nod and try to slow my breathing.

"You deserve to rest. Release your breath, release all the tension you're carrying, and let go. You're safe here."

I can't get the images out of my head. "I can't do it," I say, my voice shaking. I'm scared.

"Yes, you can. We're going to take a deep breath together, and when we exhale, you're going to let go. Deep breath in," he says.

I inhale again, and my magic waits.

"Let your body get heavy, release the tension, and exhale."

I see myself at the top of the waterfall. Afraid, worried, hurt. And then I see myself giving in to the current, flowing over the edge, eyes closed, water roaring. I'm falling.

Power rushes out of me in an unrestrained surge. It's so strong, it feels as if all my insides are going with it, my muscles and organs and bones. I gasp from the force of it, but I don't seize up. I don't hold back.

I let it all go.

Wind barrels toward the evergreens, the aggressive, cold magic of winter fueling it as it charges on. I give it everything I have.

Then I open my eyes and watch.

Wind slams into the woods, toppling the first tree it hits. But it doesn't stop there. Tree after tree crashes to the ground like a row of dominoes, making the earth beneath me shake. Plumes of dust rise from the woods, but I can't look away. The wind roars as it barrels into the last row of evergreens, tossing them aside as if they're twigs used to play fetch. It happens so fast.

The ground vibrates. Silence takes over after the final thuds echo off the mountainside.

My breathing is shallow, and my heart pounds.

I stare at the path of fallen trees. My whole body shakes as I take in the destruction.

Then a rumbling sound starts in the distance, and I watch in horror as snow rushes down the side of the mountain. It starts gradually, as if it's happening in slow motion, and then all at once, it picks up speed and tears down the mountainside.

There's nothing I can do but watch as the avalanche takes out hundreds more trees before finally coming to a stop.

Clouds of snow rise into the air like smoke, mixing with the dust the fallen evergreens kicked up.

The world gets quiet again, except for my quick, ragged breaths. A sound escapes my lips, something between a groan and a sob.

Sang stands beside me, staring at the ravaged mountainside.

"There's nothing between us and the mountains other than trees?"

I shake my head. Eastern sits on thousands of acres, nestled in the valleys of the Poconos. Plenty of room for error, as Mr. Hart used to say.

My eyes are stuck on the damage I caused. I can't move. Can't think. Can't breathe.

"Hey, you're okay," Sang says, moving in front of me. He locks his eyes with mine. "Just breathe."

I take in a deep, shaky breath.

"Good, that's good. Keep your eyes on me. Right here," he says. "Good. Keep breathing."

I take several more breaths. Slowly, my body stops shaking. My mind stops spiraling, and I can think again.

"That was bad," I say.

"Well, you did *blow* past your baseline, so technically this is the best run you've had."

"You did not just make a pun."

"I did," he says solemnly.

I want to yell at him, tell him this isn't funny. Remind him how inordinately out of control I am.

But when I open my mouth, I don't yell.

I laugh.

It's a nervous, frantic kind of laughter, but laughter all the same. Then Sang is laughing too, and we're both bent over at the waist, tears streaming down our faces.

It's the first time I've laughed, truly laughed, since Nikki died.

fifteen

"Be wary of those who will let you apologize for who you are."

—*A Season for Everything*

Ms. Suntile does not laugh when we tell her what happened. She even goes so far as to tell me I've been irresponsible, but Sang defends me. He tells her it's the most power I've been able to summon yet, which is precisely what she wanted from me in the first place. And now that I've done it, I can start the hard work of learning to control it.

She doesn't have much to say to that, and so we leave with the understanding that we will replant as many trees as we can come spring.

Mr. Burrows, to his credit, agrees with us, and I'm relieved to know he won't be taking over my training anytime soon.

"Thanks for your help in there," I say to Sang as we leave the administration building. I zip my jacket up and shove my hands into my pockets.

"She's hard on you," he says.

"I think she just expects a lot from me. Eastern, and Ms. Suntile in particular, took a risk by allowing me to stay here after Nikki died, and I'm sure she just wants it to be worth it."

"That's ridiculous."

"What is?"

Sang stops walking and gives me an incredulous look. "Clara, you're the first Ever in over a hundred years. You seriously think Ms. Suntile did you a *favor* by keeping you here?"

"Yeah," I say, but my voice rises at the end like I'm asking a question.

"I won't pretend to know what happened after Nikki died, but there is no way Ms. Suntile would have let you leave this school. You're the most powerful witch alive. Having you here makes her powerful too."

"I don't understand."

"I'm not saying the school is bad or ill-intentioned or anything. I'm just saying that you're doing *them* a favor by being here, not the other way around. You should never feel like you have to make excuses or apologize for who you are."

"But I—"

Sang holds his hand to my mouth, so close his fingers almost brush my lips. "Never," he says.

Heat rises up my neck, and I take a step back. "I'm going to be late for class."

I rush to Avery Hall, where Mr. Donovan is prepping us for the upcoming blizzard. But Sang's words repeat in my mind over and over again. My hand absentmindedly drifts to my mouth, the memory of his fingers close enough to feel my breath.

All I've done for the past several years is apologize for who I am, act as if I'm fortunate that Ms. Suntile let me stay. And I am fortunate. But something nags at me, a tiny thought I can't let go. All these years that I've been apologizing for who I am, for having the gall to exist in the first place, I've been giving Ms. Suntile all the power.

And she has let me.

I'm overwhelmed that there is someone who won't accept my apologies, who doesn't want me to apologize in the first place. Who doesn't even think I have anything to apologize for.

Sang doesn't want any power over me, and every time I try to hand it over, he refuses to accept it.

Maybe he deserves a little trust after all.

"Clara, are you with us?" Mr. Donovan, along with the rest of the class, looks in my direction.

"I'm with you," I say.

"Good. Now, I know you're all waiting for your assignments for the blizzard, but that's not why we're here today." A few murmurs make their way through the class, but Mr. Donovan silences them. "I'm sure you've all seen the news. Witches are dying of depletion at a higher rate than ever before, and we think we finally know why."

It used to be rare that a witch would demand so much of their magic that they died from exhaustion. It was practically unheard of. Our bodies let us know when we're running out of energy long before we're at risk. But depletion deaths have risen so much lately that we're struggling to fill the gaps. We can't keep up.

"A report was just released by the Solar Magic Association. Every witch we've lost to depletion in the past three years has been in their off-season."

Thomas raises his hand. "What does this have to do with the blizzard?"

"I'm sorry, Mr. Black, are you bored by the unprecedented death rate that's been devastating our community?"

Thomas shakes his head and slumps in his seat.

"The reason I will not be handing out your assignments for the blizzard is because there will no longer be a blizzard next week."

"But there's always a blizzard this time of year," Jay says.

He's right. Every winter, we work on storm cells in the area to create a blizzard that lands on our campus. It's a massive storm that enables the winters to train under extreme conditions. Training was supposed to begin next week.

"This year, there will be a heat wave instead. Not of our making, of course. This has never happened before, and the witches in the region are doing everything they can to prepare for it, but it's going to be a grueling week for them." The way he says it, the worry in his voice, reminds me that there is so much going on outside our campus. We'll all graduate soon and be left to deal with the consequences of an atmosphere that's falling into chaos.

It makes guilt prick at my stomach, knowing the eclipse

is still looming, knowing I plan to render myself useless to my fellow witches.

"We've talked with the witches controlling the area, and they're going to do the best they can to minimize the damage, but it won't be enough to get us anywhere near a typical weather system for this time of year. We'll have to wait until it's over before we can plan any sort of winter training."

The room erupts as students begin to talk over one another and lob questions at Mr. Donovan.

"Quiet," he yells. "The next person to interrupt me gets detention for a month."

The room falls silent.

Mr. Donovan rubs his temples and lets out a heavy breath. "We let things get too far out of control. We should have demanded action from the shaders years ago, when we first realized there was a problem." He shakes his head. His tone is far away, as if he's talking to himself, as if he's somewhere other than this classroom. "We're starting to see extreme atypical weather, like this heat wave, in every season. The aurora borealis and the tornado we saw in autumn were both part of this pattern, and it's why our witches are dying from depletion. Winters obviously aren't effective at dealing with heat, so summers are trying to handle the weather in winter, when they're at their weakest. It's too much for them, and it's not doing enough to restore stability, even as it's killing our witches."

The room is quiet for a long time. If Mr. Donovan is right and we continue getting severe atypical weather, witches will become completely ineffectual, and the atmosphere will collapse.

"And if we can't slow the death rate of our witches..." He trails off, but we all know enough to fill in the blank.

Paige raises her hand, and Mr. Donovan nods at her. "What can we do about it?"

"We're working with the shaders to curb the damage, but it's a long process. It'll take years. And while that's ultimately the best thing we can do to restore stability in the atmosphere long-term, we have to find an immediate solution for the problems we're facing today. Our best bet is training witches in off-season magic. Winters can't deal with heat waves because they've never had to; we need to find a way to teach them. Winters must learn about summer conditions. Springs must learn about autumn, summers about winter. Basically, we need to be able to access seasonal magic year-round without our witches dying of depletion."

"But that's impossible," Paige says. "You can't train the hottest magic to deal with ice. It isn't a matter of training; the four magics are fundamentally different."

Mr. Donovan nods. "That's what we're up against," he says. "There's always going to be typical seasonal weather, not to mention harvest and botany. There is no shortage of work or need for us. But that need is growing, and we have to figure out how to meet it. For now, we will continue controlling what we can and training you to be the strongest witches you can be."

I think back to the wildfire training, how I couldn't hold the magic of so many summers. In my training with Sang, I'm working toward being able to confidently hold the power of the witches around me. But even if I master that, it won't help with this. I'll still be holding summer magic in summer and winter magic in winter.

What Mr. Donovan proposed is impossible, just like Paige said.

"So, what should we do about the heat wave next week?" Jay asks.

"Our summers will try to teach you how to manage it. That's all we can do." Mr. Donovan offers a smile, but it's unconvincing. "Once the heat passes, we'll get back to our normal training. Are there any other questions?"

No one says anything, even though there are dozens of questions written on all of our faces.

Class doesn't end for another twenty minutes, but Mr. Donovan walks around his desk, grabs his things, and says, "Class dismissed."

CHAPTER

sixteen

"Work on your relationship with your magic now, because it's going to be the longest relationship you have."

—*A Season for Everything*

"Well, Clara, I'm impressed with your progress thus far. You've got a long way to go, but this is definitely an improvement." Mr. Burrows sounds surprised, and it reinforces my dislike of him.

Knowing my progress is what allows me to keep training with Sang instead of him is the only reason I smile and say, "Thank you."

"Give me just a moment with Ms. Suntile and Sang, won't you?"

I nod and walk to the edge of the control field. There should be snow on the ground and ice covering the pathways around campus. But the ground is bare, and the pathways are dry. The heat will arrive tomorrow, bringing worry and anxiety with it.

And it's not just any heat. We're expecting a four-day stretch of temperatures in the one-tens, unheard of even during summers in Pennsylvania and supposedly impossible in the winter months. It's terrifying, this intense heat we had nothing to do with creating.

I can't help the dread that rises in my stomach, knowing this is a harbinger of what's to come if we can't get things under control.

Mr. Burrows is doing most of the talking as Ms. Suntile and Sang nod along. Every time I start to think Sang and I are building some kind of trust between us, something happens to tear it back down.

It's not his fault, of course. I know Mr. Burrows is his mentor, and they have a lot of history together. A lot of trust between them. But the way he smiles so easily with him and laughs at his jokes and nods his head... It makes me question everything again.

The three of them disperse, walking off the field. Sang smiles and waves, and I nod in his direction. Mr. Burrows catches up with me, and we walk toward the center of campus.

"I'd like to give you a test before I hand you back over to Sang," he says. "It's not ideal, given the heat this week, but it'll have to do."

My stomach feels like it drops right out of my body. A test with Mr. Burrows, with his constant judging and pacing and note-taking, sounds unbearable. I'm not going to be of much use with all this heat.

"What kind of test?"

"It wouldn't be a true test if you could prepare for it in advance, now would it?"

I readjust my bag. "I don't understand what good any of this is doing when it won't make a difference in what's happening out there," I say, motioning to the places beyond this campus.

"But it will make a difference," he says. "We need all the witches we can get, and you're our most powerful one. Or you will be, when I'm done with you."

I fight the urge to roll my eyes. "I just get the sense that nobody really knows what I'm supposed to be capable of, other than 'greatness.' What does that mean in terms of my magic?"

Mr. Burrows hesitates. "You're right, to a certain extent. We don't really know. But everything we do know points to an incredible power we've barely scratched the surface of. And we'll never discover the full extent of your abilities unless you stay committed to your training and keep putting in the work."

The vagueness of the answer frustrates me, but at least he's being honest. I nod and turn to leave, but then he says my name. I look back at him.

"I know this is a grueling process and it feels like you're going in circles. But that accident with Paige? Had that happened a year ago, it would have killed her. You're getting stronger every day, more controlled. And it's going to be worth it." He nods as he says *worth it*, and even though the mention of Paige rouses the fear inside me, it's the first time Mr. Burrows has said something even remotely encouraging.

Maybe I judged him too harshly.

"Okay. I'll keep putting in the work," I finally say.

"I know you will. Meet me at the sundial Wednesday morning at eleven, and we'll do our test. Then I'll be out of your hair again."

I nod and head to the dining hall, leaving Mr. Burrows behind. It's packed by the time I get there, and once I have my food, I walk to the winter table and find a spot at the end.

Dinner tonight is a hearty potato soup, a food I always associate with winter. But without a cold draft leaking through the tall windows and a lack of condensation on the glass, the meal feels out of place.

The dining hall is unusually quiet. Even the summers are more subdued than usual, and I'm surprised to find that I miss the constant stream of laughter that always comes from their table.

Mr. Burrows's test weighs heavily on me. My fingers itch to grab my phone and ask Sang what I'll be facing, but I don't. The last thing I need is for Sang to tell Mr. Burrows I asked and get an even harder test as a result.

And I don't want Sang knowing how nervous I am.

I've tried not to dwell on the fact that I made a vow to get stripped if I couldn't gain control of my magic. It was easier then, when I was planning on getting stripped anyway, when I hadn't felt any joy from my magic. When all I felt was out of control and scared.

But now, the thought of losing my magic is harder to accept. Even if it weren't painful to be stripped, even if I just woke up and it had vanished, I would be devastated. I don't love it the way Sang does or Nikki did, but I'm starting to appreciate it.

It's in these small cracks and erosions of my plan that hope forms. Maybe I will have total control over my magic one day. Maybe I will never hurt another person. Maybe I won't have to get stripped.

Maybe I can have both magic and love.

Maybe.

At 10:55 on Wednesday morning, I sit down at the dial and wait for Mr. Burrows. At the center of campus, a large sundial rises out of a fountain, casting its shadow across the stone encircling it. The granite benches surrounding the fountain are carved with roman numerals that mark the hours.

I love it here, but today is not the day to be outside.

The temperature has already reached triple digits, and I'm wearing shorts and a tank top. There are a few summers at the dial, but even they're having a hard time enjoying the weather.

The shaders have helped us create a world in which we have the freedom to practice magic however we want. They give us resources and support our work, and we protect them. It's a relationship centuries in the making, built on mutual respect and trust.

But it's tenuous. When we wanted to slow down, to stop pouring magic into the farthest reaches of the globe and let the Earth breathe, the shaders wanted to keep moving forward, acting as if our power could undo any amount of damage they caused. We knew we needed their trust in order to maintain our independence, so we kept our mouths shut for too long and asked for more from a world that was already drowning.

Now we're living with the consequences.

But Mr. Donovan said the shaders are working with us now. Maybe they're finally listening; maybe this doesn't have to be our new normal.

Mr. Burrows arrives at the dial at exactly eleven o'clock. Sweat is beaded on his forehead, and he pulls a handkerchief from his pocket.

"Ready?"

I nod and head for the control field, but Mr. Burrows stops me. "This way," he says, and I follow him to the north parking lot.

"Will I be back in time to watch the others train in the heat?"

"You'll get plenty of training in the heat. But our test is going to take place off-site. Practicing on campus is great; it's how we all learn. But I want to see you use your magic in an unfamiliar environment."

"Is Sang or Ms. Suntile coming?"

"It's just us today. They know you're with me, so you'll be excused from your afternoon classes."

Uneasiness moves through me. My mind tells me over and over not to get in the car, but if I don't, Mr. Burrows will have one more reason to get more involved with my training than he already is.

I open the car door and sit down. Classical music plays on the radio, and I watch as Eastern fades into the background. Sang could have at least warned me I'd be going off-campus, but maybe Mr. Burrows told him not to say anything.

After an hour in the car, I ask, "How much longer?"

"About two more hours. We've got to get far enough out so that we can work without disturbing the other witches in the area. I've arranged things so they know where we'll be."

I stare out the passenger window and try to focus on anything but the fear that's taking over. The way the bare trees look so out of place in the sweltering heat. The way the paint lines on the road disappear when Mr. Burrows turns off the highway. The way the dirt road sends dust into the air, blocking my view of the path behind us.

And finally, the way the classical music dies when Mr. Burrows cuts the engine, filling the car with a silence somehow louder than the violin concerto that was just playing.

"Here we are," Mr. Burrows says.

I look around, but I have no idea where we are. We've been off main roads for so long, we might as well be in a different state. I know we're on a mountainside, given the old winding road that brought us here, but there are no trees around. It's all empty.

The car is parked at the end of a road, and Mr. Burrows walks past the barrier in front of us and begins to climb a narrow dirt trail. I take a deep breath and follow him. Heat batters us as we walk over large rocks and through overgrown brush.

"This is an old logging property," he says. "That's why there are no trees."

I don't say anything. We continue to hike up and up and up. I'm drenched in sweat, so tired I doubt I'll be able to complete even the simplest of tests.

Then we stop. We must be close to the top of the mountain. There's a wide-open field that stretches to a rock face in the distance, with patches of grass and wildflowers that cover the dirt. It goes on for acres, stretching out in all directions, and is fully exposed to the sunlight.

It's much larger than the control field on campus, but it reminds me of Eastern. I relax a little.

"The problem with Eastern is that there's no sense of urgency driving you to get stronger," says Mr. Burrows.

"Other than the fact that you keep insisting my magic won't hurt anyone else if I do," I say flatly.

"It's not enough. You've spent your entire life resigned to the fact that people will die because of your magic. Somewhere deep down, you've gotten comfortable with it."

"To hell with what you think. It *haunts* me." My anger mixes with the heat and sweat, my breaths coming as if I've just run a marathon.

Mr. Burrows holds up his hands. "Save your energy, Clara."

The way he says it makes the hairs on my arms stand on end. "What kind of test is this?"

"You don't respect magic, and you've never had to—you're too sheltered at Eastern. When the only thing left is your magic, when that's all you have to rely on, you'll learn to respect it. And that respect will propel you forward and make you far stronger than any kind of training you receive on campus."

"I don't understand. No one else has to train like this."

"No one else is an Ever." Mr. Burrows wipes his brow and

shoves the handkerchief back in his pocket. He looks off into the distance and nods, a small movement I almost miss. I turn and follow his gaze. There's a woman on the far side of the field coming toward us, pulling two children with her. Given how frantic she looks, I'm guessing they're shaders who got caught in the heat. I can't make out many details from here, and I turn back to Mr. Burrows.

"Should we get them out of here before we start the test?"

"No," he says quickly, hardly considering my words. Then he curses and shakes his head. "I left my bag in the car; I have to go back for it. Wait here and get acquainted with the area; send out small pulses of energy and see how it responds. Once I get back, we'll begin."

I gladly take the break. He pauses when he gets to the trail, looking back at me, then at the shaders. I hear one of them yell something, but Mr. Burrows is gone. I need to calm down and clear my head so I can get through this. But nothing feels right. My mind is racing, and the heat is making me light-headed. My shirt clings to my skin, and my legs are weak.

I take several deep breaths.

Mr. Burrows's methods don't have to be traditional; they just have to work. As long as I learn to control my magic without hurting anyone else, that's all I care about.

And I would never admit this out loud, but it isn't just about making sure no one else dies. It's about the possibility that comes with having complete control over who I am.

I pace around the field, waiting for Mr. Burrows. The shaders get closer, and I can now make out the word the woman is saying: "Help."

I rush over to her, and I know what's wrong before she begins speaking. They all have heat exhaustion, her kids worse than her. They're sweating profusely, and their breaths are shallow. Their skin is red, and there's vomit on her little boy's T-shirt.

"How long have you been out here?" I ask, wincing when my words come out sounding more accusatory than I mean.

"We got stuck early this morning. I wasn't expecting it to get so hot so early. They're too weak to hike down," she says, each word slamming into the next. "I can't carry them both, and my phone doesn't have any service."

"Okay, we'll get you out of here," I say. "Wait here."

A car engine starts in the distance.

I whip around to face the trailhead. Mr. Burrows is nowhere in sight.

"Stop!" I yell, rushing to the trail, but I stumble back when a small glimmer catches my eye. I look closely, and the glimmer gets bigger and bigger, distorting the area it covers, almost like a wall of water reflecting sunlight.

That's when I realize what Mr. Burrows is doing. He's creating a sunbar, a tool we only ever use in summer as a warm-up before we train. It's a concentrated wall of sunlight a shader could never get through. It would burn them instantly.

I survey the field. Walls of rocks rise up around the far end, so steep we'd need climbing equipment to scale them.

He trapped us here.

But I question myself as soon as I think it. There's no way he'd leave me here, and certainly not with innocent people.

The sunbar gets wider and higher, rays of sunlight sparkling on its surface. Soon, it's blocking not only the trail but the entire south side of the field. I look at it in wonder. Mr. Burrows is a winter; there's no way he'd be able to command this much sunlight. Even a summer would have a hard time creating a sunbar that large.

There have to be other witches involved, but I can't imagine anyone going along with this awful plan. There's no way Ms. Suntile would sign off on it, no way Sang would help.

I'm sure of it.

Almost.

The sound of Mr. Burrows's engine fades into the distance.

There's just silence.

I pull my cell phone from my pocket, but I know even before looking that I have no service. I lost reception an hour into the drive.

My breathing gets faster, and the world spins around me. I sink to the ground.

The midday sun is unrelenting, stagnant, heavy air that suffocates. Every part of me feels the rising temperature—105, 110, 115 degrees.

Mr. Burrows trapped a family and left me here to deal with it alone in the worst heat wave Pennsylvania has ever seen. A heat wave our winter witches cannot manage.

I have no supplies.

No food.

No shelter.

There may or may not be water in the ground, depending on when the last rain was. My magic may or may not be strong enough to find it.

And a family will die if I don't do something.

seventeen

"You are stronger than you think."
—*A Season for Everything*

My clothes are damp with sweat. My jean shorts are soaked through, and my tank top clings to my skin. It is so hot.

For a while, I don't move from my spot in the field. The winter sun makes me feel as if I'm hallucinating, it's so eerily low in the sky. It should be high above me to produce this kind of heat, but it stays close to the horizon. It's so bright.

Too bright for winter.

I push myself up. My legs shake when I stand, and everything spins. I take several deep breaths and walk over to the woman. Each step is work, as if my ankles are bound in weights. I curse myself for not eating breakfast this morning and try not to think about how the last time I ate or drank anything was last night.

"What's your name?" I ask when I reach the shader. Neither of her kids is standing anymore; they're both lying on the ground, chests rising and falling rapidly. They can't be more than eight years old.

"I want to go home," one of them cries. They either don't notice me or are too weak to care that I'm here.

"I'm Angela," the woman says. "I need help getting them down, please." Her words are fast and strained. "It kept getting hotter and hotter, and they just got too weak to move." She's crying now, large tears running down her cheeks.

There's an empty water bottle on the grass between her kids. "Do you have any more water?"

She shakes her head.

"Okay, Angela, I'm Clara. I'm going to help you." There's a sweatshirt hanging out of her day pack. "You have to get your kids out of the sun. Take them to the rocks, and find a stick to use as a pole— you can shove the hem of your sweatshirt into the crevices between the rocks and put your hood over the stick to create some shade. You don't want them to burn any more than they have already."

"No, no, we need to get them down the mountain, to the main road. They can't stay in this heat."

I glance over at the sunbar and lower my voice. "Unless you want to climb the rock face, we can't. The only other way out is blocked. Do you see that glimmer in the distance? The way the air looks somewhat distorted?" She nods. "It's called a sunbar. Witches use it to train; it's basically a thin wall of intensely focused sunlight. You can't walk through it."

"But I saw someone with you—I know I did. Can't he help us?"

I take a deep breath, and rage roils inside me as I think of Mr. Burrows and his reckless test. "He's gone," I say.

Angela's eyes get wide. She angles away from her children.

"Are you saying we're stuck here?" She gets the words out through clenched teeth.

"Yes."

Her breaths come quickly, and she chokes. "We have to get them out of here. You have to help me."

Their skin is red, and they look lethargic, fully exposed to all 115 degrees of heat.

"There isn't anywhere for us to go," I say as gently as I can. "Get them in the shade, and I'm going to look for water."

"Where?"

"In the soil. In the grass. Over the rocks. Wherever I can."

Angela stares at me for a few seconds before realization hits. "You're a witch."

I nod. "Get them into some shade."

One of her kids starts crying as she coaxes them up and moves them to the rocks. I grab their empty water bottle and turn away. I'm getting dehydrated, and with how much I've been sweating, everything's accelerated.

There is nothing I can do in this heat. I can barely think. But the sun will set soon, and the long winter night will cover us.

Water. I need to find water.

Witches can't be burned by the sun, but we can still suffer from exhaustion and heatstroke. In this kind of heat, without any shelter, I could survive without water for three days, if I was lucky. But the shaders don't have that kind of time.

Mr. Burrows will come back before the risk to them is too great. He has to.

When the only thing left is your magic, when that's all you have to rely on, you'll learn to respect it.

That's when I fully understand the test. Mr. Burrows purposely put shaders at risk to force me to use my magic, knowing they won't survive without it.

Part of me wants to die out here just so Mr. Burrows has to deal with the consequences, but he's not worth it. And I refuse to let this family suffer.

I turn back and see Angela hurrying toward her kids with a long stick. She pounds it into the dirt and gets her sweatshirt stretched out between the rocks and the stick. She carries her kids under the makeshift tent.

I walk farther away, listening for anything that sounds like water. But there's nothing.

I reach for my magic. It's faint and weak, but at least there's something. Maybe I just need to sit down again.

I lower myself to the ground and shove my hands into the dirt. I take a few deep breaths and send my magic into the earth, the icy feeling cooling my insides. It makes my thoughts just a little sharper. But it doesn't have the aggressive rush I'm used to during winter. It's slow and heavy, reacting to the heat. My body is so busy trying to cool itself down that there's hardly any energy left for magic. It crawls out of me and along the dirt as if in slow motion.

But it's enough to sense water. I thank the Sun for the recent rain, keeping the earth full of moisture. All I have to do is extract it from the ground and form a small rain cloud.

I try not to think about the sweat lining my neck and fore-head, dripping down my chest. All the water I'm losing that isn't being replenished.

I sit back on my heels and close my eyes. My magic is a shadow of itself. In this heat, it's inefficient at best, completely useless at worst.

But still, I focus everything I have on the moisture in the ground. I pull and pull and pull, and finally, a small rain cloud appears. My arms are shaking, and my jaw is clenched, the over-whelming heat threatening to abolish the cloud before I can make it rain. I move it over the water bottle, and as gently as possible, I drain the cloud.

It's barely enough water for a single person, let alone four of us. But it's something.

I look back at Angela. She's far in the distance, but I can see her kids under the tent, can see her sitting next to them.

The sun dips below the horizon, the last rays of sunlight illu-minating the sky in oranges and pinks. Then it's gone. Everything is so quiet.

Twilight moves over the field, and soon I'm enveloped in darkness.

I take my phone out and turn on the flashlight. The low bat-tery warning pops up on the screen. I make my way toward Angela and her kids.

"That's all there is?" she asks, her voice trembling, taking in the half-full water bottle.

"For now," I say. "The temperature will go down overnight,

and hopefully my body will regulate. I'll try for more in the morning, before the sun is up."

I look at her kids. They're asleep, but their breathing is shallow.

"Wake them up. They need to drink," I say, handing her the bottle. "You too." I try to ignore her excessive sweating, the way she rubs the muscles in her calf.

Once the kids have their water and I make sure their temperatures are under control, they fall back asleep. Angela takes a small sip and hands the remainder to me.

"No," I say. "Drink it."

She nods, then lies down next to her children. I watch them for several seconds. Another day out here will be catastrophic for them—organ failure, brain damage, death; it's all a risk. The reality barrels down on me like a rockslide.

My heart races as I walk farther down the rock edge, close enough to hear them if they need me. I finally lie down. My clothes are still wet from earlier, and goose bumps form all over my body.

My stomach rolls with hunger, and my mouth is dry.

Tomorrow is a fresh start. If I can just sleep, I can regain some strength and try again. The night air is still hot, still clammy, but without the sun shining, there's a respite from the intense heat.

I shift on the grass and curl into myself. Stars shine overhead, and a crescent moon hangs in the night sky. It's clear enough to see the Milky Way.

It's peaceful here, and I think how much I'd love it if I weren't so scared. So angry. So weak.

I think Sang would love it too.

The thought pops into my mind unbidden, and I try to force it back out.

I wrap my arms around my chest and roll onto my side. Eventually, my breathing slows, and my eyelids fall closed.

It is very still and very dark.

eighteen

"*Discovery is a gift: discovering ourselves, and discovering others.*"

—*A Season for Everything*

I dream that I'm not alone. Sang is with me. He sleeps beside me with his arm draped over my side, and I am not scared.

I am content beneath the sparkling starlight.

When I wake, I slowly sit up. My skin is sticky with sweat. My head is throbbing, and I push my fingers against my temples, trying to rub the pain away.

It's still dark out.

I'm covered in dirt, and several pieces of grass are stuck in my curly hair.

I stand up and brace myself for the inevitable dizziness. Nausea roils my stomach. I take a steadying breath, but it's no use.

I drop to the earth and dry heave. With my stomach already empty, it doesn't last long. I push my hands into the dirt and spit. When I'm sure it's over, I slowly stand.

The spinning isn't as bad this time, and I manage to stay upright until it stops completely. My heart thumps rapidly.

Even in the dark, it's so hot.

But sleeping was good for me. Magic pulses beneath my skin, stronger than yesterday. It's nowhere near its usual strength—most of my energy is still going toward keeping my body cool—but it's there.

And it might be enough.

Dawn begins to stretch across the field. I rush to where Angela and her kids are sleeping, and when I'm sure they're stable, I grab the empty water bottle. Once I get far enough away so as not to disturb them, I build small rain clouds over and over until I've filled the bottle to the top.

Rays of sunlight appear from the east, painting the field in golden streaks. But everything is quiet. Animals are asleep, burrowed underground. Most of the birds have migrated south, and the world is still in a way only winter can orchestrate.

I walk back to Angela. She's awake now, watching her kids sleep. Their little chests rise rapidly, and sweat lines their faces. But that's good. Once the body loses the ability to cool itself, sweat can no longer form, and heat exhaustion turns into heatstroke.

I hand Angela the bottle of water, and she takes a small sip.

"Mommy, my head hurts," her little girl says, starting to cry.

"I know, baby, I know," Angela says, giving her some water. "This will make you feel better."

We have to get them out of here.

I look at the sunbar in the distance, the way the light glitters and moves across the field. I won't be able to dismantle it, not when it's so big. Not when I'd have to fight against the witches who are keeping it there.

"We need to talk," I say to Angela. She nods and follows me out of earshot of her children. She sways on her feet, steadying herself against the rock face.

"You all have heat exhaustion," I say. "Once it turns into heatstroke, you won't have a lot of time before medical attention becomes necessary."

"But we're stuck," Angela says, looking at the sunbar, then back at me. Her voice wobbles.

"I have to go for help," I say.

"No, you can't leave us—"

"I *have* to," I say, looking her in the eye, making sure she understands what I'm saying.

"Can you get through the sunbar?" she asks.

I look back at it and nod. "It'll take a lot of my energy, but yes. It won't burn me the way it would you." What I don't tell her is that it'll likely send me right into heatstroke, and I won't have much time before I pass out from it.

But it's the only way.

"I'm going to try and make you some hailstones. They won't last all day, but they'll help."

"Thank you," she says, her voice small and scared.

I walk to the other side of the field, a safe distance away, and get to work.

Magic rises inside me. I take a long, deep breath and hope the freezing current gives me enough energy for what I need to do. On my exhale, I close my eyes. The cold flow of winter pours through my fingers and into the earth, searching out every drop of water it can find.

When the flow of magic is heavy with moisture, almost too much to carry, I pull. I pull as hard as I can, with every bit of energy I have. My pulse is racing, and I'm dizzy, but still I pull. The cold magic stings against the sweltering heat, but still I pull.

I'm sweating, and my breathing is so shallow and so fast. But still I pull.

In one swift motion, I send the droplets of water into an updraft of air, freezing them as they rise. Once they get heavy enough, they begin to fall, amassing more water. I shoot them back into the updraft, refreezing them. I do it over and over and over again. They have to get large enough that they don't melt right away.

But it's so hard. I'm breathless. My skin is clammy. I'm lightheaded, and the ground seems to tilt beneath me. I struggle to stay upright.

I struggle against the 113 degrees of heat.

I struggle to remember why I'm doing this, why I'm here.

I keep going, but my magic falters. I'm not strong enough to hold the updraft needed for the hailstones to keep freezing. They begin to drop.

They'll all melt if I can't get them high enough, vanishing before they can do any good.

"Clara!" Angela calls in the distance. "He isn't responding to me. He just passed out!"

I can do this. I *have* to do this. My hands shake, and my face is tense, eyes squeezed shut and jaw clenched tight.

Then I remember Sang and the waterfall. I'm in the current, rushing toward it. I have to choose to fall.

I take a long, deep breath. I inhale my fear—fear that I won't succeed, fear that Angela and her children will die out here. Fear that the Earth has been hurt so badly that we can never make it whole again. Fear that I will never be enough.

Then I let it all go. I release all the tension in my body, tilt my head back, let the current push me over the edge.

I'm in a free fall of magic, power bursting from my fingers and into the air, tossing the hail higher and higher as if it's weightless. I create as much hail as possible, stones dropping out of the sky in rapid succession.

When I open my eyes, I'm stunned. The field is covered in them, hailstones the size of peony blooms.

My head is pounding. All I want to do is sleep.

I gather as many as I can and rush them to Angela. I hand her a hailstone. "Hold this to his mouth," I say. Angela takes it, hands shaking. "Come on, baby," she whispers over and over.

I grab more hailstones and pack them all around the boy, against his neck and armpits and legs. His eyes slowly open, and I breathe out in relief.

But he isn't sweating, and when I put my hand to his forehead, I can feel the heat rolling inside him. Angela and her daughter aren't far behind.

I have to get them out of here.

I gather more hailstones and pile them up around both kids. "Stay with them. Keep putting ice around them, and yourself too. I'm going to get help."

"Clara," Angela whispers, touching my arm. "You don't look well."

"I'm okay," I say.

She grabs my hand and looks into my eyes, worried and scared and red with tears. "Thank you."

I nod and walk toward the sunbar, keeping my steps as steady as possible so Angela doesn't see how drained I am.

My cell phone is dead, but if I can get to the road, I have a chance of seeing another person. All I have to do is walk.

The sunbar warps the space in front of me, and nausea coats my stomach.

I take a running start, close my eyes, and jump through it.

I gasp when pure sunlight pierces my skin and cradles my organs. My temperature rises like a balloon that's slipped through my fingers, going up and up and up.

I collapse when I get to the other side.

I choke on the air and claw at the earth.

Maybe I could sleep right here. I want to sleep.

My head throbs.

I force myself to stand.

I step over rocks and through underbrush, following the path I came up yesterday. I'm careful with each step I take.

I'm not sure how much time has passed when I finally see the tire marks left by Mr. Burrows's car. We were on the dirt road for a long time, but a road is easier to follow than a narrow path.

I keep going.

My shoes kick up dust, and my legs are caked in dirt. My shallow breathing is the only sound disrupting the perfect silence of the mountainside. The day gets hotter.

My legs get heavier and heavier until I'm sure each step will be my last.

I have to cool down. With everything I have, I pull just enough magic to the surface of my skin that it produces a cooling effect throughout my body. The bite, the perfect cold of winter, settles in my skin, and I breathe out in relief. It feels as if I drank enough ice water to permeate my whole body. I walk faster.

A slight breeze moves through the air, and I kick up my magic enough to get a stronger current going.

I close my eyes and breathe some more.

My heart is pounding fast and hard. I wish I could slow it down. It's taking everything I have just to stay awake, just to keep breathing.

I follow a bend in the road, and in the distance is sharp, blinding sunlight.

I trip and stumble toward it. I'm not sweating anymore, and my lungs hiss from the effort it takes to breathe.

With shaking hands, I release some magic to the earth and form one more rain cloud. It's small, barely enough for a full drink. It will have to do for now.

I stare at the main road, at the sunlight hitting the pavement, and I steady myself. I can do this.

With one shaky step after another, I walk to the end of the dirt road.

Everything looks distorted, as if there's an Earth-sized sunbar between me and the rest of the world.

The temperature ticks up now that I've lost the elevation of the mountain.

One hundred and twenty-one degrees slam into me, and for a moment I think I will ignite upon impact.

But I don't. So I keep walking.

One foot in front of the other.

Left.

Right.

Breathe.

nineteen

"I've had moments of despair and deep resentment. But then I stand outside and touch the earth, feel the magic in my fingertips, and understand that this is how it's meant to be. The sun and stars conspired for me, and I am filled with gratitude."

—*A Season for Everything*

I have been walking for hours. I think it's been hours. Maybe it's been minutes. I don't know. The heat wave must be keeping people indoors, because only a handful of cars have passed me. I waved at them all, but none of them stopped.

Then again, maybe I'm delirious. Maybe I didn't wave at all.

My vision is blurry, and the road stretches out so far in front of me that it fades into the horizon.

My magic is the only reason I've been able to make it this far. It moves underneath my skin, keeping my body as cool as it can. But even magic is finite, and when it runs out, so will I.

Headlights appear in the distance, blurry white orbs moving toward me.

"Help." I try to yell the word, but it's inaudible. I clear my throat. "Help," I say again. This time, the word is a whisper.

I can't think straight.

I have to wave, get the driver's attention somehow. My brain tries to send the signal to my arms, but they don't move.

"Help," I say again, and with every ounce of strength I can gather, I lift my arms above my head. It feels as if I'm lifting the weight of the whole world.

But it works.

The truck slows and pulls over.

Sang jumps out, and now I'm sure I'm imagining things. He's running toward me.

I want to yell at him. I want to scream and push him away for not warning me about this test, for not trying to stop it.

I want to collapse in his arms. I want to cry and cling to him because I'm so relieved he's here.

He rushes to my side and wraps an arm around my waist. He is searching my face, and his lips are moving, but I can't hear what he's saying.

He's so blurry.

"Family. Mountain," I manage to get out.

I can't support my head anymore, can't support anything. All at once, my strength is gone, and my legs give out.

My magic is the last thing I feel, still working when everything else has stopped.

Then darkness.

When I open my eyes, I'm in a truck. It's moving quickly, trees passing by the window in a blur. There are cold, damp cloths on my forehead and chest.

I roll my head away from the window. Sang is focusing on the road, squeezing the wheel so tightly his knuckles are white. The edge of his hand is covered in faint pink paint.

I reach out my hand, run my fingers across his jaw. He looks stunned. His eyes get teary.

Then he places his hand over mine.

I can't hold my arm up anymore.

"I wish I hated you," I say.

Then I'm gone again.

I'm admitted to the hospital with a temperature of 111 degrees. Nurses and doctors swarm around me and get me in an ice bath less than ten minutes after Sang carries me in. I convulse in the tub.

Once my temperature lowers, they put me in a bed with cooling blankets and hook me up to an IV. The doctor taking care of me, Dr. Singh, looks at me in wonder and tells me I'm "miraculously stable." She stays past her shift to monitor me.

A nurse takes my blood pressure and pulse, then asks me if I'm up to seeing a visitor.

I nod, and few moments later, Sang walks into the room.

He doesn't hesitate. He rushes to the bed and puts his hand on my arm. His eyes are bloodshot, and his skin is splotchy. He brushes the hair out of my face, looks me up and down as if to reassure himself that I'm real.

"The family—" I start, but Sang cuts me off.

"They're okay. Mr. Burrows picked them up this morning."

"He came back?"

Sang takes a breath. "He was staying at a motel not far from the logging property. The test was much more controlled than he let you believe—he only started to panic when he showed up this morning and you were gone. He thought you'd never get through the sunbar."

Anger rises inside me, and a machine to my left beeps as my heart rate increases. Mr. Burrows let me believe Angela and her children would die. That I was their only hope.

I shake my head. I'm angry, but I'm also embarrassed. I fell for it.

Sang looks so upset. "Mr. Burrows called me this morning when he realized you were gone. It took hours to find you—you went the wrong way on the main road," he says. "You were delirious from the heat."

"Angela is okay? Her kids?"

"Yes," Sang says, and my whole body calms with that single word. "They'll be fine, entirely thanks to your hailstones. There were so many. How did you do it?"

"I imagined myself in the river," I say quietly.

The gold in Sang's eyes blurs.

But then I remember him talking with Mr. Burrows, and I'm angry again.

I pull my arm out of his reach and sit up straight.

"How could you not warn me?"

Sang doesn't respond right away. He looks confused. When he finally speaks, his voice is strained. "Warn you? I didn't even know it was happening."

"He said you knew I was with him."

"I did, but that's all I knew. If I had known what he was planning, I never would have let it happen." His hands are balled into fists on my bed, so tight they're shaking.

I don't want to believe him. I remember the way he stood on the field with Mr. Burrows and laughed with him, and I'm ready to yell that I never want to see him again.

"But I saw you with him and Ms. Suntile right before he told me we'd be doing the test."

"If you can only trust me if I never speak with Mr. Burrows, we may as well give up now."

"It isn't just that. He's your mentor, Sang. You respect him."

"I need to talk with him when we get back. See where his head was at." Again, I almost yell at him, demand that he leave. But then he hangs his head and says, "I might have to reevaluate some things." And the pain in his voice is so apparent that it takes all the fight out of me.

He respects Mr. Burrows the way I respected Mr. Hart. Seeing the person you've looked up to morph into someone so different would be devastating.

I'm quiet for a long time. "I'm sorry. I thought you knew about the test."

Sang looks directly at me. "I'm sorry for whatever I did to make you think I would be okay with something like that."

I'm not sure what to say, so I don't say anything at all.

Dr. Singh comes in to check on me once more before leaving for the night. She listens to my heart and checks my IV, then pulls up a chair.

"Are you family?" she asks Sang.

He shakes his head. "Should I leave?"

Dr. Singh looks at me. "He can stay," I say.

"We're going to do some blood work in the morning, once you've had more fluids and remain stable through the night. At a temperature of one hundred and seven degrees, multiple organ failure can occur. At one hundred and ten, brain damage and death. Your temperature was one degree higher than that when you showed up, and quite frankly, I didn't think you'd make it."

I take in a sharp breath.

"We won't have the full picture until we run your labs in the morning, but your vitals are good, and you're not showing any signs of distress. You're extremely lucky, Clara, even for a witch. Try to get some sleep tonight, and I'll see you in the morning."

Dr. Singh walks out of the room, and I hear her tell my nurse to page her if anything changes overnight.

I turn to look at Sang, but his eyes are on the chair Dr. Singh was in just moments ago.

"I'm tired," I say.

Sang stands. "I'll go."

But the thought of being alone terrifies me, as if I could end up back in that field at any moment, completely exposed and so weak I can hardly stand. I reach out and touch my fingers to his. I fight the urge to pull him into me, to fold into him. To press my head to his chest and let the beating of his heart lull me to sleep.

"Maybe don't?"

Sang looks down at his hand, then back at me. Something like relief flares in his eyes. He nods, leaves the room, and comes back a few minutes later with a pillow and blanket.

He doesn't say anything. He simply turns out the light, walks to the couch, and lies down.

I can't see him, but his presence is enough. If I weren't so tired, if I weren't so angry, it might worry me that him being here matters to me. That it matters more than it should.

The machines in my room beep in time with my heart, and for some reason I can't explain, it comforts me.

"Thank you for coming for me," I say into the darkness.

A pause. Then, "Always."

twenty

"There is nothing more powerful than being understood."
—A Season for Everything

All of my blood work comes back normal, and I'm sent home the next day. Dr. Singh says mine is one of the most surprising cases she has seen in all her years of medicine, witch or shader.

The car ride back to Eastern is long. Sang asks repeatedly if I'm comfortable, fidgeting with the temperature control and telling me multiple times how to adjust my seat. But other than being weak and tired, I'm fine.

Both of our hands sit open on the center console, just inches apart. The space feels alive, as if there's an electrical current running between us. I've never been more aware of my hand in my life.

I finally move it to my lap and look out the window.

"Do you know what the most frustrating thing about this is?" I ask after a particularly long stretch of silence.

"What?"

"Mr. Burrows said the reason he was leaving me on the mountain was because I didn't respect my magic and that I'd learn to if I was forced to rely on it. And he was right. My magic is what kept Angela and her kids alive, maybe even me. The reason I didn't go into organ failure is because it never stopped pulsing through me. It cooled me down. It couldn't do a damn thing to stop the heat wave, but it's the only thing that kept me alive."

"He didn't have to leave you on a mountain to teach you that." Sang's voice isn't aggressive or angry. It's sad.

I don't say anything, because I'm not sure he's right. I've hated my magic for so long, it's hard to imagine that I could have learned to respect it without something drastic like what Mr. Burrows did. But then I think back to my training sessions with Sang, and I'm not actually sure I hated it anymore. I didn't love it—I still don't—but I was learning to appreciate it. Maybe I was learning to respect it too.

"Maybe not," I finally say. "But I think I was starting to learn it from you."

Sang doesn't respond, but the smallest hint of a smile forms on his lips.

It's lunchtime when we pull into the Eastern parking lot, but everyone is inside. No one wants to be out in this heat, not even the summers.

I step out of Sang's truck and groan. Today is supposed to be the last day of the heat wave, and then we can get back to winter. But this has been another reminder that things are shifting, that we don't have as much control as we used to. That we need help if we're going to undo all the damage that's been done. The witches in charge of this area must be exhausted from trying to deal with the heat.

I think back to Mr. Donovan's class, to what he told us about witches dying from depletion, and I finally understand it.

Winter magic is useless in a heat wave, and the summers are too weak for their magic to be effective right now. But they try to help anyway, because this world is everything to them.

And they die because of it.

Ms. Suntile rushes out to meet us. Her forehead is creased with worry, and her lips are pulled into a frown. "Thank the Sun you're here," she says. "How are you?"

"I've been better."

"Mr. Park said the doctor released you with instructions to rest, but otherwise you're fine?" Her eyes move from me to Sang.

"Fine? I was left in the middle of nowhere by a teacher during the worst heat wave in history. I'm not fine."

Ms. Suntile winces. "Of course not. I'm sorry. I just meant that I'm glad you'll make a full recovery."

I'm already sweating from the temperature outside. "I'm going to my cabin to rest."

"Good, that's good." Ms. Suntile walks beside me. "Mr. Burrows would like to see you when you're feeling up to it." Her tone is uncertain.

I stop walking. "He's here?"

"Yes, and I can imagine you're displeased with him. Those circumstances were too perilous for a test, and we are working out the appropriate—"

"Where is he?" I cut her off.

Ms. Suntile checks her watch. "I believe he's in the dining hall eating lunch."

I change direction, no longer interested in getting to my cabin. Ms. Suntile and Sang follow me, struggling to keep up.

"You should rest before speaking with him," Ms. Suntile says, but I keep moving.

Sang keeps pace with me, and we burst through the dining hall doors at the same time. The hall is packed and noisy, and it takes several seconds before I spot Mr. Burrows in the far corner.

My entire body responds, shaking with rage. My heart slams against my ribs. The noise of the dining hall fades until all I can hear is the rush of blood surging through my arteries.

I storm across the room. Mr. Burrows stands when he sees me, and before he can say anything, before I even have time to think, I punch him in the face so hard I feel his nose crack under my knuckles.

He staggers back and hits the wall behind him. He covers his face with his hands, but there's so much blood rushing from his nose that it runs through his fingers and dribbles to the floor.

My hand throbs, and I want to cry out, but I bite my tongue and force the pain aside. It was worth it.

The dining hall gets very quiet. Everyone is staring.

"Ms. Densmore, in all my years—"

I whip around to Ms. Suntile. "I don't know who helped him or who signed off on what he did, but I will *never* be put in a situation like that again. I will sit in my cabin all day every day until you expel me before I do another test like that." I try to keep my voice steady, but it rises and rises, piercing the air. I sound hysterical.

But I get my point across. Ms. Suntile clenches her jaw and nods once.

"And yet, somewhere in the back of your mind, you wonder if this exercise wasn't exactly what you needed. No other winter could have produced that kind of hail in these weather conditions. You were extraordinary out there." Mr. Burrows says it through bloody fingers, but his tone is confident.

I look at him. "Who helped you with the sunbar? I know you couldn't have done that on your own."

"I told the witches controlling the area that a sunbar of that magnitude would help mitigate some of the effects of the heat wave, which isn't entirely untrue. The sunbar did end up absorbing enough sunlight to lower the temperature by a few degrees." Mr. Burrows still manages to sound condescending, even with his face bloody.

"You let me believe that family would *die*," I say.

"And look how well you did because of it. You were in total control out there."

Ms. Suntile hands him a towel, and he holds it up to his face.

"You should get that checked out," I say.

I turn and walk out of the dining hall. The weight of hundreds of eyes follows me.

I rush to my cabin, and as soon as I'm inside, I hold my crushed hand to my chest. All the adrenaline drains out of my system. I scream.

Tears burn my eyes and rush down my cheeks. I grip my aching hand. A large bruise spreads across my knuckles and turns my skin the color of twilight.

I kick off my shoes and crawl into bed with Alice's memoir. Even though she loved her magic in a way I'm not sure I ever will, her words have become a comfort for me, a security blanket. They're the first thing I reach for.

I throw the covers off. The cabin is so hot, heat clinging to the stale air as if the Sun herself resides here. It intensifies the musty smell.

Nox runs in through the cat door and launches himself onto the bed.

"It's so good to see you," I say, pulling him close to my chest. He wriggles away and walks on top of my side, purring.

There's a knock at the door. I don't say anything, but Sang steps inside anyway. He's carrying a bag of ice and some crushed lavender. I give him a grateful look and set the book aside.

He pulls over a chair, and I place my hand down in front of him without saying anything.

"Clara," he starts, and I think he's about to reprimand me for punching his mentor. But he doesn't. "That was *amazing*. I wish you could have seen what happened after you left. There was just this bewildered silence, then Mr. Burrows walked out and the whole room erupted into conversation."

"I admit it would have been better to do that in private."

"Maybe," Sang says, wrapping the ice in a towel. "But it was pretty spectacular as it was."

We're both quiet for a minute.

"That test—it was too big a risk," Sang says. "He couldn't have known for sure that the shaders would survive."

"You didn't think I'd save them?" I ask, my tone playful, trying to lighten the mood.

"I don't gamble with people's lives," he says. "But if I did, I'd put my money on you." He looks up at me. "Every. Single. Time."

Sang is gently holding the bag of ice against my hand, but I swear I can feel his fingers as if the bag doesn't exist.

His words are so genuine I have to look away.

I remind myself that I just went through something traumatic. The way my insides tighten when he looks at me like this, the way I want him near—it isn't real.

It can't be real.

It's a product of going through an awful experience and having him here at the end of it.

I clear my throat. "For a minute there, I thought *you* were going to hit him," I say, another attempt to make the space between us lighter.

He smiles this time. "Nah, I saw the look in your eyes and knew you had it."

We both look down at my bruised hand. And at the exact same moment, we burst out laughing.

"The horror on Ms. Suntile's face..." Sang starts, but he can't get the rest of the sentence out.

"I'm such a mess," I say, still laughing.

I punched a teacher in the face. In front of the entire school.

"A mess is something that needs to be cleaned up. You're not a mess." He looks at me then, and his face turns oddly serious. He is no longer laughing. "You're a force to be reckoned with."

Sang gently places the lavender on my skin. It reminds me of the day we met, when he helped me after the tornado.

Before he was assigned to train me.

Before trusting him wasn't so complicated.

I used to think Sang's openness was a way to manipulate me, to wield power over me the way Eastern and Ms. Suntile and Mr. Burrows do.

Maybe I was wrong.

Maybe what Sang wants isn't power.

Maybe it's to help me regain all the power I've ever given away.

"I am?" My voice is quiet.

"You are the most magnificently disruptive thing that's ever entered my life."

I stare at him, stunned by his words. I swallow hard. "What happened to that bit about the sleeping orange and only opening up if someone tries to see you? You're an open book with me." I say it lightly, like a joke, trying to clear the air of what he just said.

But it doesn't help. His words slide into my core and drop anchor, securing themselves to me forever.

I'm not a mess. I'm a force. A magnificently disruptive force.

"I feel seen by you." He says it simply, as if it's obvious and not an incredible admission.

But the thing that terrifies me, that makes me want to run from this room, isn't that Sang feels seen by me.

It's that I feel seen by him.

"I think I should probably get some rest," I say.

"That sounds like a good idea."

Sang finishes wrapping my hand with the lavender and puts some extra on my bedside table. "Sleep with this on. It'll help keep the swelling down."

I nod.

Sang scratches Nox on the head, turns on my fan, and heads to the door.

"Hey, Sang?"

He turns to look at me. The floor creaks beneath his weight.

"Thank you."

He smiles and shuts the door behind him. I feel his absence as soon as he leaves, a heaviness that makes me question what he is to me.

But I can't question it. He can't be anything to me.

I'm making progress with him, more progress than I've ever made with anyone. And that's when I realize that what I'm feeling is nothing more than gratitude for helping me get stronger. Respect for his patience with me. Appreciation for his own abilities.

That's it.

I need to rest. I close my eyes, relieved to have worked out my feelings.

But it's a fitful sleep.

twenty-one

"You are more than your magic. Spend time with people who know that so they can remind you of it when you forget."

—*A Season for Everything*

Weeks pass. Mr. Burrows keeps his job because I've gotten "so much stronger under his guidance" and "he was close by for the whole test."

The bruise on my hand heals.

There is snow on the ground.

There's frost on the trees.

The temperature drops below freezing and stays there, as if guarding against another heat wave.

My training goes back to normal, and Mr. Burrows still makes the lesson plans. I hate knowing he has sway over what I do, but the silver lining is the weekly updates Sang gives me on the state of his bruised face.

Ever since getting back to campus, I've plateaued. Sang hasn't mentioned it, but I'm sure he's noticed. It would be impossible not to. I'm worried the heat wave had some kind of permanent impact on my magic, but I can't figure out how that could've happened. It scares me.

Witches continue to die. Pennsylvania isn't the only place in the world experiencing atypical weather, and witches in their off-seasons keep stepping up to help. They die of depletion while the witches whose season it is stand by helplessly.

And it will get worse. The fewer witches we have controlling the atmosphere, the more erratic the weather will become. It's one thing for heat waves and hailstorms to occur during seasons whose witches can't help, but what happens when it's hurricanes and famines and droughts? If the atmosphere devolves into chaos, civilization will follow.

Maybe that's why I've plateaued—I've seen firsthand the effects of unseasonal weather, and I can't do anything about it. The fact that I can supposedly combine the power of dozens of witches into one intense stream of magic doesn't mean anything in this evolving atmosphere. Right now, I'm a winter witch, but what good is a powerful thread of winter magic when the only way to address a heat wave in February is with the magic of summer? And I can't help with that.

Maybe that's why Sang hasn't said anything about my lack of progress. Maybe that's why the administration has gone easy on me—because they know my power wouldn't do any good.

A year ago, that would have been an incredible relief. But now it fills me with dread.

I take a deep breath and slowly exhale. Tonight is one of my favorite nights of the year, and I want to enjoy it.

It's our Celebration of Light, and while I love all the season-end celebrations at Eastern, this one is my favorite. Ms. Suntile even let me join the rest of the winters to prepare, and we spent the past week constructing a massive ice dome for the occasion.

It's sitting in the middle of the control field, a place where I have experienced so much failure and disappointment and fear. And recently, a place where I have experienced success and contentment and pride. I wish I could get those successes back somehow.

The ice keeps most of the sound from drifting out, a low murmur of voices and music all I can hear. The night is clear, and the sky is black. A waxing moon provides enough light to cast the dome in a blue glow, and stars poke through the darkness like needles through fabric, sharp and bright.

But the amazing thing is that because the dome is thin as glass, the stars are visible from inside as well. I walk in and look up, and sure enough, they're on full display, along with the moon. It takes a lot of magic to make ice that clear, and I'm amazed by the effect.

A large chandelier hangs in the center of the dome with hundreds of crystals carved from ice. Small birch trees line the perimeter, their branches bare and covered in frost that sparkles in the light. A dance floor sits in the middle of the dome, and it feels as if we're in a snow globe.

At first, I thought we were going overboard, trying to compensate for the week we lost to the heat, but seeing it now, I don't think that anymore.

I think it's perfect.

Sang did the floral arrangements in shades of deep purple and white. The room is dim, and a live quartet plays instrumental pieces. All the winters wear shades of crimson, and the rest of the witches wear anything but.

That's something I like about Eastern: when it's your season, you get the spotlight. The different seasons may not always understand one another, but they certainly respect everyone's turn with the sun.

I walk to the bar and get a sparkling cider, careful to hold up the bottom of my long velvet dress so it doesn't drag on the floor. I find an empty table and sit down.

Sang is standing on the opposite side of the room, tending to some flower arrangements. He's in a black tux, bent over an orchid, turning the vase and then taking a step back to evaluate his work. His fingers hover over the deep-purple petals, and for some reason, the image takes my breath away. If I could choose ten things to keep sharp in my memory for the rest of my life, I think maybe this would be one of them.

Someone sits down next to me, but I barely register it. I want to love something, anything, as much as Sang loves his flowers.

"Careful, or you'll burn a hole in his back." Paige is sitting next to me, but she isn't looking at me. She's looking at Sang.

I instantly avert my eyes and look at the tablecloth instead. I don't say anything.

"He's had an effect on you," she says.

"Who?" I ask, not wanting to acknowledge her words, but it sounds stupid. I obviously know who she's talking about. She knows it, too, and rolls her eyes.

"You're calmer. More self-assured." Page twirls the straw in her drink and finally looks at me. Her eyes are the perfect shade of blue. They're dark, almost navy, the color of the sea when the shallows turn to depth.

"He's a good training partner," I say.

Paige shakes her head and looks back at Sang. "Is that all?"

"Of course that's all."

"You look at him as if he's magic."

"I do not." I try to keep my voice even, but it rises with defensiveness.

"Whatever you say." She finishes off the last of her drink. "By the way, seeing you punch Mr. Burrows is my new favorite memory of you."

Paige stands, but pauses before she walks away. She leans down, her mouth so close to my ear that I can feel the warmth of her breath on my skin. It's tinged with the sharp smell of alcohol. "Well, almost my favorite."

The comment catches me off guard. I never saw her coming, which is one of the cruelties of love. I couldn't protect her. And now, memories of the way she used to look at me in the middle of the night flood my thoughts.

She didn't mind my changes. She called them my ebbs and flows.

She said I was her ocean.

When we started dating, she said she wanted to drown in me. I wanted to drown in her too.

Then Nikki died, and we drowned in grief instead of each other.

A cold, prickly feeling nips at my skin, but it's not the memory of Paige. It's what she said about Sang, her implication that he means something to me. Paige snuck into my heart long before I realized she was there, and it's why she was struck by lightning earlier this year. It's why I can't let my magic anywhere near her.

It's why I have to ensure that I never get too close to Sang.

Then it hits me all at once, the answer to the puzzle I've been trying to solve since our first session after the heat wave: I've plateaued because I'm afraid we've gotten too close.

I've plateaued because seeing the worry on his face made me feel something.

Because the way he wrapped my hand in lavender made me think for a fleeting second that this is what love is.

I've plateaued because I'm afraid my magic knows about all those passing thoughts and short-lived feelings and has turned them into something they're not.

I'm afraid he'll be hurt because of it.

Ms. Suntile says something to Sang, and he nods and leaves the dome. I finish my drink and follow him outside. The cold air makes me shiver, and I hug my shawl closer to my body, hurrying after him.

"Hey," I call.

He turns around and smiles as soon as he sees me. His dimples are showing, and his eyes are bright. "Hi. You look beautiful."

My heart pounds. His words mean nothing.

"You can't say stuff like that to me."

The smile falls from Sang's face. "I'm sorry." His voice rises at the end, as if he's asking a question. "I didn't mean to make you uncomfortable."

"I'm not uncomfortable. You're just seriously confused about what this is, and I need to make sure you understand." I motion between the two of us.

I need to make sure my magic understands.

"Why don't you explain it to me then." His voice is calm but strained at the edges.

"There is nothing between us. You just happened to be the person assigned to train me." I laugh, and it sounds mean. "You were tricked, Sang. You were brought out here and forced to work with me because Mr. Burrows thought your calming magic would help me. It was never about botany."

Sang's expression falters. "I came out here *by choice* to continue my studies under Mr. Burrows," he says, but it isn't convincing. He knows I'm right.

"Some mentor, huh?"

Sang shakes his head. "You never know when to let things go, do you?"

"I just thought you should know the real reason you aren't able to fuss around with your plants all day."

Sang looks at me as if I'm unrecognizable to him, and I

instantly regret the words. The image of him tending to his orchids just minutes ago pops into my mind, and pain blooms in my chest.

"Fuss around with my plants," he repeats, tasting the words I threw at him.

I feel my cheeks redden with heat, but I don't say anything. If I do, I'm afraid I'll back down, apologize, tell him Mr. Burrows was wrong for tricking him. Tell him that even though it was wrong, I'm glad I met him. So glad I met him. But I can't. I have to make sure he knows there's nothing here.

I have to make sure my magic knows there's nothing here.

"I've always been on your side, terrible mentor or not," he says. He does not look away from me, not for a single second, and I force myself to keep my eyes on his.

I won't be the one to look away first.

I shrug. "You never had a choice. Neither of us did."

"Why are you doing this? Did you seriously follow me out here just to pick a fight with me?"

"I'm not picking a fight. I just need to make sure you understand." My voice rises, and I try to keep it together.

"I understand perfectly. I never even wanted this, for Sun's sake. I moved here to study, not be your babysitter." He pauses, looks at me. "And between the two of us, Clara, I'm not the one who's confused. I never was."

Sang turns and walks away.

"I'm not confused," I shout after him, but my voice sounds shrill and unsteady.

He throws his hands up and keeps walking.

I can't believe I let Paige worry me over Sang. If he were more to me than a training partner, the sight of him storming off wouldn't be a relief. It wouldn't be okay.

But it is.

And even though I wish I didn't have to say those things to Sang, I feel better. Because now I know with absolute certainty that there will never be a reason for my magic to seek him out.

We can keep training together.

I can keep getting stronger.

Strong enough that my magic never hurts anyone else ever again.

twenty-two

"There will come a time when you believe you no longer need to be challenged. And when that time comes, you'll be wrong."

—*A Season for Everything*

Sang is standing on the control field when I arrive for our last training session of the season. His stance is rigid, and he doesn't smile when he sees me.

He's still mad.

There's a large, dark rain cloud hovering next to him, and I assume we'll be working on hail or sleet. But he doesn't say anything.

With one swift motion, he shoves the cloud at me, hard, and the energy from it knocks me back.

"What the hell?"

He shoves the cloud again.

"Seriously, Sang, what is wrong with you?"

"You're not the only one who can pick a fight," he says. "Or did you think that was a talent only you had?"

Now I'm angry. "Wow, get over yourself." I shove the cloud as hard as I can back in his direction.

He's expecting it, though, and he stays where he is. He closes his eyes and fills the cloud even more, this huge, dark presence between us.

This time, he throws the cloud over my head, and before I have time to move, he squeezes his hand. The cloud bursts, and I'm drenched in rain.

I stalk over to him and shove him hard on the shoulder. He stumbles back.

"Use your magic," he says. His voice is low but rough, and it causes a weird sensation deep in my core.

I yell in frustration. As quickly as I can, I pull moisture from the snow-covered grass until a thunderstorm cloud sits heavy in front of me. It takes just seconds. Winters aren't as capable with thunderstorms, but I can control a small one.

Besides, I'm not using it for thunder or lightning.

I send an intense current of air straight up into the storm, pushing droplets of water into the coldest part until they freeze. Hailstones form, dozens of them, and I let the storm take over. The hailstones descend into warmer air, gather more water, then lift and freeze again, over and over, until the updraft of air can no longer support their weight.

I throw the storm at Sang at the exact moment hail starts to drop. The hailstones are larger than I intended, and one after another, they pelt him in the face. He jumps out of the way and covers his head with his hands, but it's too late. There's a huge gash on his lip, bright red with blood, and another cut on his forehead.

"Sang, I'm sorry—" I start, but before I can get to him, a small tornado, no larger than a person, slams into me.

If it were spring, Sang never could have done that safely. His magic would be too strong, and the tornado would be too powerful. Lucky for me, it's winter.

Still, it's enough to knock me off my feet. I hit the snow, and my whole body gets hot with anger. I push myself to standing. With shaking hands, I form a tiny snowball, then roll it onto the ground.

I close my eyes and send my magic chasing after it. The snowball picks up speed, getting larger and larger as it goes. I send it around the perimeter of the field, picking up layer after layer of snow until it's taller than I am.

I'm about to send the giant snowball tearing toward Sang, wanting to knock him to the ground and bury him in snow, when he motions to the trees.

At his command, they bend over and block the path directly in front of the snowball. I don't have enough time to change its course, and it slams into the trees and explodes, sending snow everywhere.

"Not bad for someone who just fusses around with plants, huh?"

I don't answer. I'm so mad I can't think straight. In the time it takes for Sang to throw my words back at me, winter magic pours from my fingers in a flood of rage. I build a small, intense blizzard.

I throw it at Sang, knowing he can't do a thing about it. Spring magic can't touch blizzards.

He falls to the ground as the blizzard hammers him with snow and wind. Soon he's almost buried, and I walk over and look down at him.

"Not good enough."

Sang rolls out of the way and stands, sending a shower of warm rain over the blizzard. It dissipates the storm and douses me in the face.

Then I think of our drill, the wind I've summoned over and over with him. I close my eyes, and the air answers instantly, building up a current I send directly at Sang. He dodges it and steps toward me, and I quickly change the wind's course. It's stronger than I thought, though, and it catches Sang in the back and tosses him toward me.

We both fall backward. He lands right on top of me.

It's so windy that the snow on the ground rises into the air, swirling all around us. Sang tries to move off of me, but I'm not done yet, and soon we're rolling around in the snow, me on top of him, him on top of me.

Snow gets in my hair and down the neck of my jacket, sending cold water running down my skin. My hat fell off ages ago, and my hands are freezing.

Our magic follows us around like shadows, his trying to help him, mine trying to help me. Even the calm that's laced with his magic isn't enough to relieve the anger between us. We grunt and grab and get tangled up in each other, refusing to relent.

My magic pulses inside me, waiting to be used. With all my might, I roll and send Sang onto his back. I pin his arms with my chest and use everything I have left to pummel him with magic.

I don't pause at the top of the waterfall; I barrel over it with unrestrained fury, reaching for my magic to end this. To win.

But something isn't right when I take hold of it.

It feels different. Familiar, but different. It isn't aggressive or deliberate or cold. It's patient, in a way, waiting for whatever I'll ask of it.

I shake my head and refocus.

I reach for my magic once more and send all my energy into it, creating the biggest flood of power I can.

Sang screams.

Then, all around us, tiny green plants push through the snow. I scramble back.

My hands are shaking, and my eyes are wide.

Sang sits up, so close to me his shoulder touches mine. Our legs are tangled together, but we don't move.

The magic. It felt like spring.

"What..." I start, but my voice fades. I don't even know how to ask it. "Did I hurt you?"

"No." There's wonder in his voice. "But I felt it." I lift my gaze from the small green sprouts encircling us, and instead focus on the gold in his eyes. "I felt you pull it out of me."

"But that's impossible." I watch him closely, aware of every breath he takes. I don't dare look away.

"I know," he says, shaking his head. "But look around us.

Those sprouts could only come from spring magic, and I would never be strong enough to grow new plants this quickly in winter. They had to come from you." He pauses. Then, "Try again."

"No," I say, shaking my head. Whatever this is, it terrifies me. "No," I say again. There is no way to pull magic from a witch without them handing it over, without them weaving it in with yours. And even then, it can only be done between witches of the same season.

A winter witch pulling magic from a spring is unimaginable.

Sang takes off his gloves and grabs my hands. "Try again."

Almost instantly, I feel Sang's magic moving through his veins, pulsing beneath his skin. I'm desperate to touch it, as if it's life itself, and before I know what I'm doing, I close my eyes and reach.

It responds, and I pull it from him in one strong motion.

Sang gasps.

The earth shifts as a birch tree shoves through the ground and grows right next to us, tall and white and real.

Spring magic heightened to its full strength in the dead of winter.

Impossible.

I want to reach out and touch the smooth, white bark, feel it against my skin, but I'm scared it will vanish.

Sang opens his eyes, and we stare at each other. Our chests heave, our breaths heavy between us.

The magic beneath his skin still reaches for mine, our hands vibrating with the force of it.

It's unlike anything I've ever felt before, as if I've seen his soul, read his mind, touched every single part of him.

He is as good, as genuine, as I thought he was, distilled into the most perfect stream of magic.

I cannot tear my eyes from his.

He swallows hard. "Clara," he says, his voice rough with something that sets my insides on fire. "If you don't want me to kiss you right now, you're going to have to stop looking at me like that."

But that's exactly what I want. I don't care that his lip is bleeding and I'm out of breath. I want it so badly it doesn't feel like a want. It feels like a need.

I keep my eyes on his for several seconds, the idea of looking away as impossible as the birch tree standing next to us.

I lean toward him, ever so slightly. He does the same.

Then I pause.

If I kiss Sang after what just happened, I don't think I'll be able to control myself. And if I can't control myself, I can't control my magic.

I slowly look down and pull my hands from his. Sang leans back, the cut on his lip bright with blood.

We're silent, our legs still tangled, our breaths still coming shallow and fast.

The birch tree beside us is tranquil and quiet, as if it has lived in the center of this field forever.

I can see my breath in the cold winter air. I watch it mix with Sang's in the space between us.

His magic is still wrapped up in my own, winter and spring colliding as if it was always supposed to be this way. I could push my magic down, break the connection.

But I don't want to.

So I don't.

primrose

spring

twenty-three

"And just when the world is certain it cannot handle
another day of winter, the vernal equinox arrives in
a rush of sweet rain and awakening color."
—*A Season for Everything*

The vernal equinox has come and gone. The days are getting longer, and the Earth is beginning to warm. The quiet and stillness of winter is replaced with the bustle of spring as birds return home and animals wake from sleep.

It's been two weeks since Sang's and my discovery, and I haven't told a single soul. We tried it several more times before the equinox, just to be sure, and each time confirmed the impossibility that I can summon off-season magic.

Not even Alice's memoir alludes to this kind of power, and I'm unsure if it's because she never discovered it or if she simply referred to it as "magic" because she was always able to do it. Or maybe it's that the Earth was happier when Alice was alive and hadn't yet been pushed too far. Maybe this kind of magic wasn't needed.

Sang uprooted the birch tree and replanted it somewhere else on campus, along with the sprouts that pushed through the soil around us. The control field is back to normal. No one else knows what we discovered that day.

I try to concentrate on what Mr. Mendez is saying at the front of the classroom, but all I can think about is the way it felt to be tangled up in Sang's magic, as if I'd been wandering alone for seventeen years and finally came home.

Sunlight reaches through the windows and reflects off Mr. Mendez's glasses. His black hair stays perfectly in place when he looks down at his book to close it. He leans back on his desk and twirls his wedding ring around his finger.

"We have one bit of housekeeping to discuss before you're dismissed," he says. "We've finalized the arrangements for the total solar eclipse this summer."

I look down at my desk and shift in my seat. I've ached for this eclipse ever since I learned it was coming, years and years of counting down to my way out.

But now the eclipse fills me with fear instead of relief.

I don't want to be stripped.

I let the thought sink in, roll it around in my mind, decide if it has a place here. I feel it take root and settle into my skin.

I'm amazed and happy and terrified to realize it's true. I don't want to be stripped.

But the impossibility of it is heavy. It isn't only that I don't want to be stripped; I don't want to be stripped, *and* I don't want to be isolated.

I don't want to be stripped, *and* I don't want my magic to target the people I care about.

I don't know if those things can coexist. The eclipse is coming, and if they can't, I will be forced to make a choice.

And that scares me.

"We will be evacuating the night before and staying in upstate New York. We'll be out of the path of totality and can see the partial eclipse from there."

"Doesn't it bother you that you'll never get to see a total eclipse?" Ari asks thoughtfully. "I think it would be amazing to see."

"It would be incredible," Mr. Mendez agrees. "Some shaders say it's life-changing." His voice is far off and wistful, like he's forgotten he's teaching a class. He clears his throat. "But being unable to see a solar eclipse is a small price to pay for being a witch."

All witches in the path of totality are required to evacuate. It's illegal to be stripped on purpose—the atmosphere would fall into disarray if witches were stripped of their magic every time a total eclipse occurred.

Still, it would be remarkable to see.

"Are there any other questions?" Mr. Mendez asks. He looks around the room, and when no one raises their hand, he dismisses us.

I stand up and shove my books in my bag. When I leave the room, Paige pulls me aside. She's holding a stack of books to her chest, and her hair is in a ponytail.

"I remember what you told me," she says simply. She doesn't have to elaborate for me to know what she's talking about.

I look down, my heart racing.

It was before. Before we broke up, and before Nikki died. She'd asked me what my parents were like during a long, sleepless night where we shared secrets and kisses and laughter. I told her all about them, about how Dad thought it was the coolest thing in his life that I'd been born a witch. About the way my mom would ask me to make it rain in summer just so she could dance in it. She loved the rain.

I told her about how they died, how my magic roared out of me in a burst of lightning and sunlight and heat, incinerating them on the spot.

I told her how sometimes I wake up in the middle of the night and hear their screams.

That was before I knew my magic sought out the people I loved, rushing toward them until it swallowed them whole. I didn't make the connection until Nikki died and Ms. Suntile dove into research. That's when I ended things with Paige and moved into the cabin in the trees.

But still, I knew my magic was dangerous. I knew it was a power I might never learn to control.

So that night in my bed, with my fingers laced through Paige's and her hand in my hair, I looked her in the eye and whispered, "I might stay for the eclipse."

She didn't gasp in horror or lecture me or pull her hand from mine. Instead, she brushed my hair behind my ear and said, "I might try to stop you."

That was all. We never spoke of it again.

I look at her now, the image receding to the corner of my mind where I hold all our broken promises and memories too vivid to forget. "I know you do."

"Do you still feel that way?" she asks.

I think about what I discovered with Sang and how it could stop witches from dying. I think about all the good it could do.

And I think about how, if I can't learn to control my magic fully, I will have to isolate myself for the rest of my life because of it. That's a life I'm not sure I can commit to.

"I don't want to be stripped," I say. It isn't a lie.

She studies me, and it's clear she knows there's more I'm not saying. "Good," she finally says, "because I don't want to have to stop you."

Then she walks off without another word.

I'm still trying to shake the memory off when I get outside. Sang is leaning against a brick wall and stands up when he sees me. He gives me a crooked smile that pushes all the tension from my body, all the tight knots and clenched muscles.

And he's not even using his magic.

"Hey," he says, walking over.

Spring has washed over him. Everything about him is brighter, as if I'd only ever seen him in shadow and he has finally stepped into the light. The rings of gold in his eyes are richer and deeper, an ocean of sunlight I can't look away from.

He looks perfect.

If I were the Sun, I'd choose to live in his eyes too.

Neither of us has mentioned his comment about kissing me, but I think about it all the time. I'm convinced it was a product of the moment, a comment brought forth by the intimacy and shock and absolute wonder of what we'd just experienced. It would have been odd if we *hadn't* felt a need for each other.

And yet it lingers. The way his eyes were locked on mine, our tangled limbs and tangled breath and tangled magic. The way his voice felt like sandpaper lightly trailing across my skin, awakening a yearning I've only ever felt in summer.

"I was hoping we could chat about something before our session today." His words bring me back to the present, and I hope he doesn't notice the heat that has settled in my skin.

"Sure, what's up?"

Sang waits to speak until we're out of earshot of anyone else. "I think we should tell Ms. Suntile and Mr. Burrows about what you can do."

I knew this was coming. Of course it was. We need to figure out the extent of this power, learn if it's something I can do in all seasons, with all witches.

But the thought of telling them causes my stomach to twist with worry. I'd be handing over an incredible amount of control to people I'm not sure I trust. Eastern has done so much for me, but between the way Ms. Suntile acted at our training session with Mr. Hart and the fact that Mr. Burrows is still around even after his test, I wonder if they really care about me or if all they care about is my power.

"I know we need to," I start.

"But?"

"But it feels like handing something over that I can never get back."

Sang nods. "Believe it or not, I know exactly how you feel."

"You do?"

"Yeah, I do."

I want to ask him what he means, but the words are stuck in my throat. We don't need something else binding us together, another shared secret that makes him feel essential to my life.

When we get to the control field, I put my bag down and wait for him to pull out a lesson plan. But he pauses and looks around as if he's thinking.

"What would you think about bailing on our session today? There's something I want to show you."

My brain yells at me to say no. To stick to the lesson plan. To ensure that our relationship doesn't build into something my magic can sense.

But a small voice tells me to go. Tells me it's okay. Reminds me I'm going to be strong enough to control my magic.

Sang fills me with contradictions. I'm torn between wanting to experience his openness and wanting to run from it as fast as I can. Part of me thinks he's weak and foolish for giving so much of himself away.

But the more I get to know him, the more I wonder if maybe it's a gift too few of us have. Maybe it isn't a weakness at all.

Say no.

Go with him.

I pause. I'm not sure how many moments it takes to form a closeness that's *too* close, but I'm sure we're nowhere near it.

Which is why I say, "Let's do it."

I pick up my bag from the grass and follow him off the field.

twenty-four

"When magic courses through my body and bursts into the world, I know this was always the only option for me. I was fated for this."

—*A Season for Everything*

I follow Sang through the gardens. A group of springs are kneeling on the ground, pushing their fingers into the dirt. They can plant their emotions in the earth, where they'll grow as flowers. It's my favorite part of spring magic because it has nothing to do with control; its sole purpose is bringing beauty into the world.

Sang keeps walking past the gardens and deep into the surrounding woods, so far from campus I can no longer see the buildings of Eastern. Evergreens and oaks stretch for acres in every direction, and I step over tree roots and duck under branches.

Birds chirp high above us, and a light breeze rustles through leaves as if they're whispering secrets as we pass. Sunlight reaches through gaps in the trees and bathes the forest floor in streaks of gold.

Sang and I walk in a comfortable silence that strikes me as strange. Even Paige and I were always filling the silence with *something*, but Sang makes me feel as if my presence is all he wants.

He stops when we come to an old brick building covered in ivy and overgrowth. It's square and small. The stone walls are crumbling, and the right side is half caved in. Moss coats the roof, and ferns rest against the base.

"Here we are," Sang says. He opens the weathered door, and it creaks with the movement.

The first thing I notice is the smell. It isn't musty like I thought it'd be. It's sweet and strong, like someone took all the flowers in the entire world and put them in this old, abandoned building.

I walk inside. Rays of sunlight stretch through the holes in the roof and walls, giving the room a soft glow. Every color of the rainbow comes into view, hundreds of flowers and plants lining tables and crawling up the walls and hanging from the ceiling. There are more species than I could ever identify, and for a moment, I'm speechless.

There's a narrow walkway through the center of the room, the only space that isn't covered in something living. It feels like I've stepped through a portal to another world, a rain forest and greenhouse and enchanted garden all in one.

"What is this place?"

"It's an abandoned immersion house, and Ms. Suntile agreed to let me use it for my research." Sang reaches out and touches the leaves of a nearby plant. "But I also come here to think. To be alone. I wanted to keep its history intact, which is why there are so many plants here that have nothing to do with my research. I want it to feel like one of the old immersion houses."

"You don't really believe in immersion, do you?"

"Why not? The shaders have wishing wells and four-leaf clovers. I kind of like believing this place can make all my dreams come true."

I look around the room. The earliest witches believed it was good luck to immerse themselves in a space with so many plants and flowers, so they created immersion houses. Over time, these houses became their own kind of churches, witches flocking to them with their fears and desires and hopes and dreams.

Being here with Sang, I fully understand it.

"Maybe it can," I say.

Sang looks at me then, a small smile pulling at his lips. My heart beats faster, and my body is restless, standing in this small space with him. I look away.

Loose papers sit on the edges of tables and on the floor, under pots and stained with dirt. I pick one up and study it. It's beautiful, a hand-painted illustration of wild larkspur. The species name is written in cursive, and different parts of the flower get their own close-up illustrations. Glass jars of brushes and watercolor paints are jammed in between plants and flowers around the room, and a large case of colored pencils sits underneath a table.

"Did you do all these?" I ask, holding up the picture.

Sang nods. "I've been really into botanical illustration since I was a kid. It relaxes me," he says.

So that's why his hand is always stained different colors. I smile to myself.

The pictures are all so intricate and detailed, beautiful but scientifically accurate. "These are amazing. You could publish your own textbook."

"Maybe one day," he says. "I mainly just do it because I love it."

"You're really talented."

Sang looks away, but I notice the blush settling in his cheeks.

"So, what kind of research are you doing in here?"

Sang leads me to a table in the far corner. Rows of sunflowers are lined up under UV lights. Dozens of dead plants are in a bin beside them.

"I'm working on a better way of getting rid of harmful plants and weeds. Witches are so tied to nature that it physically hurts us to rip plants out of the earth, and even though we're used to it, that kind of stress takes its toll. It's the same for the plants; they're still alive when they're torn from the ground, and it's incredibly jarring for them. Spraying them with chemicals isn't any better. This is basically a more compassionate alternative to weeding."

"If the Sun played favorites, I'm pretty sure you'd win," I say.

"Says the Ever."

"What have you come up with?" I ask, looking at the flowers.

"It's basically reverse photosynthesis. If you extract the sunlight from a plant before it's converted to energy, you halt the plant's growth. The plant will die, but peacefully; it's the equivalent of a human not getting enough oxygen and simply falling asleep."

"How do you harvest the light from the plant?"

"That's the tricky part. You have to ignore all the other sunlight in the area and isolate only what's in the leaves. Once you've found it, you can slowly extract it. But the force of extraction must be exact in order for it to work, and the smallest variation can cause the light to flood back into the plant. I'm still working on it."

"Incredible," I say, studying the sunflowers.

"One day, I'd like to get my research published by the Solar Magic Association so other witches can adopt the practice. This would give them a way to remove plants without the pain and stress that goes along with it. I'm also seeing a lot of indicators that the soil becomes healthier with this kind of weeding. When a plant dies in this way, all of its nutrients are absorbed by the earth, creating a richer growing environment; it becomes its own kind of fertilizer. It's still early, but I'm excited by the possibilities." He turns away from the table and looks at me. "You're the only person I've told about it."

Now I understand why he brought me here. He wants to protect his reverse photosynthesis project the way I want to protect my ability to summon magic that's outside my season.

"Thank you for showing me. I'm blown away, truly."

"Thanks. It's a labor of love," he says with a smile.

This room is so small, and Sang is so close. It would be easy to let the back of my hand brush his, to let myself lean into him. I am pulled toward him like a magnet, and it takes so much effort not to let go and snap into him.

"Do you know what the most common use for these houses was?" His eyes find mine, and I can't look away.

I shake my head. I try to remember what I learned in class, but I'm too distracted.

"People would come here to fall in love," he says.

His eyes are searching mine, sending pulses of heat through every square inch of my body. I clear my throat and look down.

"I made something for you." Sang walks to a table in the corner of the room. He picks up a small vial of liquid and brings it back to me.

"Is this some kind of potion to make me fall in love with you?" The words fly out of my mouth before I can stop them.

A smile tugs at the corners of his mouth. "Why?" he asks. "Would it work?"

He's trying to keep his smile small, but his dimples give him away.

"My resolve is rather strong."

"Is that so?" he asks, stepping so close I can feel his breath on my skin.

I want to remove the space between us, closer and closer until we snap together.

Then I think about Paige and striking her with lightning. Paige and the way she looked when I ended things, betrayed and angry and broken.

I can't do this.

I break eye contact and step back. "Are you going to tell me what's in the vial or not?" I ask.

"It's a dream elixir," he says. "We don't use them much anymore, but the earliest witches believed there was an elixir for everything. Talent, courage, strength. Different plants create different elixirs; they're meant to be worn like perfume."

Sang holds the vial between us, the amber liquid glinting in the light. "You don't need a talent elixir," he says. "You're already talented."

I will myself to look anywhere other than his face, but it doesn't work.

"You don't need a courage elixir," he murmurs. "You're already brave."

He hands me the vial, placing it softly in my palm. I shiver when his fingers brush mine.

"You don't need a strength elixir. You're already strong."

"Then what's it for?" I ask, forcing my voice to stay steady.

"There's an old belief that if you take a small sample of every plant in an immersion house and speak your wildest dreams out loud as you apply it, it will make them come true."

I look around the room, at the hundreds of plants surrounding us.

"There's a sample from every plant in this elixir?"

"Yeah, I've been working on it for a while." His voice is quiet, shy. His confidence from earlier is gone, and his cheeks betray him with a dark shade of red.

I roll the vial around in my hand. It is the best gift I've ever been given.

"I don't know what to say. I love it. Thank you."

"I can't imagine what this year has been like for you. The rest of us get to try and fail on our own, but you're expected to do everything in front of others. And who knows how things will change once the school learns about your new power."

I swallow hard.

Sang leans against a table but never takes his eyes off mine. "I guess I just wanted you to know you're not alone. I wanted to put myself out there the way you're forced to do on a daily basis."

I don't say anything. It hurts to swallow, and my throat aches with all the words I'm holding in. I'm overwhelmed, afraid I might cry if I speak.

Sang seems to take my silence as displeasure, because he quickly adds, "I know it's nowhere near the same thing. I just thought—"

"Thank you," I say, cutting him off.

Slowly, I walk over to Sang and wrap my arms around his neck.

"Thank you," I say again, my voice nothing but a whisper. My breath hits his neck, and goose bumps rise on his skin.

Sang wraps his arms around my waist and pulls me closer, so close our bodies are perfectly aligned, touching at every point. He smells like black tea and honey, and I rest my head on his shoulder and close my eyes.

"I like you, Clara Densmore." His tone is defeated, as if he has done something wrong, as if he's scared I'll be disappointed in him. "I like you so much."

Tears sting my eyes. I force them back and fight against the words rising in my throat. We hug each other for a long time, his admission hanging in the air like the fog at dawn.

And in this moment, I'm too tired to fight. I'm too tired to swim against the current.

I lean back and look into his perfect eyes. The air between us is charged, and before I can talk myself out of it, before I can marvel at a desire I've only ever felt in summer, I let myself be swept away.

I kiss him.

At first he's stunned, still. Then his arms tighten around me, and we're fall-fall-falling over the edge of the waterfall, his hands in my hair and his lips against mine.

He kisses me as if it might never happen again, slow and deep and deliberate. There's a gentleness to the way he opens his mouth and twists his tongue with mine, the way he traces his fingertips down the sides of my face and onto my neck as if he's memorizing me. He touches me the way he does his flowers, with confidence and awe and adoration. It showers me in warmth, and I push into him, trying to get closer still.

We stumble back into the table behind him, pots shaking from the movement, but our lips never part. I'm breathless with a desire I didn't know I had. Kissing him feels like hunger and standing in the rain and falling from the peak of a roller coaster all at once. I'm desperate for him and push further into him, never close enough. A pot falls from the table and shatters on the floor, but we do not pause.

If I were capable of melting, I think I'd melt right here on the floor of this immersion house, because there's not a single worry propping me up.

The worries will come later. I know they will.

But right now, with Sang's mouth on mine and his arms wrapped tightly around me, I revel in the fall.

twenty-five

"I love the way rain is accepted in all its forms. Sometimes it pours. Sometimes it sprinkles. And sometimes it hangs back and watches the world before it falls."

—*A Season for Everything*

I couldn't sleep last night, kept awake by the ghost of Sang's lips on mine, by the way his hand felt pressed against my lower back. By the worries that got louder and louder as the seconds ticked by. I'm so angry at myself for letting this happen, and yet I can't bring myself to wish it hadn't.

Sang is at risk. He was before we kissed, and he is now. The only difference is that I can't deny it anymore.

There's this tiny hope in the back of my mind that maybe I'm in control now. We've been training together for so long. My magic knows him. If it were going to seek him out, it would have done so already. We pummeled each other in the snow, for Sun's sake. If it were going to hurt him, that would have been the perfect chance.

But it didn't hurt him.

Instead, it showed us a new kind of magic.

And maybe that's what Sang is: a new kind of magic.

I feed Nox and rush to meet Sang outside the administration building. He's already waiting for me, and I can't help the way my eyes drift to his lips, the way the back of my hand brushes against his. I look away to stop myself from closing the space between us.

Spring has brightened everything, as if the trees and flowers and grass were covered in plastic that's been ripped away. It's all still here, even after frost clung to it and the earth froze and harsh winds cut through brittle branches. Everything survived and is waking up again, being coaxed from sleep by gentle rain and warmer earth.

"Ready?" Sang asks.

I nod, and we walk into the administration building together.

"Go on in," Ms. Beverly says.

Sang and I sit down across from Ms. Suntile and Mr. Burrows, and it feels good to have him on my side of the desk instead of theirs.

Sang starts, telling them about his reverse photosynthesis project and the progress he's making. He tells them how he's successfully been able to pull the exact amount of sunlight from plants to let them die peaceful deaths. He explains how this method of weeding eliminates the pain it causes witches, how it's easier on the witch, the plant, and the earth. His voice gets faster as he talks, his excitement and love for what he does filling the room with a lightness that is undeniably spring.

220

Ms. Suntile leans back in her chair, listening, and I'm surprised when she smiles, a real smile that touches her eyes and shows her teeth. I've never seen her smile like that the entire time I've known her, and I almost laugh; I'm not the only one Sang has had an effect on.

"I would very much like to see your research, Mr. Park. It sounds remarkable."

"I look forward to showing it to you." There's relief in his voice, and he relaxes beside me.

"It sounds like you've been able to pick up right where we left off at Western," Mr. Burrows says.

No thanks to you, I want to say, but I keep my mouth shut.

Sang nods. "I'm glad I've been able to find the time for it."

Sang did this for me. He told them about his research before he wanted to so I wouldn't be the only one who was vulnerable today. So I wouldn't be alone. It makes me want to wrap him in my arms right here, right this second, in front of Ms. Suntile and Mr. Burrows.

But there's something else, too, a hot, prickly sensation that runs up my spine. My stomach feels as if it drops ten feet. I'm jealous. Jealous that I will no longer be the only person who's seen Sang's immersion house and his project. Jealous that my eyes won't be the only ones on his botanical illustrations. Jealous that the secret we shared is no longer secret.

And now I have to let them in on the other secret, the other unseen rope tying me to Sang. I'm afraid telling them will erase our moments, erase the things that make us *us*.

"Now, was there something else?" Ms. Suntile asks, her voice returning to its usual sternness.

Sang looks at me expectantly. I twist my hands in my lap, and my heart hammers inside my chest. "Yes. But it's something I need to show you."

"What is it?" Impatience edges her voice, but I want to do this my way. Keep at least a semblance of control.

"It's something that's worth leaving your office for."

Ms. Suntile exhales, not bothering to hide her irritation. "Well, then, let's go see it."

She stands, and the four of us walk out of the administration building and toward the farm at the edge of campus. The air is cool, and the sky is clear, a perfect shade of blue convincing the plants to come back to life.

Mr. Burrows talks with Sang about his project as we walk, his voice enthusiastic and supportive, asking questions and presenting hypotheticals. It's a glimpse of what they must have been like at Western, and it makes me angry that Sang's experience here has been so different from what he was promised.

And yet I'm so thankful for it—thankful it's him waiting for me on the control field every time I train, thankful he's the one by my side as I fail and succeed and everything in between.

Thankful for him.

The farm is quiet when we get there, acres of land patiently waiting for autumn's harvest. If Ms. Suntile is surprised that we're here instead of at the control field, she doesn't show it.

"All right, Ms. Densmore, the floor is yours."

Mr. Burrows stands beside her, and they wait with expectant expressions on their faces. I look at Sang, and he gives me an encouraging nod. But I feel frozen in place, everything stuck except the racing of my heart.

I can never go back from this. As soon as they see what I can do and realize what it means, everything will change.

And the thing I've spent my life avoiding will *become* my life.

I take a deep breath and close my eyes. I made my decision long ago, when Mr. Hart died and Mr. Burrows put me through that test. When Paige called me a waste and Sang told me I was made for this.

When I started to believe him.

"Ms. Suntile, would you please get ready to use your magic? Don't actually do anything, just call it to the surface." I don't open my eyes; I don't want to see the look on her face or the way Mr. Burrows watches me with doubt.

Ms. Suntile doesn't say anything, but I feel the slow, somewhat sad flow of autumn and know she is doing as I asked. But when I try to reach for it, I can't.

I can feel it, but I can't get to it.

I try again and again, but nothing happens.

I open my eyes and see Ms. Suntile looking at me with a cross between pity and annoyance. I will never get a smile from her.

"Well?"

That's when I understand. I can't grab her magic, tie our seasons together, because I don't trust her.

"I need a second," I say. I take Sang by the arm and pull him aside, ignoring Mr. Burrows as he leans into Ms. Suntile and whispers something.

"I can feel her magic, but I can't create the tie I need because I don't trust her."

I expect Sang to list off the reasons why I should trust her or explain the ways this power is good for all of us, but he doesn't say anything like that. After thinking it over, he says, "Is there an autumn you do trust?"

"I trusted Mr. Hart."

"Try focusing on him. The same magic that is in Ms. Suntile was in him too, so pretend you're working with him."

Ms. Suntile checks her watch. "I don't have all day, Ms. Densmore. I do have a school to run."

I walk back over to her. "I'm ready now. Please call up your magic," I say.

I close my eyes and start again. I picture Mr. Hart and his patient demeanor, the way he never lost his temper or demanded more than I could give. The way he always met me where I was and never lost faith in me. The way he thought my changing with the seasons made me powerful instead of weak, extraordinary instead of volatile.

I slowly send my magic out, and this time, it grabs hold of Ms. Suntile's. I pull and pull and pull. Ms. Suntile gets stiff and fights against me, every part of her resisting. But I keep pulling, going with the current.

When I have a solid stream of autumn magic, I send it into the earth beneath us and wrap it around the seeds of winter squashes. I gently tell the seeds to grow, drenching them in magic that makes them sprout through the ground.

The sprouts grow into vines, long and dense with large green leaves that cover the earth. The vines snake between us and wrap around our legs. The squashes grow and grow until they're ripe for harvest. Even the early spring chill can't contend with autumn magic.

I open my eyes and slowly break my hold on Ms. Suntile's power. It flows back to her in a steady stream, then it's gone.

Ms. Suntile is looking at the ground. She bends over and touches the leaves, runs her fingers over the variety of winter squashes that should be impossible to grow in spring. Her eyes glisten, and her hands shake.

"The reason you were disappointed with my performance during the wildfire training is because I'm not supposed to hold the magic of witches who are in their season. They're already doing what they were born to do; why take their magic away from them and give it to me?"

I bend over and pull a small squash from the vine, then throw it to Sang. He catches it, his face full of wonder and adoration and awe, though I'm not sure if it's for the squash or for me. Probably both.

I grab another squash and hand it to Mr. Burrows, who gapes at it, then one more for Ms. Suntile. She takes it in her hands with care.

"The witches who are waiting for their turn with the sun, whose magic is weak and ineffective because it isn't the right season—that's something I can help with."

"Clara, do you understand what this means?" I bristle at the sound of my first name in her mouth. "All of the witches dying from depletion, the atypical weather we've been powerless to deal with..." Her voice trails off.

"I understand," I say.

"We never could have predicted this kind of magic," Mr. Burrows says, staring at the ripe squash, his voice quiet. Reverent. Ms. Suntile startles when he speaks, as if she forgot he was here. "How did you discover it?"

I think about fighting with Sang, throwing magic at each other and rolling around in the snow. How angry we were. How desperate we were. Heat rises to my cheeks, and I look down.

"We got in a fight," Sang says simply, and I look at him. His eyes lock on mine, and there's something in them that makes me curse the fact that we aren't alone. I want to tackle him right here in this field among the winter squashes and feel his mouth on mine. From the way he looks at me, I know he's thinking the same thing.

"A fight?" Ms. Suntile asks, interrupting our moment.

"We were mad at each other," I say, keeping my eyes on Sang. "I tried to throw a storm cell at him, and when I reached for my magic, I somehow ended up with his."

A shiver runs down my spine. I need Ms. Suntile and Mr. Burrows to leave.

"Incredible," she says, going back to studying the squash in her hands.

"I'd like for you to demonstrate on me so I know how best

to structure your training going forward," Mr. Burrows says after we've been quiet for a while.

I walk toward him to get started, but then I stop. I don't have to do this for him. I step back. "No, I don't think I will. It isn't necessary for you to experience it firsthand to make effective lesson plans. I appreciate that you know more about Evers than anyone else at this school, and I will follow your plans when it comes to my training, but I don't owe you this." I say the words as evenly as possible. I don't sound angry or upset, and my heart beats in its normal rhythm.

It makes me feel as if my magic isn't the only thing getting stronger.

Ms. Suntile raises her eyebrows but says nothing. If I didn't know her better, I'd say she looks proud. Mr. Burrows starts to say something, but Ms. Suntile speaks over him. "That sounds fair to me."

To his credit, he recovers quickly. "Maybe some other time," he says. "Sang is a spring, so we'll need to get you practicing with other seasons right away." Mr. Burrows turns to Sang. "I want you to oversee as she begins training with other witches. There's clearly something about working with you that has helped her reach her full potential."

Ms. Suntile nods. Mr. Burrows isn't wrong, but something in the way he says it feels as if he's invalidating all the effort I've put in.

"I'm happy to oversee," Sang says, "but she did all the work."

"Sang, if I'm going to practice with other witches, are you sure you don't want to get back to your studies?" I turn to Mr. Burrows. "You brought him out here to study botany and do research, not train with me."

"I think I've got a few more sessions in me," Sang says, and I give him a grateful look. I want him to do his research and study what he loves, but I'm not ready to train with someone new.

"Then it's settled," Ms. Suntile says. "Mr. Park, come with us. We need to create a new training schedule. You know more about Ms. Densmore's capabilities than we do."

Ms. Suntile drops her squash to the ground, as does Mr. Burrows, and they walk off the field together, talking over each other.

But the memory of my fight with Sang—and what came after—has yet to fade, and we look at each other with the same need. The same want.

"Later," he whispers, kissing me softly before he follows Ms. Suntile.

The squash I gave him is tucked safely beneath his arm, and the way the image undoes me lets me know I'm in deeper than I should be.

Because if I'm wrong, if I'm not in total control of my magic, it will find him.

And I'll be powerless to stop it.

twenty-six

"When in doubt, plant something."
—*A Season for Everything*

It's six thirty in the morning. Early enough to have the campus to myself, late enough to hear the birds chirping and animals waking. Every day, there are new blooms to look at and different scents in the air, longer grass to step through and thicker hedges to walk around.

Training is going well, and Ms. Suntile is beside herself with what I can do. It scares me, her belief that I can steady the atmosphere and keep witches from dying of depletion while we work with the shaders to heal the Earth.

I think about Alice's quote, about making sure her magic was worth something. And I know that I have made sure mine is.

Each time I use it, each time I call out-of-season magic, the hope inside me grows that I've found my control. That my magic will never hurt another person ever again. The hope is so thick, so full, it's as if my organs are wrapped in ivy, as if climbing hydrangeas have made their way up up up until my entire body blooms with it.

But a new thought, a darker one, finds me in moments of fear and uncertainty: if I don't have control over my power, if Sang will never be safe as long as I'm a witch, I could still stay for the eclipse. I could get stripped of my magic. And Sang and I could be together, knowing he would be safe.

It's a selfish thought, one I don't dwell on, but it's there, lurking in the back of my mind. And it brings with it a question that hurts so badly it steals my breath each time I think it: *If I weren't a witch anymore, would Sang still want me?*

I exhale. I need to outrun the thoughts that refuse to quiet.

I follow the path in the woods, far from the center of campus. I have the trail to myself, though I'm sure Paige is out here somewhere, her feet pounding into the wet dirt, her breathing heavy. She's been a runner as long as I've known her, waking up before the rest of campus and running for miles, regardless of the weather.

A low layer of fog hangs in the trees. It's uneven, giving way to tree trunks and brush in the distance. The fog is one of my favorite weather conditions. Most of the time, witches are the ones to greet the weather. We pull the clouds down closer to us or form our own. But fog is the atmosphere's way of greeting us, getting low enough to the ground that we can touch it, feel it on our skin and breathe it in our lungs.

Everything is calm. Peaceful.

I run over roots and rocks, and ferns reach out and nip at my ankles. The trail begins to incline, and I climb with it, my breath coming faster than before. The higher I get, the colder the air becomes, a refreshing chill that pushes me farther. The fog gets dense, and I run through it until I'm higher than the clouds. Then the thick mist is replaced by sunlight that cuts through the branches and coats the air with lines of gold. The distinct sound of sighing carries on the breeze, the way flowers sound when they bloom. It gets louder and louder, and I run toward it until I see a clearing in the distance.

The trail is poorly defined now, and I jump over branches and push through underbrush until I escape from the cover of the trees. The clearing is large, several acres, and the half closest to me is covered in wildflowers. Bull thistle and baby blue eyes, Woods' rose and bloodroot, trillium and chicory cover the dirt like paint on a canvas. Pinks and blues and whites and reds float atop green grasses and damp earth. Sunlight drenches the field in yellow, drying the sweat from my skin. I stop and put my hands on my hips, letting my breath slow.

In the middle of the field, a large white birch tree rises up from the sea of flowers. Bright-green leaves hang from its branches and rustle in the breeze, and I know without a doubt that this is *our* birch tree. Sang's and mine—the one that grew when I used his magic for the very first time.

It's larger now and covered in leaves, but it's ours.

I knew he had uprooted the tree and replanted it somewhere else, but I can't imagine how he possibly got it all the way up here.

I want to go to the tree, touch it and prove that it's real, but

I'm stuck at the edge of the meadow. It's so full of flowers that there's nowhere for me to walk without crushing some. I feel inexplicably drawn to this place, as if the flowers were sighing just so I'd come. The air is cool and fragrant, and I sit down on the dirt, not caring that it's damp enough to soak my running tights.

I've been at Eastern for ten years, and while our gardens are lovely, this is something else entirely.

The sound of humming startles me, and I quickly stand and step back toward the trees until I'm concealed in their shade. I stay perfectly still.

The humming gets louder, and I recognize Sang's voice moments before I see him. He took a different way up, and he steps into the clearing many yards to my right. He walks toward the side opposite where I'm standing, and I instinctively take another step back.

I want to run to him and wrap my arms around his waist and kiss him beneath the branches of our tree, but something keeps me rooted in place. He walks in a way that tells me he knows this field, that it's his.

Sang drops his messenger bag on a boulder and sits on the grass. He looks so perfect here, surrounded by flowers and grasses and trees, and it makes me feel guilty, knowing he's being pulled from something he loves so much just because his magic flows on a current of calm. He's amazing with weather; his magic rivals that of everyone I know. But this is where he's at home, and it fills him up in a way that nothing else does.

I know I should say something, announce myself in some way,

but curiosity keeps me from moving. He bends over and pushes his hands into the grass. Primroses rise up and bloom right in front of him. They cover the far edge of the clearing in delicate yellow petals that sit atop deep-green leaves.

Primroses grow from contentment, and I realize with a rush that this field was built entirely from Sang's magic, planting his emotions in the dirt and watching them grow into wildflowers.

I think of all the trips he must have taken up here to cover the clearing so completely. His flowers range from love to loneliness, happiness to anger, desire to frustration. I'm overwhelmed looking at them, this map of Sang's heart plotted before me like stars in the sky.

Heat rises up my neck, and I step back as noiselessly as possible. This place is undeniably his, every flower, every sigh, every color representing a hidden part of himself. I want so badly to know what prompted each flower—what he loves, what he's mad about, what makes him happy and frustrated. I want to know it all.

But none of this is for me, and if I knew all the emotions that brought this field to life, I could never pull back from him. This meadow is Sang when he's all alone, when he's sure no one else is watching, and the beauty of it takes my breath away.

I shouldn't be here anymore. Every motion he makes—the way he plants his feelings in the dirt like seeds, the way his eyes brighten with every new flower that blooms, the way he sighs when he looks out over the field—is too much.

It's everything.

He stands and pulls a thermos, sketchpad, and plastic container from his bag, then slowly makes his way to the birch. He steps carefully over flowers and sits at the base of the tree. He leans back against it, takes a sip of what I'm sure is black tea, and closes his eyes. After several moments, he flips open his sketchbook, grabs a pencil from the container, and begins to draw. I wonder what species he's illustrating today, what plant will come alive with the strokes of his hand.

As quietly as possible, I step farther into the woods and begin my descent. And when I'm sure Sang won't hear me, I start to run. I run hard and fast, fighting against my aching muscles and burning chest, fighting against my own desires, my own frustrations, my own fears. I run down the trail and through the center of campus, all the way to my tiny cabin in the woods, the place that was supposed to prevent something like this from happening.

This feeling is entirely new to me. All I've ever known of romance is racing pulses and passionate nights, high highs and low lows, restlessness and impatience and anxiety. Everything I had with Paige.

Everything I've only ever had in summer.

And that's when I'm hit with a new fear, one that's completely separate from my magic. I'll fall even harder for Sang come summer—that's what the season has always been for me. But the first day of autumn sucks those feelings up and tosses them aside as if they're leaves on the wind.

Gone.

The dread that moves through my body feels a lot like the dread of falling for him and not being able to do anything about it.

Even if I have my magic under control, even if it never goes after him, never hurts him, my feelings are something else entirely.

And come autumn, I'll have no control at all.

CHAPTER

twenty-seven

"People, shader and witch alike, will surprise you if you let them. Some surprises will be bad, but some...some will be brilliant."

—*A Season for Everything*

A week later, I'm walking to the control field for my first test using my new magic. It's a perfect spring day, bright sunshine drenching the field and the earth damp with recent rain. Color is everywhere, greens and blues and pinks and yellows. Winter has been all but forgotten.

Sang is waiting on the field when I get there, but Mr. Burrows and Ms. Suntile aren't with him.

"Hi," I say, dropping my bag and reaching for him. He takes my hand, but he's tense and distracted. "What's wrong?"

He kisses my knuckles and gives me an apologetic look. "Mr. Burrows thought it was time for you to do another off-site test. He's waiting for you with Ms. Suntile; we're supposed to meet them there."

Dread stirs in my stomach, but I force it down. Sang will be there. Ms. Suntile will be there. And I'm more in control of my magic now than I've ever been.

"Where is it?"

"I mapped it out—the whole area is farmland."

"Great," I say, grabbing my bag from the ground. "Let's get this over with."

Sang laces his fingers with mine, and we walk to the parking lot. It's such a simple thing, walking through campus holding hands with the boy I like, but it feels monumental, significant in a way I can't explain.

He doesn't mind holding my hand in front of everyone because he believes he'll get to keep holding it. Even as our connection gets stronger and my magic recognizes what we have. Even as the seasons change and the eclipse grows nearer.

I swallow hard and tighten my grip on his hand. He must think I'm worried about the test, because he stops and looks at me. "You're going to do great," he says, and I nod, because I don't want him to know I'm distracted by what the future—what my magic—has in store for us.

I'm distracted by a decision I don't feel ready to make.

But I know I'm getting stronger. And I'm demonstrating a level of control that would have been unthinkable a year ago. Maybe I won't have to choose after all.

Today is the perfect opportunity to prove to myself that the hope I feel rising within me is justified.

We get in Sang's truck and drive to the farmlands east of us.

Sunlight reflects off the windshield and bathes the surrounding fields in its warmth, coaxing the crops from the earth.

Sang pulls off the highway and onto a narrow dirt road where Ms. Suntile and Mr. Burrows are waiting. There's a small red house in the distance and infinite rows of barley stretching out to each side. Mountains border the northern edge of the farm, the last of winter's snow dusting their peaks.

Sang turns off the engine and squeezes my hand. "You've got this. They'll be blown away, just like I am."

I raise an eyebrow. "I hope not *just* like you are."

He laughs. "You never can keep it strictly business, can you?"

"That seems to be a weakness of mine when it comes to you."

Sang leans into me. "I'm glad," he whispers. Then he opens his door and gets out of the truck.

"Welcome to your second off-site test," Mr. Burrows says when I walk over to him, as if it's something I've looked forward to. As if the first one wasn't completely outrageous.

"We've got a pretty simple test for you today," he continues. "If you do well, this will be your last until summer."

That alone is enough to make me stand up straighter and focus. "That sounds good to me," I say, hoping he doesn't miss the meaning in my words.

"You're not going to like it though," he says, going on as if I haven't spoken. My heart beats faster, and I look to Ms. Suntile for some kind of reassurance, but her expression gives nothing away.

"Why is that?" I ask, keeping my tone even. Calm.

"Because it requires the use of winter magic."

"Seriously? Don't you think it's a little pathetic that you're using a test to get your way? I told you I won't use your magic, and I meant it."

"It's your choice," he says casually. "You don't have to participate."

I look from him to Ms. Suntile and back again. "I don't?"

"No," he says. "We'll come up with another test if you choose not to do this one." He pauses. "But you will not always like the witches you have to work with. If you're going to move to the next level of your training, I have to know we can trust you to work with everyone. If not, it doesn't make sense for Sang and me to be here anymore."

I ball my fists at my sides.

"The work you've been doing with Sang has led up to this. You know how to control your magic in a calm, comfortable environment. Now it's time to control it when you're angry and upset," Mr. Burrows says.

He gestures to the mountain. "That snow is right on the edge, hovering just below the freezing point. It will take hardly any magic at all to heat it up a degree. It drains into a river as it gradually melts, but if it all melts at once, the river will flood. And if the river floods, so will this field, drowning the crops. When it does, you'll be the only one of us strong enough to stop it."

"*When* it does? You said I don't have to participate."

"You don't," he says simply.

But I hear the words he doesn't say: *This field will flood regardless.*

"These crops are someone's livelihood." My eyes burn, and my throat aches from the effort it takes not to cry. I hate how upset I sound.

I can't let him win.

"Let's go," I say to Sang.

I walk back to the truck and open my door, but something stops me from slamming it shut. I still and listen. Then the air fills with the sound of rushing water. It barrels down the mountain, taking out plants and trees as it goes, and it will destroy the farmers' crops if I don't do something.

I jump out of the truck and rush to Mr. Burrows's side. I close my eyes and find his magic darting to the surface. It's weak, but there's enough for me to follow his instructions.

I latch on to it and pull it away from him as hard as I can, freezing power slicing through the warm spring air. Mr. Burrows inhales, rapid and shallow, and he stumbles back.

With the full force of winter, I throw his magic to the clouds and gather as much cold air as I can. I shiver, and my hands shake. When my thread of magic is full of ice crystals, I send it barreling toward the mountainside and toss it into the rushing water, freezing it on impact.

I hold my hands out, keeping the magic right where it is, ensuring every last drop of water has been turned to ice.

The water comes to a halt, and everything falls silent.

I stay where I am for several seconds, breathing heavily, making sure no more water melts and no more trees fall.

I stare at the mountain, at the trail of water frozen to the side,

240

clear of the trees and brush that stood there moments ago. I slowly release Mr. Burrows's magic and send it shooting back at him in a rush that makes him lose his balance.

The barley looks golden in the sunlight, and it sways in the light breeze, unaware of how close it came to death.

Spring surrounds me again, and I'm no longer cold.

"That was truly impressive," Mr. Burrows says when he's regained his composure.

"I didn't do it for you," I say.

"Clara, you can make me out to be the bad guy all you want, but these tests are meant to stretch your magic, to challenge your control. And they work. Look how far you've come."

He begins to say something else, but I storm off toward Sang's truck and slam the door behind me. Sang gets in a moment later and starts the engine, leaving Mr. Burrows and Ms. Suntile behind.

After miles of neither of us saying a word, he takes my hand and looks over at me. "Okay, but that *was* truly impressive," he says.

I shove him in the side, but then I pause. "It was, wasn't it?"

"It was," Sang says.

He catches my eye for the span of a breath.

And before I know what's happening, he pulls over to the side of the road, and I'm closing the distance between us, crawling onto his lap and wrapping my arms around his neck. I kiss him with the urgency of the water roaring down the mountainside and my magic rushing out to meet it.

His arms are tight around my waist, and we breathe each

other in, desire edging out all my anger from before. His hands find my hips and his lips drift down my neck. My head falls back and I arch into him before returning my mouth to his.

I kiss him until the sun sets and the moon rises, until my entire body hums with want. Until it's so dark that I feel him more than see him, fingers trailing over skin, lips following in their wake.

And when we're both out of breath, our bodies aching from the cramped space, we crawl into the bed of his truck and watch the stars.

twenty-eight

*"Plants have a way of discerning between good and bad.
They will not grow and bloom for just anyone."*
—*A Season for Everything*

The days get progressively warmer. Campus is so vibrant with color and fragrance, it's hard to believe winter ever touched us. Flowers are blooming and grass is growing and the air smells of petrichor, sweet and fresh and earthy, the unmistakable scent of rain.

During periods of little rainfall, plants secrete oils that build up in the dirt and rocks, and when the rain finally comes, those oils mix and release into the air, filling it with a scent reminiscent of the forest floor. That's why spring smells so crisp, so fragrant and new. It clings to my skin and my clothes.

When I walk into the greenhouse for class, the room is already full. I look around and find a place next to Paige. I drop my bag to the floor and slip off my sweatshirt. Mr. Mendez heads to the front of the room and dives into a discussion of weeding and extraction.

The greenhouse door opens, and Sang walks over to Mr. Mendez, smiles, and shakes his hand. I knew he was coming, and yet my heart still races. My face heats with the memory of his body under mine, his face tilting up to me, his mouth on my neck and his hands in my hair. I feel Paige's eyes on me and pretend not to notice.

"Great, our special guest is here," Mr. Mendez says. "This is Sang, our advanced studies student. You've probably seen him around campus or in the field, training with Clara." Sang looks at me and smiles, and it feels so intimate even with all my classmates around. "What you probably don't know is that while he's unquestionably talented on the field, his passion lies in botany."

Botany is usually looked down upon by the witches who focus on weather, but Sang's unbridled joy in what he does makes that impossible. Even Paige keeps her mouth shut, sitting still next to me. She respects greatness in people, regardless of where it's focused. I hope she can't hear the way my heart began pounding when he walked through the door. I hope she can't feel the electricity radiating from my skin, the way it used to do for her.

I take a deep breath and try to relax.

"My Sun, Clara, get your shit together," Paige says out of the side of her mouth. "Are you this much of a mess when he trains with you?"

"Ms. Lexington, is there something you'd like to share with the class?" Mr. Mendez asks as I die from embarrassment.

"No, sir," Paige says.

Sang quirks a brow at me, and I shake my head. I'm mortified. I want to tell Paige that, for the record, I haven't always been such a mess. It's only started happening recently, when echoes of his mouth on mine and his fingers on my skin and the way he breathes out when I kiss the notch in his neck flood my mind when I see him.

And it's only spring. I can't image what summer will be like.

Mr. Mendez continues. "Sang has been working on a project that is going to revolutionize the way we uproot weeds and aggressive plants. You are the first group of witches ever to see his method, so pay attention. One day it's going to be huge, and you'll all get to say you remember the time you saw his first demonstration at Eastern. Take it away, Sang."

I try to ignore the blush that's settled in Sang's cheeks, the shy smile that forms on his lips at Mr. Mendez's praise. Sang is the perfect embodiment of spring, gentle and warm with a quiet confidence that radiates from him.

He begins his demonstration, first talking about the emotional toll of pulling plants from the earth. Springs are devastated when plants die because so much of our magic is focused on life. Death is to us what heat is to winters and ice is to summers: something we're ill equipped to handle.

Sang turns to the table at the front of the room, where one healthy sunflower sits in a clay pot.

"When we tear plants from the ground, it's very jarring for them. They leave behind a kind of stress that permeates the soil and creates suboptimal growing conditions. It's hard on the plants, hard on the earth, and hard on us. But imagine if we could simply put them to sleep and let their energy and nutrients seep into the soil, creating a richer environment than before, without causing them the trauma of being ripped from the ground or sprayed with poison." His voice makes the whole world slow, as if it's the sound of the ocean or rain falling on palm leaves.

His hands are caked in dirt, but even from here, I can see the faint stain of watercolor on his skin. The room falls perfectly silent as Sang brushes the yellow petals with his fingers and closes his eyes. At first it doesn't look like anything is happening, but then a trail of golden light bursts from the sunflower and stretches toward Sang's hands. The class inhales in unison as he gently pulls the sunlight from the flower. The light pulses, dims, and finally vanishes.

Sang turns to the room. "Now that the sunlight is extracted from the plant, it has no more energy left. We can remove sunlight faster than a plant can absorb it, weakening it so much that it's no longer able to grow." Sure enough, the sunflower has already begun to wilt.

"That's amazing," Paige says beside me.

"How do you differentiate between the sunlight in the plant and the sunlight everywhere else?" Ari asks.

"With a ton of practice," Sang says with a laugh. "I've been working on this for eight months now, and there's been a lot of trial and error. That's why I'm demonstrating on a sunflower—the stem is really large, making the sunlight within it easier to target. I'm still working on smaller plants and flowers."

Several more students ask questions, and Sang answers them with enthusiasm and grace. I want to jump up and shout that I saw this before anyone else, that it was our secret first. I wonder if he feels that way when I train with other witches, using their magic instead of his.

Paige leans toward me, breaking my train of thought. "I can see why you like him," she says.

I want to tell her she's wrong, that I don't like him in that way, but lying to Paige has never made sense. She can always see right through me.

"Yeah," I say with a sigh.

The greenhouse door opens, and Mr. Burrows rushes in.

"Pardon the interruption, Vincent," he says to Mr. Mendez. "Clara, please come with me."

There's something in his voice that worries me, and it makes me want to stay right here, safe in this greenhouse with Sang and his sunflower. I've completely ignored Mr. Burrows since the test last week, but he speaks with an urgency that forces me to move. I shoot Sang a quick glance before walking toward the door.

"Grab your things," Mr. Burrows says. I walk back to my seat and get my sweatshirt and bag.

I catch Sang's eye again on my way out. "Okay?" he mouths, and I nod.

It's been a long time since someone has looked out for me like this, and it fills me with warmth. It's these little moments I'm terrified of losing, terrified my magic will destroy in the span of a single heartbeat.

I don't want to lose him, and in my weakest moments, I feel overwhelmed by the reality that I very well might.

I pull my eyes from his and leave the greenhouse.

"This better not be another test of yours," I say to Mr. Burrows.

"It's not."

When we get outside, I understand what's happening. The sunny sky has been replaced with layers of dark clouds, and the temperature has dropped by thirty degrees, something I would have thought impossible prior to our winter heat wave.

"As I'm sure you can see, we're about to be hit by a substantial blizzard we didn't create. We're working on getting everyone inside for the afternoon and evening." Mr. Burrows leads me to the dial, where Ms. Suntile is waiting for us. I wrap my arms around my chest.

"I'll get in touch with the witches in the area and make sure they defer to us while the blizzard is on campus. We may not have planned this, but it's an opportunity for you to try out your magic in a real situation and see how you do. We won't force you, but I think it's worth using this chance to see what you're capable of," Mr. Burrows says.

I'm instantly reminded of the tornado I couldn't stop, the tornado that killed Mr. Hart, and even though my pulse is racing and I'm filled with dread, I want to try. It won't erase my failure in autumn, but maybe it will bring me some peace, knowing I've done what I set out to do: get stronger.

"He's right," Ms. Suntile says, but I cut her off.

"I'll try," I say. "But not with him."

Ms. Suntile nods. "Understood. Mr. Burrows will coordinate

with the witches in the area. Is there a particular winter you would like to work with?"

"Paige," I say without hesitation. Images of her being struck by lightning fill my head, but I force them away.

I have to start trusting myself and trusting my magic.

I have to stop living in fear that I'll hurt the people I care about.

"You're sure?" Ms. Suntile asks.

"Yes. And I'd like Sang there, too, if possible."

"Of course. Go get a jacket and whatever else you'll need, and meet Mr. Burrows at the control field in fifteen minutes. I'll engage the emergency system and make sure everyone is indoors before meeting you there."

I rush back to my cabin and find Nox pulling at the hem of my sheets. I breathe out in relief and pet his head before locking his cat door. I put on my winter coat and a hat, and just as I leave the cabin, five loud bells ring in the distance.

Here we go again.

CHAPTER

twenty-nine

"Trusting people is hard. Trusting no one is harder."
—A Season for Everything

Mr. Burrows is waiting for me on the control field when I get there. I feel the temperature as it drops with each passing second. I watch the nimbostratus clouds as they move over campus and cover the entire sky, a thick gray blanket that blocks out the sun. I shiver when the first snowflake touches my skin.

The wind is picking up. The spring flowers and green fields that brought our campus back to life are disappearing under the snow, their stems shaking with cold. Soon, I won't be able to see much in front of me, the visibility decreasing as the snow gets heavier and the winds blow faster.

I hope Ms. Suntile is able to get everyone inside.

Mr. Burrows doesn't look worried. He watches the sky and paces the field as if in anticipation.

Paige and Sang jog onto the field, and seeing them together does something weird to my heart. A huge scarf is wrapped around Paige's neck, blowing out behind her in the wind. "Ms. Suntile sent us here. What's going on?" She looks up at the falling snow, her jaw tense.

Sang goes to stand with Mr. Burrows and squeezes my hand as he passes. I don't understand how even in the worst conditions, he can make everything pause—my worries, my fears, the whole world.

I look at Paige. "We're going to try and stop the blizzard."

"And how do you propose we do that? You can deal with frost, but nothing like this," she says, motioning around us. "And I'm too weak and would prefer not to die of depletion."

The wind is getting faster, and snow is blowing every which way. I can no longer see the end of the control field, and my face is getting colder by the second. I tug my hood over my ears to keep warm.

"I'm going to pull magic from you and use it myself."

Paige laughs. "Oh, yeah? Are you going to ripen all our crops and bring on a heat wave while you're at it?"

I'm about to answer when Ms. Suntile rushes onto the field. She's out of breath and saying something, but I can't make out the words.

"What's going on?" I ask her when she's finally within earshot. Mr. Burrows and Sang come over and stand by my side.

"Our first graders," Ms. Suntile says. "The whole class is studying trees in the hills. They can't make it down in time. I was able to reach Stephanie by phone; they're all together, but visibility is low. If they try to get down, she won't be able to keep track of everyone. They aren't dressed appropriately and have no provisions with them."

Terror claws at my stomach as images of Angela and her children flood my mind. I close my eyes and try to calm down. There weren't supposed to be any stakes attached to this—it was just supposed to be a way for me to practice on a storm we didn't create. The pressure sits heavy on my chest.

"Mr. Mendez and Mr. Donovan are working on getting to them, but they're pretty far out." Ms. Suntile takes a shaky breath, and it unnerves me to see the cracks in her composed exterior. "Even with all the progress you've made, we don't expect you to be able to dissipate this storm. That class is not your responsibility; it is mine, and I failed to get them down soon enough. But if you're going to try, Ms. Densmore, now is the time."

"I don't know if I can do it," I say, my voice breaking at the end. I'm terrified of making things worse for them, the way I did for Mr. Hart.

"You can try. That's all you need to do," Sang says, stepping in front of me. "Just try."

"But trying is what killed Mr. Hart," I say, quiet enough that only he can hear me.

"A tornado killed Mr. Hart," Sang says, "and the blizzard is already here. It's already on top of them." He looks at me so intently, so gentle and sure, that everyone else fades away. I focus on his eyes, on the sun inside them, and nod.

Then the wind slams into me, throwing snow every which way until he's just a blur.

I find Paige beside me, her eyes wide. Scared. "It won't hurt," I say. "It'll be unsettling, though, and your initial reaction will be to fight me. But don't."

She looks at Ms. Suntile, who nods. "Okay," Paige says, her voice uncertain. I barely hear it above the sound of the wind.

The blizzard is fully formed now, dropping so much snow that the world around me is pure white, the greens and pinks and blues of spring hidden once more beneath winter. The wind is howling, gusts blowing fast enough that I have to plant my feet farther apart so I don't stumble back.

I worry for the kids stuck in the woods with their teacher, huddling together, freezing. The branches will provide some shelter, but with winds reaching fifty miles per hour, the trees aren't the safest place to be. And since they left when it was spring, a warm day of almost seventy degrees, there's no way their clothing will protect them from this.

"Ready?" I call to Paige. Her body is tense, and she's shaking.

She nods, and it's the first time I've ever seen her look truly scared.

I close my eyes, and Paige's magic rushes to the surface of her skin, aching to be let out, to help in some way. I recognize it instantly—the bite of winter, aggressive and deliberate. It's weak, but there's enough to grab hold of, and I send my power chasing after it.

Paige inhales a sharp breath, and I know she feels it now. She takes a step away from me and tries to hide her magic, but I step closer and catch her hand in mine.

"You're okay," I say, hoping my words find her through the wind. "Don't fight it."

"That's all I know how to do with you," she says.

The words slam into my chest and reach for my heart, threatening to break it. But I know exactly what she means, because it was always that way. We fought against our pull toward each other, our desire and love and want. We fought when we were together, each always wanting more than the other could give. We fought sleep so we could stay awake for one more kiss, one more sentence, one more touch.

And when we broke up, we fought against the feelings that didn't understand, that stayed where they were even though we had long since left.

"I know."

As soon as I say it, her hand stops pulling against my own, and her body relaxes, letting her magic flow toward me in a solid rush of power.

I think about Sang's sleeping orange and how maybe that's all anyone really wants: to be seen by another person, to be validated even when we work so hard to hide certain parts of ourselves. Maybe especially then.

I let go of Paige's hand. She's still shaking, but her magic responds right away. I pull as much as I can, the gentle, patient nature of spring replaced with the precision and force of winter. Magic wraps around magic, spring summons winter, and when I cannot hold the strength of it any longer, I direct it at the storm.

The blizzard shifts, trying to get away, but I grab hold of the wind and drape it in freezing magic that calms it down. It fights, moving left and right, up and down, trying to break free, but I hold it steady.

The thrill of cold moves through my veins, and I see myself on the river, calm and peaceful and steady. When I get to the waterfall, I don't hesitate or try to swim against the current.

I fall.

Magic rushes toward the blizzard and blasts inside. Finally, it responds. Draped in power, the storm calms and the winds slow. In one swift motion, I pull more magic and send it chasing after moisture, absorbing it all until the earth and air are dry.

I focus on the water, eradicating each drop I encounter. Without moisture, there can be no clouds, no precipitation, no blizzard.

I've never used this much magic in my life, and even though I'm pulling from Paige, my entire body shakes, and I get light-headed. The storm fights against me, and I fight back.

I fight because for so long, I hated who I was, hated my power, hated how I change from season to season. But standing here with shaking hands, using magic that isn't mine? It doesn't feel bad. It feels cleansing.

There's so much wind and snow that I can't see anyone else on the field. The blizzard howls around me as if begging me to stop, begging me to let it be.

Only one of us can win.

With one final surge, I send freezing magic rushing through the air, attracting cold right to it, making way for warmth.

The temperature begins to rise.

Snow stops falling.

There is no more wind.

And then it's over.

I can see all the way to the edge of the field.

Everything is silent, the world just as shocked as I am.

"Holy shit, Clara," Paige breathes.

Her voice sounds distant and jumbled.

"That was extraordinary," Mr. Burrows says, walking toward me. I squint, try to make him clearer, but I can't. He's blurry.

The air gets warmer, melting the snow that had started to accumulate. Spring takes over again, green grass and bright flowers peeking through the white earth.

I drop to the ground, no longer able to support my own weight.

I watch the remaining snowflakes melt and the sun punch through the clouds as if it was never hidden in the first place.

"Are you okay?" Sang kneels beside me, tilting my chin up so I look at him. I'm dizzy and weak and utterly exhausted. But I'm also shocked and filled with pride.

I used to think being alone was the answer, that letting Eastern isolate me was the only way to protect everyone else. But being in this field with Paige and Sang and my teachers, I know we were wrong. Being kept from other people was the very reason it took me so long to learn about this power, a power that is wholly dependent upon the strength of others.

I convinced myself I was okay being alone, that things were better that way.

But I'm not okay with it.

A life of isolation is too high a price for magic. A life of constantly worrying about those I love is too high a price.

And I don't want to pay it.

Sang came into my life and opened me up to a magic I never would have known without him, and I refuse to give him up. I will keep him safe, whatever it takes.

"Paige says I look at you like you're magic," I say to him, not caring who hears me.

He laughs, and his eyes get teary. He searches my face and touches my skin, and I know that as long as he's in the world, I want him beside me.

"You're my sun," I say.

Then I pass out.

thirty

"There is nothing riskier than handing your heart to another person and trusting them to keep it safe."
—*A Season for Everything*

When I come to, the field is warm, not a single crystal of ice remaining. Sang is saying my name, and Mr. Burrows is rushing over with water. I hear Ms. Suntile talking frantically to someone, and Paige is standing several feet away, watching.

"Hi," Sang says when the world comes into focus and my eyes find his.

I blink several times. "Hi."

He brushes the hair out of my face and helps me sit up.

Mr. Burrows hands me a glass water bottle, and I take several long sips. I'm not in pain anymore, and my vision is back to normal; I just feel overwhelmingly tired.

"Are you hurt?" Mr. Burrows asks.

"What do you care?" I know the words sound immature, but I say them anyway.

Mr. Burrows looks startled. "Clara, I know you don't agree with my methods, but you must see that everything I've done is because of the sincere belief I have in you and your ability to make a difference in the world."

But I don't see it, and when I don't respond, Mr. Burrows keeps talking. "We'll get you back to your room so you can rest. What you just did..." he starts, then trails off. He shakes his head.

"Was fucking wild," Paige says.

Mr. Burrows looks at her. "Yes. Precisely that."

Paige looks down at me. "You're okay?"

"I'm okay."

"Good." Then she turns and walks away.

The moment lodges in my throat, making it painful to swallow. The way she made sure I'm okay while standing several feet from me, guard up but not all the way, sears itself into my mind. The way she stayed long enough to ask, even though Sang is beside me with his hand on my back. She did it despite herself, and that means something.

"Would you help me stand up? I want to get to my cabin and take a nap," I say.

Sang helps me to my feet, and I hear Ms. Suntile tell someone to get a cart.

"I could always give you a piggyback ride," Sang suggests, his voice light.

"That won't be necessary, Mr. Park," Ms. Suntile answers for me, but I swear she tightens her lips to keep from smiling. Mrs.

Temperly comes into view and stops the cart next to me. I get on the back.

"Ms. Densmore, we'd like someone to stay with you for a while to make sure you don't have any delayed reactions. That was a significant amount of magic you used, and I'd feel better knowing you're being looked after. I can send the nurse down, or Mr. Park can stay with you. It's your choice."

"Do you want to take the afternoon off? Work on your research?" I ask, but Sang grabs my hand.

"My nephew tells me I'm the best tucker-inner he's ever seen," Sang says.

"The best?"

Sang nods. "The very best."

"I'll be the judge of that." I look at Ms. Suntile. "I'd like Sang to stay with me."

She nods. "Mr. Park, if her condition changes, you're to call the nurse and myself right away."

"Understood."

"And Clara," Ms. Suntile says—the second time she's ever used my first name—"thank you for what you did."

She turns away before I can answer, and Sang sits on the back of the cart next to me.

When Mrs. Temperly drops us off at my cabin, Sang opens all the windows and turns on my fan. He waits with his back to me while I change into a camisole and boy shorts, and then I crawl into bed.

I watch him as he pours me a glass of water and brings it to my nightstand, this simple gesture that causes my heart to ache. The blizzard makes me hopeful that my magic is under control, that it's done targeting the people I care about. But in the quiet of my cabin, seeing Sang doing something as ordinary as getting me water, my confidence wavers.

I want these moments with him, these routine, everyday moments that have nothing to do with magic. And the selfish part of me wonders if we could have this even if I were stripped.

Staying for the eclipse would give me absolute certainty that my magic would never hurt him, never go after him. And watching him right now, hope doesn't feel like enough.

I want certainty.

My eyelids are heavy. I'm so tired.

Sang pulls my sheet up to my chin and goes down the length of my body, shoving the sheet under me until I'm tightly tucked in. Then he drifts his fingers all the way back up until they reach my mouth. He gives me a soft, slow, lingering kiss. Then he pulls away.

"How'd I do?" he asks.

"I do believe your nephew is right," I say. "The best tucker-inner I've ever seen."

He kisses me on my forehead, and I close my eyes.

"I remember what I said before passing out," I whisper. "I meant it."

"I know."

I'm so glad he knows.

I sleep for fifteen hours.

Rumors about the blizzard tear through campus like a gale-force wind, and the classmates I've worked so hard to barricade myself from keep coming to chat with me as if we've been friends forever. I don't mind it; if I heard about magic like that, I'd want to know more too.

But I feel awkward and uncomfortable, not exactly sure how to react. I smile at odd times and force myself to laugh, the sound of it foreign in my ears. I'm invited to the dining hall and crowded by groups of witches who want to know what it feels like, looks like, sounds like. They ask me to take them to the control field and summon their magic, aching to see their power used in a season not their own.

But that's where I draw the line, and Ms. Suntile lets me use her as an excuse to repeatedly say no.

After two weeks of nonstop questions and stares, I'm happy to be eating lunch in my small cabin. Nox is sitting under my desk, and the window is open, letting in a warm spring breeze.

I sit down on my bed with a bowl of soup, and just as I'm about to start eating, there's a knock at the door. I almost don't answer it, but with the window open and music playing, it would be obvious I'm ignoring whoever it is.

I set my soup on my nightstand and open the door. I'm surprised to see Paige on the other side, mouth set in a straight line, hair smoothed back into a ponytail. She steps inside but doesn't say anything.

"Hi," I say, walking back to my bed and picking up my soup. "I was just eating lunch."

Paige looks around the cabin, and I turn off my music. The floor creaks as she moves through the small room.

"I can't stop thinking about the blizzard," she finally says.

"I know. I'm still surprised we were able to dissipate it."

She shakes her head. "That's not what I mean. I can't stop thinking about the way it *felt*." She sounds angry, but I can tell she's embarrassed, the way she was when she asked me to kiss her almost two years ago.

I know what she means, though.

"The first time it happened, it felt like I was falling in love, but instead of taking months or years, it was compressed into a single moment." I say it as if it's normal, but the truth is that I haven't stopped thinking about that first time with Sang, even though I've practiced this magic dozens of times now.

Untangling my legs from his, standing up, breaking eye contact—it all felt insurmountable, as though I'd have to die right there in that field because I'd never work up the strength to leave.

"With Sang?" Paige's voice brings me back to the present.

I nod.

"Did you—" She shakes her head and abandons her question.

"Did I feel it with you?"

She's still standing in the middle of my cabin, but she looks in my direction, waiting for me to answer.

"It was different. It seems to magnify any intimacy there is between me and the other person. When I demonstrated on Ms.

Suntile, it didn't feel like there was a special connection between us. It just magnified the relationship that was already there, so it was cold and impersonal. Same with Mr. Burrows. But with Sang, and you, my magic recognizes the connection we have, and it feels intense and visceral as a result."

I pause and take a sip of water. Paige doesn't say anything, so I keep going. "I think it's part feeling and part intuition. I can tell when my magic doesn't trust the person we're pulling from. I wish I could have done this with Mr. Burrows right when he arrived; I would have known he was bad from the beginning."

"But then we would have missed out on seeing you punch him, which would have been a shame." She says it seriously, and I can't help but laugh.

"I'm never going to live that down," I say.

"Never."

I set my soup on the nightstand again and shift on the bed. "It felt like remembering," I finally say.

"What?"

"When we stopped the blizzard together. It felt like remembering. Remembering when we were close friends, remembering when our friendship gave way to sleepless nights. Remembering all the things I loved about you, and remembering all the hurt and fighting and pain. It felt like our entire relationship played out over the course of one storm."

Paige breathes out as if she's relieved. "It was like that for me too. I wish I could get it out of my head."

She pauses and looks down, and I can tell she wants to say

something else. "Tell me if I'm out of line, but I got a very strong sense that you think I blame you for Nikki's death."

It's not what I'm expecting, and my throat gets tight. "Don't you?" My words are so quiet, I'm not sure if I actually said them out loud.

For the first time since she got here, Paige looks me straight in the eye. "I have *never* blamed you for Nikki's death."

As soon as she says it, something inside me breaks free. My eyes burn, and I try to hold back the tears threatening to spill over.

Paige sits down on the bed next to me. "I blame you for a lot of things, but what happened to Nikki has never been one of them." Her voice isn't soft or sweet, because she isn't trying to make me feel better. That's not her way. But she never says anything she doesn't mean, and I'm overwhelmed by the weight of her words. It feels as if I locked myself in a cage when Nikki died, and after years of being trapped inside, Paige has just opened the door for me.

"Why not?"

"Because all you did was love her." She says it so simply, and when tears slip down my cheeks, I hurry to wipe them away.

"It was my fault," I say, my body shaking with the memory of it.

"It was an *accident*. You didn't know what would happen," Paige says, her voice almost annoyed, as if she's speaking the most obvious of truths. "You have to stop blaming yourself."

"I don't know how."

"Well, figure it out, because you deserve some peace."

I look at her then. "Mr. Hart said the same thing to me once."

"He was a wonderful person."

"The best."

Paige stands and walks to my door, bends over to pet Nox. "You seem to attract the best," she says, her eyes drifting to one of Sang's illustrations on the wall.

"He's really special," I say.

"I was talking about me," she says, rolling her eyes. "But yeah, he's all right."

I barely register the way her mouth tugs up on one side before she pushes through the door, letting it swing shut behind her.

CHAPTER

thirty-one

"You're allowed to love yourself."
—*A Season for Everything*

The Spring Fling has been perfect, everything I could have hoped for in a season-end celebration. It's just winding down, the huge white tent blowing in the breeze. The linens are see-through, and hundreds of twinkle lights hang from the ceiling. Live music floats on the air and reaches far beyond the tent.

Sang has outdone himself again with the floral arrangements, but instead of brightly colored flowers, the arrangements are all made of small trees and bushes. Branches form nests with tea lights in the middle for centerpieces, and moss outlines the beverage and dessert tables.

A table at the far end of the tent holds a large planter that's filled with flowers. When we arrived, they were just seeds, and as the night went on, they fed off the magic of the springs in attendance. Now the flowers are in full bloom.

It's hard not to be swept up in it all.

These are the best parts of Eastern.

The sun has set, pinks and purples giving way to midnight black. A crescent moon hangs low in the sky, and stars make their debut for the night.

I catch Paige's eye from across the room. She looks beautiful. Her long hair is loose and easy, and she's wearing a navy gown. I smile because I can't help it, because when we dissipated the blizzard together, we weren't broken. We were us again.

She nods in response.

"Please join us on the dance floor for the last song of the evening," the vocalist says into her microphone, and my heart drops a little. I don't want it to end.

Sang wraps his arm around my waist and whispers, "Shall we?" His breath tickles my skin, and I have to shift away before the rest of my body notices.

He's in a blue suit and a crisp white shirt, and even though I've been looking at him all night, it hasn't been enough. His hair is slightly disheveled from all the dancing, and the top two buttons of his shirt are undone.

"I'd love to," I say, letting him lead me to the floor.

The piano starts, a slow, aching song I don't recognize. I wrap my arms around Sang's neck, and his hands find my waist. When I'm here with him, I don't think about what will happen after I graduate, about the expectations that will be placed on me and my magic. I don't think about the harm I've caused or worry about whether I'll do it again. I don't think about what will happen to us come the first day of autumn.

I stay with him in this exact moment, when it's just us two. Music fills the tent, the dance floor crowded with witches, the sweet smell of daphne drifting in from the shrubs outside. I press my face against Sang's, and his hand floats up and plays with my hair.

I close my eyes and sear this moment into my memory, making sure it'll be with me for the rest of my life.

The last line of the last verse keeps repeating as the song quiets, the words *please be my forever, ever, ever* carrying on the wind.

"You're my Ever, ever, ever," Sang whispers along to the song, lips brushing my ear. "Please be my forever, ever, ever." With one of his hands against the hollow of my back and the other in my hair, I beg myself to believe it. To believe we can have a forever, one that will survive my changes, one that will last long past summer.

I've always believed that being an Ever, being who I am, is incompatible with lasting romance. And maybe that's true, but I sure as sunlight know what it means to adore someone for no other reason than that they exist, for no other reason than that the universe created such a perfect person from the dust of the stars.

And tonight, I choose to believe that this will last. That we will get past my magic and the eclipse and the first day of autumn, and we will last.

The music fades out, but Sang keeps swaying with me, holding me close, so I stay right here, dancing with him to the silence that has washed over the tent, to the breeze that rushes in.

It's isn't until Ms. Suntile walks to the front of the tent and starts speaking that we finally step apart. She thanks us all and formally closes out the evening, and I lace my fingers with Sang's.

"Good night?" he asks, pressing a kiss to my temple.

"The best," I say.

"Good." The way he says it, quiet and rough, makes me pull his hand and lead him outside.

"Where are you taking me, Ms. Densmore?" he asks, following me, the voices in the tent fading into the background.

"Away."

I hold the hem of my dress as we walk into the east garden, the emerald-green fabric draped loosely over my arm. Cobblestone paths wind between shrubs and maple trees, and a small fountain sits in the center. The constant splashing of water drowns out everything else, making it feel as if we're miles away from the dance.

Just us.

A few dim lights illuminate the pathways, but otherwise it's dark enough for the moon and stars and fireflies to shine brightly around us. We weave through the garden until we reach the end, where it's bordered by tall pines and oaks.

When I turn to face Sang, there's a smile playing on his lips, his eyes the brightest thing here.

"You're my Ever, ever, ever," he sings softly, his voice just barely reaching me over the breeze. He breaks into a full smile, wrapping his arms around me and laughing into my hair.

"Why are you laughing?" I ask, holding him tight.

"Because I'm happy," he says.

"Me too." But the admission scares me, because I know how easily this feeling can be taken away.

He leans back and looks at me, the smile on his face transforming into something heavier. For a moment, we watch each other, each daring the other to close the space between us.

I'm not sure which of us breaks first, but suddenly his mouth is on mine. I drop the hem of my dress and pull him into me. Kissing him under the light of the stars makes me feel as if he is who I was always meant to find. I've never felt this way in spring, never *wanted* to feel this way in spring, and I start to think of Sang as my exception.

My spring exception.

My magic exception.

Maybe he'll be my exception when summer turns to fall. If he's the only exception I ever have, it'll be enough. More than enough.

I smile against his mouth because I can't help it, because I feel like I'm finding myself for the very first time. He doesn't define me, but the way he sees me has given me the confidence and strength to define myself.

I think that's why I look at him like he's magic. Because to me, he is.

My lips part, and the kiss deepens, each of us breathing the other in as if we're the cool night breeze or the perfect scent of daphne. He trails his fingers down my face, my neck, my arms, and when I lose my balance and stumble backward, a large evergreen is there to catch me. Sang follows, his mouth back on mine, and I think for a moment how perfect it is that two spring witches are falling for each other in the gardens at night.

I slow our kiss before reluctantly pulling away.

"It's getting late," I say.

"Can I walk you to your cabin?"

"I'd like that."

He takes off his blue jacket and drapes it over my shoulders, then wraps an arm around me. When we leave the garden, the lights in the tent are off, but I hear several voices nearby.

"Clara!" Someone hisses my name, and I squint into the darkness.

I stop walking, and Paige comes into view.

She looks me up and down, then looks at Sang. A mischievous grin spreads across her face. "You guys up for a little fun?"

"What kind of fun?" I ask, my voice skeptical.

"The ring of fire," she says.

"No way. Ms. Suntile will kill us if she finds out."

"That's why she's not going to find out. How about it, Spring?" She looks at Sang.

"I've never played before," he says.

"There's a first time for everything." Without waiting for a response, Paige grabs his arm, he grabs mine, and we're being pulled to the control field in our formal wear. I'm tripping over my dress and clutching Sang's hand as I try to keep up, my heart pounding.

"Do you know the rules?" Paige whisper-shouts over her shoulder.

"Vaguely," Sang replies, laughing as we go.

Paige finally stops pulling us when we get to the control field.

At least a dozen of our classmates are here, all seniors, and I wonder how many things I've missed out on because of my small cabin in the trees.

"Clara! Sang! You guys came!" Ari says, bouncing up and down.

"My money's on the Ever," someone else says, but they're too far away for me to see who it is.

"Is everyone here?" Paige asks.

"Yep," several people reply.

"Okay, spread out in a circle," she says, and we all do as we're told. "You want to be several yards away from your neighbor."

I'm holding Sang's hand, and we wait until the very last minute to let go.

Paige stands in the middle. "Remember: if the lightning dies with you or touches you, you're out."

Then she gives me a wicked grin.

"I'll start."

thirty-two

"Never let anyone make you feel bad about the things you're capable of. Some will insist you step into the shadows to make them more comfortable. But I'll tell you a secret: there's enough light for us all."

—*A Season for Everything*

I wish I could watch the game from above, surrounded by darkness and thousands of twinkling stars. I'd look to the Earth and see more than a dozen witches in a huge circle, still in formal gowns and suits and makeup and updos, passing a lightning bolt around so quickly I wouldn't know where it began or ended. A ring of fire in a dark, peaceful night.

My heart is racing as I track the lightning around the circle, my magic thrumming in front of me, catching the charge and keeping it going before it burns out or strikes my skin. The lightning bolt is the lowest voltage we can manage, but it still hurts if it catches your hand before you're able to send it to the next witch.

Paige stands next to me in the circle, and I toss the lightning to her, watching as it illuminates her face before moving on to Sang. The lightning never sputters or flickers when it's in his control; he sends it to the next person as if it's the most natural thing in the world, easy as breathing.

"Shit," Jay yells from the opposite side of the field. The lightning bolt crackles in front of him before vanishing. He was struck, and his skin will burn for the next day or so. As Paige would say, it hurts to lose.

"You're out," Ari says. Jay moves away from the circle and sits on the grass to watch the rest of the game. We all move in a little closer.

"Your start, Ari," Paige calls across the field. Fifteen seconds later, Ari is turning her lightning bolt horizontal and sending it off toward Thomas. But he isn't ready for it, and it dies out before he has a chance to push it forward.

Jessica laughs from beside him and announces that he's out, and he joins Jay on the grass. We all take another step closer.

Jessica creates her lightning quickly, and soon it's racing around the circle at a speed that's hard to keep up with. My magic is ready when it gets to me, and it passes by easily, never threatening to hurt me, never threatening to die out.

Around and around it goes until Melanie yells, "Ouch!" and darkness takes over the field once more. "I caught it a second too late," she says, leaving the circle. She's rubbing her hand but still high-fives the others before she sits.

Another step in.

We keep playing, the lightning coming faster and faster as

people are disqualified, and soon we're down to six players: Paige, Sang, Ari, Jessica, Lee, and me.

"Down to the wire," Lee says as he crafts our next lightning bolt. He turns it on its side and sends it flying around the circle, a brilliant, glimmering line of light connecting us all. I love watching it illuminate the faces of the witches it passes, everyone in contented concentration, laughing and focusing and challenging each other.

It doesn't feel like work. It doesn't constantly remind me that our atmosphere is hurting or that our witches are dying. It's just fun, a group of witches enjoying that we're witches.

"Damn it," Jessica yells, jumping back and clutching her hand.

"Good run, Jess," Lee says, but she shoves him when she passes, rolling her eyes.

"Oh, stop gloating," she says, and Lee holds his hands up, laughing.

Jessica sits down with the others who are out, and it's my turn to start the next round. My hands get to work, pulling water from the soft dirt until it vaporizes and a heavy thundercloud hangs high above me.

It waits for me, the patience of the season obvious even within the storm. Spring is the epitome of patience, waiting out the cold and frost and death of winter until everything comes alive again.

I smile, because I think maybe I came alive again this spring too.

The energy builds, a current that prickles my skin and moves through my body in jolts. Lightning flashes before me, and I flip it on its side and send it flying toward Paige.

But when it makes its first pass around the circle and gets back to me, it's clear it's too strong. Way stronger than the others. I try to catch it, stop it with my hand or let it vanish in front of me, but it's as if it has its own magic, circling around us as if it's the one in control.

Paige grunts under the weight of it, but it refuses to go out, spinning around and around and around.

"Move back!" I yell. "It's too strong."

Everyone does as I say, rushing back, but the lightning follows them, unwilling to die out.

I watch in horror as I realize what's happening.

The lightning bypasses Paige and weaves around Ari, flying straight toward Sang. It follows our connection, leaving a shimmering trail in its wake, crushing my hope that I'd learned to control my magic.

I was so wrong to hope.

"No!" I scream, but it's no use.

Lightning enters his chest and shoots down his left arm, exiting out his fingertips. He convulses and is thrown several yards before slamming into the ground, shaking shaking shaking.

"No!" I yell again, running toward him.

I drop to my knees and say his name, but he doesn't respond. A superficial burn is already forming on his skin, an intricate, fractal-like pattern that's deep red and looks like the leaves of a fern. It covers all the skin I can see on his chest and neck.

"Sang!" I yell, but there's still no reply.

I look at his chest, but it doesn't rise and fall.

It's motionless.

My fingers tremble as I check for a pulse, and I almost cry when a faint, rhythmic beating meets my fingertips.

"He has a pulse, but he's not breathing," I say as Paige drops to the ground beside me. I tilt his head back and begin mouth-to-mouth, taking huge gulps of air and filling his lungs. I watch his chest rise as I breathe into him, up up up before deflating again.

Another big breath, another rise of his chest.

I keep going until finally, *finally*, he chokes and gasps for air.

"I'm here, you're okay," I say, tears streaming down my face. "You're okay."

His movements are slow, and his eyes drift back in his head before locking on mine.

"Tell me what hurts," I say, searching him for signs of trauma.

"My skin," he says, his voice garbled.

"Okay. Anything else?"

"My muscles are sore."

I nod. "Do you know who I am?"

A small smile forms on his lips. "My Ever, ever, ever," he says, so weak I can barely hear it.

I choke back the tears and nod hard. "Yes, good," I say. "That's good. Do you know what happened?"

"I was about to win the ring of fire when I was struck by lightning instead."

I laugh and help him sit up. "Yes, I'm sure you were going to win."

"I would have given you a run for your money," Paige says beside me, but I can hear the relief in her voice.

Sang looks at her. "I believe that," he says.

Paige stands and goes to the rest of our classmates, tells them Sang's okay and that they're not to tell anyone else what happened unless they want to open themselves up to Ms. Suntile's punishment.

"Can you walk?" I ask, my voice shaking.

Sang reaches his hands to my face and looks me right in the eyes. "I'm okay, I promise. Just a burn and some sore muscles. I'll be fine." He wipes the tears from my cheeks and gives me a soft kiss.

"This was my fault." It's a terrifying realization that I whisper more to myself than him.

"What? No, it was a stupid game that got out of hand. That's all."

"Sang, I watched it go after you. It sought you out." My breath gets quicker and shallower as I realize the full weight of what happened. "I can't keep you safe," I say between sobs.

"Hey, let's talk about this later, okay? It's late, and it's been a long night." He slowly gets to his feet, and I stand with him, ready to catch him in case he falls. But he's steady, his vision and breathing back to normal.

"That burn's going to hurt like hell," Paige says. "I still have some cream left over from when I was struck earlier this year. Hey, we could start a club."

"That isn't funny," I say to her through clenched teeth.

"Not even a little?" Her mouth quirks, and I know she's trying to lighten the mood, trying to keep me from spiraling into thoughts of my parents and Nikki and how I have no control over who I am.

But it's too late. I'm already there.

"He's right," Paige says, removing all teasing from her voice. "It was just a game that got out of hand. That's all."

"You saw how it passed right by you," I say. "It *chose* him."

"Well, you know what they say: lightning never strikes the same place twice." She pauses, letting her horrible joke hang in the air between us. Then her mouth quirks up again, and I can't help but laugh.

Sang laughs, too, pulling me into his side and planting a kiss on the top of my head. But dread moves through me and sits heavy in my gut.

I thought I had gained control over my magic, thought I'd finally mastered it. Thought it was no longer a threat to the people I care about.

But I was wrong.

If I don't separate myself from Sang, keep my magic far away from him, he will always be at risk.

The realization breaks my heart in two, but it's the only way.

I wrap my arm around Sang and get him home. I tend to his burns and tuck him in with perfect tucker-inner technique. I kiss him softly in the darkness and watch as he drifts into a heavy sleep.

And as his breaths come and go, the only sound interrupting

my thoughts, I plan out the words I'll say in the morning, when I'll end the best thing I've ever had.

My heart aches, knowing it's something I'll never heal from.

And for the very first time, I hope that when autumn comes, it makes my feelings vanish. Gone, as if they were never here at all.

thirty-three

"The pain of love is almost directly inverse to the joy of it."

—*A Season for Everything*

I wake up to early morning light filtering in through thin curtains. Birds chirp outside the window, and Sang breathes softly in his bed, fast asleep. I tried to stay up all night, to make sure Sang was okay, but I crawled into bed next to him sometime after three. I didn't even bother to change out of my dress.

His back is pressed up against my torso, my arm wrapped around him, clutching him as if he's the most precious thing in the world. The night before floods into my mind, images of dancing with Sang while he whispered in my ear, kissing in the gardens, playing the ring of fire, being so incredibly happy. Then lightning. I ache with the memory of it, with how quickly the night turned.

I was so sure I'd mastered my magic, so sure it was within my control. Even now, I don't know where I went wrong. I was able to use more magic than I ever had to stop a blizzard, and Sang was safe, but a stupid game with zero stakes turned into a nightmare. I don't understand.

Maybe I've approached my magic all wrong; maybe I'll never have total control over it. Maybe it will always be a risk to the people I care about most.

Suddenly, I'm angry that I've devoted so much time to training, given so much of myself to the process. And now I'm stuck. Before I knew I could pull off-season magic, the eclipse was always my answer: get stripped, stop hurting people.

But it's so complicated now.

If I don't get stripped, my magic will save countless witches from depletion, but Sang and anyone else unlucky enough to be cared about by me is at risk.

If I do get stripped, witches will continue to die needlessly, but I could have relationships. I wouldn't have to be alone.

It makes me want to scream in frustration.

I know I need to get up. Start the day. Talk with Sang. But the thought of removing my arm from his body, of creating a space between us that will never be closed again, threatens to undo me. It makes everything hurt, my heart and stomach and head and throat. So I stay. For another hour, I keep my arm draped over him, my forehead nestled into his back, and I memorize the rhythm of his breathing. I match my breaths to his, count the seconds between inhales, so that even when I'm alone in my cabin, I can breathe with him.

In, out. In, out.

Sang stirs beside me, and I quietly slide off the bed. It's the first time I've been in his apartment, and it's so perfectly him that it's hard to look at. I didn't see any details last night, when it was dark and I was solely focused on Sang.

But now it's bathed in golden light, and I see him everywhere. There are dozens of houseplants hanging from the ceiling and covering most of the horizontal surfaces. Species I recognize and species I don't. There's an old wooden desk covered with half-completed paintings and drawings, watercolor staining the wood, and dirty water with brushes in it.

There's a framed picture of him with a little boy, whom I assume is his nephew. Another framed photo from his graduation, his parents on either side of him, proud smiles on their faces. It stings, knowing I'll never meet them. Knowing I expected that one day, I would.

I walk into the kitchen and put the kettle on, but when I look for tea, I'm met with an entire cupboard of loose-leaf varieties I have no idea how to prepare. Jars and jars of Assams and Darjeelings and oolongs, teas I've never heard of before. I don't think I've ever had tea that didn't come in a bag, and if this were a normal morning, I'd ask Sang what the differences are and watch as he prepared some. I feel as if I'm already missing out on all these things that could have been.

There's a jar of ground willow bark on the first shelf, and I grab it and dump some in water to simmer on the stove. Willow bark is a natural pain reliever, and Sang will have a nasty headache when he wakes. Once it's done simmering, I set it aside to let it steep.

I wrap my arms around my chest and walk into the living room, sinking into the only chair. There's an easel in the corner with a half-finished painting on it, a large pine tree in an otherwise urban setting. The detail is incredible, so realistic and vivid it could be a photograph. A book of poetry sits on one side of the chair, a huge science fiction novel on the other. I page through the poetry, paying special attention to the poems Sang has marked. They're all about nature. My fingers trace the paper, and I only put it down when I hear the floor creak.

I jump up and rush into the bedroom. Sang is sitting on the side of his bed, wearing a T-shirt and sweatpants, holding his head. His eyes light up when he sees me. "Hi," he says, voice still groggy with sleep.

The pain in my chest gets worse.

"Hi," I say. "Headache?"

He nods, and I walk to the kitchen and strain the bark from the water before pouring it into a mug. I hand it to him, and he takes a long sip.

"I found your stash of willow bark," I say.

He gives me a grateful smile. "I would have cleaned up if I'd known you'd be coming over." His voice is shy, and I almost laugh. There isn't a single thing out of place.

"How are you feeling?" I ask, sitting next to him. My dress pools on the floor around my feet, and I wish I had changed into something of Sang's. But the thought of having to give it back to him makes me glad I didn't.

"My skin feels like it's on fire, and my muscles are really sore. Otherwise I'm fine."

I take a deep breath and try to erase the memory of him being struck by my own lightning, but I know I'll never forget it. It will stay with me and haunt me the way the images of my parents and Nikki and Mr. Hart do.

"I'm so sorry," I say. I can't look at him.

He rubs his hand over my back. "It was an accident," he says, the words so gentle.

"It was foreseeable," I say.

"You had no way of knowing. It was just a game that got out of hand. That's all."

"That isn't all, and you know it."

We're silent for several moments. "Why don't we get you some tea first, and then we can talk about it?" He stands up and offers his hand to me, but I don't take it. He looks at his open palm and frowns, then walks to the small kitchen. I follow behind him.

"I started the water, but I got overwhelmed by the selection," I say.

He laughs, but it's superficial and small. "Do you like black tea in the morning?"

I nod, and he grabs a jar from the cupboard labeled ASSAM. "This one's my favorite," he says, scooping the leaves into a porcelain teapot, a routine that's clearly second nature to him. It's soothing, and I think it would be nice to start the day with the clinking of teapots and scooping of leaves.

Nice to start the day with him.

And not just today. Every day.

When he's done, he pours me a mug. He motions for me to sit

down in the living room, and he brings out his desk chair and sits next to me, sipping his willow bark tea.

My eyes catch on the painting on the easel. I could have an entire house covered in his art, and it still wouldn't be enough of him.

"It's for my mom," he says, following my eyes. "Her birthday is coming up."

"It's beautiful."

"It's a Korean pine; she had a huge one that she loved in her backyard when she was growing up, but since she moved to the States, she's never lived in the right climate to grow one herself. She still has a jar of preserved pine cones sitting on her dresser that she took from the tree before she moved."

"She's going to love it," I say, and I force my voice to remain steady. I want all these stories, all these moments, all these details that make him *him*. I don't want to lose them.

"Talk to me," he finally says, looking at me with such tenderness that I think I might cry as soon as I open my mouth.

I swallow hard.

"I thought I had control over my magic, but I clearly don't. If I can lose control like that during a stupid game, I can't even imagine what could happen during a dangerous event where I'm using all the magic I can." I take a sip of tea, and the warmth feels good as it slides down my throat. "My magic went after you last night, and I can never let that happen again. I would never forgive myself if—if—" But I can't make myself say the words. My unfinished sentence hangs in the air between us.

"We'll be extra careful going forward," Sang says, touching my arm.

"Careful how? There is no careful with you," I say, my voice rising. "I care too much."

"I don't know, but we can figure it out. I know we can."

"We've already figured it out. The solution is isolating me in a cabin in the woods and making sure I never use my magic around people I care about. Making sure my magic never even *knows* there are people I care about. That's the solution."

Sang shakes his head. "That is not a solution. We'll find another way."

"There is no other way!" I practically shout the words. "As long as I care about you, I can't—we can't—" But I don't know how to finish the sentence.

I can't come near you.

We can't be together.

We can't be anything.

I set down my tea and stand up, pacing around the room.

He stands as well and reaches for my hands. "Clara, we can make this work. Please."

I shake my head, back and forth and back and forth. I finally look him in the eye, hold his gaze. "You are everything to me. And that's why we can't be together."

"Clara, please," Sang says, his face crumbling. "Please don't do this."

"You have been more to me than I ever could have imagined. I owe so much to you."

"No," Sang says. "Don't you do this." Tears spill from his eyes and run down his cheeks, and I force myself not to reach out and wipe them away. "I love you," he says, his voice breaking. "I love you," he repeats, this time in a whisper.

A sob escapes my lips, and I turn away from him and cover my mouth. I think I've known for a long time; I think maybe his love for me is what enabled me to love myself.

Then a thought—a selfish, dark thought—edges its way in, the total solar eclipse becoming vivid in my mind. I turn back around and meet his eyes, red and swollen and wet.

"Would you still love me if I weren't a witch?" The words catch in my throat, so quiet and weak, barely a whisper. I can't believe I've spoken them out loud.

Sang's eyes widen. He watches me, and it's clear he's warring with himself, trying to figure out how to respond. But his silence is for the best.

I don't want to know if his answer is no, and he would never tell me if his answer were yes. He thinks I'm too important.

"I—" he starts, but I cut him off. I put my hands on either side of his face and kiss him through my tears and his.

When I pull away, he looks defeated.

"I would rather die than cause you harm," I say with so much finality I can practically see the wall forming between us, an impenetrable barrier that's impossibly vast.

"Don't I get a say in this? Don't I get to decide if it's worth the risk?" he asks through gritted teeth.

"No," I say.

I look at him for several more seconds, then walk out the door.

As soon as I do, I know I will never, not for a single moment, forget the way his face collapsed and he stared into his willow bark with swollen, angry eyes.

I wonder if there will ever come a time when I can think of it without breaking.

But Sang has turned me into glass, so strong, yet with the tiniest crack that's spread from every kiss.

Every touch.

Every look.

And when that crack comes under pressure, I will shatter every time.

spotted wintergreen

summer

thirty-four

"You weren't born to be isolated."
—A Season for Everything

The air is sweet, and the sky is bright. Summer rolls through campus on a wave of sunshine and heat and long days fading into short nights. The grass grows taller, flowers bloom brighter, and the sun sits higher in the cerulean sky.

The past two weeks have gone by in a blur of training with new witches and dreaming of lightning and trying to remember the cadence of Sang's breathing when I can't sleep. I get up in the mornings, go to classes, and solemnly nod at the other witches involved in the ring of fire as if we're in on some sort of conspiracy together. Then I do it all again.

I let Mr. Burrows oversee my sessions, because the animosity I feel toward him is easier than the pain I feel with Sang. I train with other witches and convince myself it's better this way. I take the long route to class so I can pass the greenhouse and make sure Sang is there, safe.

Safe from me, and safe from my magic.

The first time I see him feels like being crushed by a wave of longing, swept out to sea and gasping for air. Every part of me aches for him—my fingers and skin and mouth and hair, my veins and heart and lungs and bones. Summer overwhelms me, making the pain of losing him greater than it already was and the misery of wanting him stronger than before.

I don't know if I can make it through three months of this.

I walk to the east garden, where my first group training session is taking place since the one in winter, when I struck Paige with lightning. I don't feel ready for it. The ring of fire proved I haven't mastered my magic the way I thought.

I let my guard down, and it resulted in injury that could easily have been death.

A group of springs is already at the edge of the garden when I get there, and even though it's a bright, sunny day, I see the garden cast in darkness. The ghosts of Sang and me kissing, touching, holding each other send a chill down my spine.

I blink and refocus, setting my bag on the ground and waiting for Mr. Burrows to arrive. Mr. Donovan will be running the exercise, but Mr. Burrows will watch and judge.

"How are you feeling? Excited?" Mr. Donovan asks. He was elated when Mr. Burrows decided we'd use spring magic for my first group exercise. He's been counting down the days.

"I'm nervous," I say, answering honestly. "I just want to do a good job."

"I'm sure you will," he says. "Try not to put too much pressure on yourself, Clara. We're only working with flowers—nobody's life is on the line."

He says it to be reassuring, but the ring of fire was a game too—a silly, no-stakes-attached game that went wrong. So horribly wrong.

I don't feel any safer using my magic to grow daffodils than I do using it to stop a blizzard.

Still, I smile and shove my worries aside. I have to work with other witches if I want to realize the full extent of my power. I might as well start now.

Mr. Burrows arrives at the garden just as the bell rings, but Sang is with him, a jar of seeds in his hand. Every part of me tenses up. I want to run to him, touch him, hear his voice and feel his calming magic.

But more than that, I want him to leave, because he can't be anywhere near me. Can't be anywhere near my magic.

I walk over to Mr. Burrows. "What is he doing here?" I ask. My words sound almost frantic. I wish Sang would look anywhere other than my face, but he doesn't—he keeps his eyes on me.

"We're using spring magic for your exercise today. It makes sense for him to be here," Mr. Burrows says.

But I take a step back.

"He can't be here," I say, my voice quiet but urgent.

"Clara," Sang starts. I cut him off.

"No," I say.

Mr. Burrows looks between us, and understanding sparks in his eyes.

"I thought you may have gotten close," he says, more to himself than to me. I wince anyway. "That's not a judgment, Clara. He's easy to like."

"Please," I say. "I can't do this exercise with him here."

"He'll be off to the side with me, observing—"

"He can't be here!" I shout, cutting him off and surprising myself with the shrillness in my voice. The springs stop talking, and everyone stares at me, waiting to see what will happen next.

Mr. Burrows holds up his hands and nods. "Okay, whatever you're comfortable with." He doesn't mean it. He's only saying it because he got his way, because I've already used his winter magic.

Sang's jaw is tense, and his eyes are still trained on me. I look at him, desperate, pleading. He swallows hard.

"The last thing I want is for you to be terrified of who you are," he says, his voice quiet and sad. He hands the jar of seeds to Mr. Burrows and walks away, and I'm relieved and devastated at the same time.

Would you still love me if I weren't a witch?

It was an impossible thing to ask. Sang would never be okay with me giving up my power for him, which is one of the reasons I fell as hard as I did, one of the reasons I'm sure my heart no longer belongs to me.

But I still wanted to hear a yes slip from his lips.

Impossible.

I shove away my question and shove away his silence.

Mr. Burrows clears his throat. "Shall we begin?" he asks, looking at Mr. Donovan.

Mr. Donovan nods and starts to explain the exercise. It's easy enough: we'll dampen the soil with rain, plant the seeds, then accelerate their growth, using only spring magic. Once we're done, we should have a pretty row of daffodils bordering the garden.

I stand next to Ari, and the rest of the springs line up on the other side of her. The goal is to find Ari's magic, and once I have a solid grasp on it, try to pull from the others as well until I have a strong, powerful stream of spring magic.

I've only ever pulled magic from one witch at a time, and my heart races even though we haven't started yet. I take a steadying breath; nobody's life is on the line, like Mr. Donovan said.

Except it always feels like there is when my magic's involved.

"Okay, Clara, take it away," Mr. Donovan says.

I glance at Mr. Burrows, who's standing off to the side with a clipboard, taking notes. For some reason, it enrages me—he treats me as if I'm a lab animal being used for research. It's all about how far he can push me and push my magic. He gets excited when I accomplish something new, and then it's on to the next maze, the next exercise, the next test.

I'm so tired.

I take a breath and tell Ari to call up her magic. Her short, curly hair bounces with her movements, and I feel when she settles into herself and brings her magic to the surface.

Then I get started.

I find her magic right away, calm and steady, and she laughs when I pull it toward me, as if she's utterly delighted.

I get to work on forming a basic cumulus cloud that we can

fill with rain and use to dampen the soil, but before I've even tried to add another witch's magic, I tense up.

Ari and I have been at Eastern together for over ten years. We've never been particularly close, but we've always been friendly. Does my magic recognize her?

And what about Mr. Donovan? He's been my teacher since I was in middle school.

Then there's Melanie, who photocopied all her notes and brought them to my cabin the week I had the flu last year. She even brought soup with her. We don't know each other well, but did her generosity and thoughtfulness create a connection between us that my magic can sense?

It's overwhelming, the worries and what-ifs and questions I might never have the answers to. I'm so afraid of hurting another person.

I try to hold on to the cloud, but all my fear makes it vanish, as if wrapped in warm air.

Ari gives me a questioning look.

"Start again," Mr. Burrows says with irritation.

I shake out my arms, trying to dispel the nervous energy coursing through me. Then I do as I'm told.

I close my eyes and let the impulsive, fiery magic of summer be replaced with the peaceful stillness of spring, a held breath in no rush to discover where I'll send it.

It waits for me, and when I start to gather moisture in the air, it flows from me in cautious streams, as if it knows I'm scared.

Finally, another cloud forms.

"Everyone call your magic to the surface," Mr. Donovan says. "It's there when you're ready, Clara."

I nod and slowly feel for the other springs, their magic rising to greet me the way dogs greet their owners, excited and happy and eager.

I start pulling, but this entire garden reminds me of Sang, of the moments we spent together before we played the ring of fire and everything changed.

Sang being chased by lightning.

Sang flying through the air.

Sang slamming into the ground.

I don't trust anything anymore, don't trust that a single person here is truly safe.

I can't do it.

I drop my hands and open my eyes.

"I'm sorry," I say to Mr. Donovan. Then I turn to Mr. Burrows. "I'm done. I'm not doing this."

"Yes, you are," he says. "This exercise is a necessary part of your training. You're ready for it."

"It's not up to you." I grab my bag and sling it over my shoulder.

"We aren't done here," he says, each word strained and tight, ready to snap. Everyone is watching us; even Mr. Donovan doesn't look away.

I don't say anything as I pass him and leave the garden.

"This is a failing grade," he calls, his last attempt to bring me back.

"Then fail me," I say without slowing my steps.

For a moment, it's freeing, acting as if I don't care, acting as if the consequences don't matter to me. And maybe they don't, not when it comes to Mr. Burrows.

But I have a very powerful, very volatile magic inside me, and I have to figure out how to live with it.

And if I can't, I must decide if I can live without it.

thirty-five

"In the summer, I fall in love with every soul I come across, even if just for a moment."

—*A Season for Everything*

Mr. Burrows calls me into his office first thing the next morning. Ms. Suntile is present as well, and he says that I must make up the session I walked out on. He tells me I wasted everyone's time and that I owe Mr. Donovan an apology.

When Ms. Suntile interrupts him to ask why I left, I tell her the truth: I didn't feel ready. I didn't feel in control.

And to my amazement and gratitude, she says I did the right thing, that I should never be forced to use my magic if it feels erratic in any way. She says they've pushed me hard this year and that perhaps I'm due a break.

I'm not sure why she has come to my defense so strongly, but it matters more than she knows. She says I can make up the group session after the eclipse and that I don't have to worry about it until then.

And while I don't know how to stop worrying about it, I'm grateful for the days off from training and the days away from Mr. Burrows.

I walk back to my cabin feeling a little lighter than I did when I woke up this morning, and that's something. It's small, but it's something.

When I get inside, I change out of my jeans and put on leggings and a tank top. I lace up my running shoes and take a long drink of water. I rarely exercise in autumn or winter, favoring late nights and long novels to early mornings and cold temperatures. But spring and summer drive me outside, and I step out of my cabin and run. Run from the image of Sang's face when I left his apartment; run from the memory of his mouth on mine; run from the way the world slowed and my mind stilled when I was with him.

Run from everything.

It's a warm morning, and I start sweating right away. I pass the houses and the dial, the library and the dining hall, and weave through the gardens until I'm out past the control field and see the trails in the distance.

Birds are chirping, and a slight breeze moves through the trees, rustling the branches. My hair is in a ponytail, frizzy curls hitting my back as I go. I wish my legs could carry me faster, could outrun my mind.

My breaths are even and deep, getting heavier by the time I finally reach the trail that's become my lifeline.

I run along the path, my legs burning and my lungs heaving

as I climb the mountainside. I jump over rocks and exposed roots, getting higher and higher.

When I finally reach the meadow, I stop and catch my breath. It gets denser every day, new wildflowers popping up, and I know they must be from Sang because of how quickly they appear, how fast the meadow changes.

I walk to the birch tree, careful not to crush any flowers, and sit in the dirt surrounding its trunk. I lean against it and close my eyes, listening to the way the leaves move with the wind, the way my breath mixes with the sounds of nature.

And then, because I can't help it, because I miss Sang so much it physically hurts, I get on my knees and press my hands into the dirt, feeding all my emotions to the soil. A single spotted wintergreen rises up from the ground, a bright-green stem giving way to tiny white flowers. They open up in unison and sigh as if perfectly content.

Spotted wintergreens are the flowers that grow from longing.

It is the only flower in the dirt surrounding the birch, and I know he'll see it.

I check my watch and slowly stand. I stretch my legs and roll my shoulders, getting ready for the run back to my cabin. I look at the wintergreen once more, then step through the meadow until I'm back under the cover of the trees.

I begin my descent, but the sound of a twig breaking in the distance stops me. I know I should keep going, should run down the trail and not risk being seen, but I can't. I slowly turn and tuck myself behind a large evergreen, watching the meadow.

Sang appears in the distance, his bag over his shoulder. He walks around the far end of the meadow and through to the birch, *our* birch, and sets his bag on the dirt. He pushes his palm against the trunk of the tree and exhales, so heavy I can hear it from here.

He turns and stops, his head tilted toward the ground. He stands there for several seconds, staring at the spotted wintergreen, then crouches beside it and touches the petals. He stands up and looks around, and I duck behind the evergreen, out of sight.

My heart pounds, my legs aching to go to him.

But I stay where I am.

I take a deep breath and risk another peek at the meadow. Sang is no longer looking around and instead sits in front of the flower cross-legged, watching it. He shakes his head. Then he carefully pushes his hands into the soil next to it, and a cardinal flower punches through the surface, long green stem rising toward the sun, vibrant red leaves spilling every which way. It's so close to my spotted wintergreen that its leaves brush the white petals.

Cardinal flowers grow from frustration.

I lean back against the evergreen and close my eyes.

I'm relieved, so relieved that we have this secret way of communicating. Fully separate from one another, perfectly safe.

Sang is frustrated, and I almost laugh at how glad I am to know it.

Maybe it will be tortuous, communicating in this way. Maybe the whole meadow will soon be filled with cardinal flowers that do nothing to ease the hurt inside us.

And yet, the next morning, I run the same route, through

campus and up the trail to this perfect meadow beyond the trees. I kneel beside the cardinal and touch the earth, a perfect purple coneflower rising to greet me. The deep-orange center is perched upon delicate purple petals that point to the ground, the perfect flower for apologies.

I look at the three flowers side by side. Other than yelling at him to leave the group session, it's our only conversation since that day in Sang's apartment.

I miss you.

I'm frustrated.

I'm sorry.

Over the next three weeks, we add to our conversation, wildflowers taking over the dirt surrounding our birch tree. Baby blue eyes to say I'm relieved, bull thistle to say he's angry, blanketflowers to say I'm ashamed, Queen Anne's lace to say he's hurt, chicory to say I'm sad, more chicory because he's sad, too, and so much spotted wintergreen, longing everywhere.

We go back and forth, planting our vulnerability and hurt and desire for the other to see. We're honest with each other. We open ourselves up, each trusting the other to see us for who we are.

And we do.

We see each other. I think we always have.

A new flower punctuates the end of our conversation—a single iris to say he loves me.

Every emotion beautiful, every reaction valid, each flower stunning in its own way.

It doesn't erase the hurt or pain or fear or longing. But it makes it more manageable, knowing we're in it together.

I think deep down, he understands that this had to happen. He knows I could never keep him safe, and he'd make the same decision if our roles were reversed. And while I'm so mad at the Sun for cursing my magic the way she has, I can't regret that she brought Sang to me.

The eclipse is in two days, and while I still let myself consider what it might be like to get stripped of magic and live a new life, I don't know if I can go through with it. I used to be so sure, but this past year has complicated everything, and part of me mourns for the certainty I once had. Stay for the eclipse, get stripped, never let another person die from my magic.

Be with Sang, knowing he would be safe. If he still wanted me, that is.

I'd lose a lot, but I'd gain a lot too.

But now I think about all the witches who have died from depletion, risking their lives by stretching their magic in the off-season, something that is entirely natural for me. Something that feels right, like all my pieces fall into place when I'm pulling power from a season that's fast asleep.

And I think about the shaders who are finally having conversations with us, who are finally accepting their roles in all this and looking for ways to reverse their course.

I could help bridge the gap, stabilize the atmosphere now while we work to heal it in the future.

It's a messy, complicated choice that has a clear right answer.

But I'm a messy, complicated human, and I'm selfish and tired and want more for myself than a life of longing and isolation.

I look down at the iris, and my eyes fill with tears. I know Sang would still love me if I weren't a witch—I know it the same way I know that hot air rises and broccoli is a flower.

Next to the iris, I touch the earth and pour one more feeling into the soil. Wild bergamot rises up before me, a perfect lavender flower that grows from absolute adoration.

I adore you.

I watch as the pompom bloom sways in the breeze, completing the conversation until we return after the eclipse.

Then I run down the trail, leaving part of myself for Sang to find.

thirty-six

"It is not your job to protect the people who hurt you."
—*A Season for Everything*

I'm rushing around my cabin, packing my bag for the evacuation today. The path of totality crosses directly over Eastern, so we're heading a few hours away, where we can watch the partial eclipse and keep our connections to the sun.

Every witch has to evacuate the path, leaving it wide open to whatever the atmosphere has in store. It's risky. But totality only lasts for a few minutes, then it'll be safe for the witches to return. There's no other option.

I'm about to zip my duffel when the dream elixir Sang gave me catches my eye. I've never used it because I don't want it to run out, but I take off its small cap and smell the amber liquid every night before bed. It's part of my routine now, and I wrap the vial in layers of tissue and tuck it in the folds of my sweatshirt, not wanting to go a night without it.

Nox is following me around like a shadow in the sun, sensing my imminent departure. I fill his food and water bowls and give him lots of scratches. He's been with me through my worst, and I wonder if I'd be okay if it was just Nox and magic and me.

I wouldn't be as happy as I could be, or as content, or as joyful. But maybe I'd be okay. And maybe okay would be enough.

I zip my bag and sling it over my shoulder, then open the door. A small package sits on the mat outside, and I bend to pick it up. It's wrapped in brown paper and twine with an envelope taped to the front that has my name on it.

"Who's this from?" I say to Nox as I walk over to my bed, tearing the envelope open. I scan the bottom of the letter and find Lila Hart's name—Mr. Hart's wife. I inhale slowly.

Dear Clara,

We've only ever met in passing, but I feel like I know you. Richard spoke of you often, and with such high regard. He loved teaching you and counted the years you spent together among the best of his career. I've heard bits and pieces of what you've accomplished this past year, and I know Richard would be so proud of you. I wish more than anything that he were here to see it.

I recently started packing up his office and came across this. He kept a logbook of all your sessions together, but it's more than that.

It turns out that he spent many late nights, coming to bed hours after I had fallen asleep, researching Everwitches. He made a few discoveries that I think will interest you.

Please read it.

And if there is ever anything you need, I hope you will consider reaching out. Richard cared for you very much, and after years of hearing him talk about you, I suppose I started to as well.

With love,
Lila Hart

I read the letter twice. I wish Mr. Hart were here and swallow the guilt I feel that he isn't. I look at Alice's memoir, the book that was wrapped in the same brown paper. He keeps finding his way back to me, and the thought makes me smile.

I start to unwrap the package, but a loud bell rings in the distance. It's time to go. The buses have already started loading.

I set the gift down and give Nox a final kiss on the head. I put my hair in a ponytail and grab my water bottle, then pick up my duffel and leave. I'm halfway out the door when I turn back. Something tells me not to go without Mr. Hart's logbook; at the very least, it will be good to have a distraction while I'm stuck in a hotel with nothing but my own thoughts.

I grab the package off my bed and gently tuck it inside my bag.

Another bell rings, and I rush to the parking lot. I don't want to be left behind.

As soon as I think it, though, I know Mr. Burrows would never let that happen. He would drag me out of the eclipse's path with his bare hands if he had to.

When I get to the parking lot, rows of buses are lined up along the curb. I get on the summer bus, relieved I don't have to be on the same one as Sang. I haven't seen him since we started growing flowers for each other to find. I hope he's been busy with his research, spending hours in his immersion house, making up for all the time he lost when he had to start training with me.

I hope Mr. Burrows is making up for the deceit he used to bring him out here in the first place.

The buses pull away from the school one by one, and I lean against the window and watch as Eastern recedes into the distance. Even as we get farther away from campus, I know I haven't fully made up my mind. I could decide at the last minute to head back into the path of totality, to greet the eclipse I've counted on for so long.

I close my eyes and try to sleep, but the bus is filled with conversation and laughter. I grab my headphones from my bag, and Mr. Hart's logbook peeks out at me.

The drive is over two hours, so I put on some music and grab the logbook. I take it out of the brown paper and let my fingers brush over the soft cover. It's old and worn, and I gently open it and flip through the pages. He started keeping records after the very first session we had together and continued through to our last, the one where Ms. Suntile showed up and I collapsed under the pressure of her magic.

I start from the beginning. Some entries are short, logging only what we worked on and what he felt needed improvement. But there are also longer entries, pages full of research and questions and theories.

From our very first session, Mr. Hart dedicated himself to researching Evers. He dedicated himself to me.

The more I read, the more it sounds as if he was forming a plan, the pages practically moving with his churning thoughts and ideas. But I'm unclear on what he wanted to accomplish. The entries are hard to follow, broken up by tangents and thoughts that seem unrelated to everything else. And the more excited he was when he wrote the entries, the more chaotic they get.

He details how much it hurts him to hear me say I hate the sun and hate my magic. How devastating it is to hear me say that my love kills people. He never believed that, was never once worried that I might cause him harm. He writes that magic is the deepest part of a person, that he understands why it would search out those I care for most. He doesn't think it means to hurt them; he makes it sound as if it simply longs to touch the people I adore.

But he also acknowledges that it *does* kill people.

I'm struck by how deeply Mr. Hart believed there's a solution, whether it's me learning total control over my magic or something else entirely. He didn't believe I'd have to live like this forever.

But Alice did, and I will, too, if I don't stand beneath the total eclipse.

Mr. Hart is clearly building toward something, but the bus goes over a speed bump, and the small hotel comes into view. I close the book and put it back into my bag, knowing I'll read the rest after dinner tonight.

I grab my duffel and file into the lobby with everyone else. Sang is in the corner, talking with Mr. Burrows, and I look away as soon as I see him. The way my insides stir, knowing we'll both be in this hotel tonight and can't be together, sends heat directly to my face, and I turn around so he won't see.

It's more than that though. More than desire. It's also that I want to tell him about Mr. Hart's logbook and hear about his research and tangle our magic together again. It's that I want to hear him breathe and listen to the sound of his voice and be in comfortable silence with him. It's all of those things.

It's all of him.

I shake my head and turn my attention to Mr. Donovan, who's handing out room assignments. There's an odd number of summers and winters, and I end up in a room with Paige.

"You've got to be kidding," she says, and I have to agree.

Mr. Donovan looks embarrassed, which only makes it worse. "Will this be okay? I'm not sure how you two ended up together. I can see if someone's willing to switch," he says.

"It's fine," I say. It's only one night.

"No lightning strikes, then, agreed?" His tone is easy and light, but it still makes my stomach drop to the floor.

"Agreed," we both say.

I take the key and haul my duffel up a flight of stairs to the second floor. Paige comes in a few minutes later and throws her bag on the unclaimed bed.

We're quiet for a few minutes. "How's Sang?" she asks, her voice filling the silence. The words are stiff coming from her mouth, but she was there when he was hurt. She wants to know that he's okay.

"I'm not sure," I admit. I pause, then say, "We're not together anymore."

She gives me a disbelieving look. "You're not together anymore," she repeats in a mean tone.

"What?"

"Let me guess—you broke up with him after the ring of fire." She's shaking her head, and it automatically makes me defensive.

"I had to," I say. "You saw the way my magic went after him. It was the only way to keep him safe."

"And how did he react to that?"

"Not very well," I say. "He thought he should have a say in it."

"Which he should have," she says, her voice sharp. That's when I realize she's speaking not just for Sang, but for herself.

When I don't say anything, she continues, "It takes a lot to trust someone in that way, and to have your control taken from you like that—it's a really shitty thing to do to someone. It's supposed to be a partnership."

I stare at her, incredulous. "It's hard to have a partnership when one person is dead," I say.

"Did it ever occur to you to try to solve the problem together? Maybe you don't use your magic when you're with him. Maybe you never work on the same storm cell. There are ways around it."

Her voice rises as she speaks, fighting with me, making up for her silence when I ended things with her.

"You know as well as I do that magic is unpredictable and can arise when you least expect it."

"I'm not saying it can't. I just don't believe that walking away makes you brave or selfless or some kind martyr the way you think it does." Her gaze locks on mine. "I think it makes you selfish, defeatist, and weak."

I'm stunned by her words, so heavy and full they take up space between us. Her jaw tenses, and she keeps her eyes on mine, daring me to say something.

I look away and swallow hard, fight the sting that burns my eyes.

"See?" she practically shouts, throwing her hands in the air. "You won't even fight for the things you care about."

I hear what she's really saying, as cold and clear as a winter morning.

You won't even fight for me.

You won't even fight for Sang.

She walks out of the room, and the door slams shut behind her.

thirty-seven

"Not all love is meant to last, but that does not mean it's not remarkable."

—*A Season for Everything*

Paige doesn't come back to our room after dinner. I take a long shower, put on sweats, and crawl into bed with Mr. Hart's logbook.

Her words have stayed with me, swirling in my mind like a cyclone, threatening to damage everything they touch. *You won't even fight for the things you care about.*

I thought that's what I was doing by training with Sang and throwing myself into my magic and telling Ms. Suntile about our discovery. I thought that's what I was doing when the tornado hit our school and when Mr. Burrows stranded me in the middle of nowhere and when a blizzard landed on our campus.

Even kissing Sang, dancing with him under the stars, laughing with him so hard I cried—that was fighting too. Fighting for myself, choosing to believe I deserve more than a life of isolation and fear.

Choosing to hope.

I put my trust in myself and my magic, hoped so badly that I'd finally learned to control it, and I ended up devastated. That's what happens when you let yourself hope. It crushes you like an avalanche, cold and heavy and suffocating.

Walking away from people I care about *is* fighting for them. It's fighting to keep them safe.

I open Mr. Hart's logbook. My argument with Paige recedes into the background as I get further in, following along as best I can as Mr. Hart explores different theories and explanations as to why my magic hurts people.

He doesn't know why, only that he believes my magic flows on a current of feeling, almost as if the people I care about enable it to exist in the first place. As if my parents and Nikki and Paige and Sang and Mr. Hart have all made it stronger. Better. He thinks it recognizes the connection I have with them as the same sort of connection it has with me, and that's why it gravitates toward them.

I think about how Sang's magic is carried on an undercurrent of calm. Maybe mine is carried on an undercurrent of feeling.

My eyes burn, and my throat aches. I've been told countless times that I feel too much, that I'm too sensitive, too in my head. Having my feelings framed this way, as if they're the source of all my power, all my magic, is one of the loveliest things I've ever encountered.

Even if it's wrong, I'm thankful to have read it.

I keep reading, not caring that the world is getting darker and time is passing. I read page after page, reliving training sessions and taking in Mr. Hart's stream-of-consciousness thoughts about controlling my magic.

I'm so moved by how much effort he put into this, by how much he wanted to help me and see me at peace. By how fully he believed I'm not meant to be isolated, how many times he went to bat for me with Ms. Suntile without me ever knowing.

How much he cared about me.

I decide here and now that I won't let the Ever who comes after me feel so alone, won't rely upon them finding their own Mr. Hart. Maybe I'll write to them—a book or a collection of letters that can be passed down, something *meant* for them, not something they'll have to work so hard to find. Anything to prevent them from feeling the loneliness and disconnect I've felt for the past seventeen years.

Even if I have to be alone for the rest of my life, I can hold on to the fact that what I write will someday find its way to the next Ever, an invisible tie I can take comfort in.

I'm getting toward the end of the logbook, the pages so full there's hardly any blank space, writing crammed into the margins and along the edges. My eyes widen as I understand what Mr. Hart has been building to: that if my magic could be "reset" in some way, it would be able to seek out the people I care about without hurting them.

And he thinks the eclipse is the way to do it.

My heart races, reading his words. He believes I'm strong enough to survive the direct exposure, that an Everwitch's magic is too powerful to be lost. He believes that when totality is over and my connection to the sun is restored, my magic will reset and find its balance.

I stare at his words, unable to comprehend the incredible risk he's suggesting. If he's wrong—if I go back for the eclipse and get stripped—I'd lose a magic we could never hope to get back. Not until another Everwitch is born.

The risk is immense, and yet I don't fully dismiss it. It swirls in my mind like a hurricane above the ocean.

I shut the logbook and put it on my nightstand. I've been so lost in Mr. Hart's writing that I haven't noticed the sunlight reaching into the room or the birds chirping outside. I've missed breakfast. Paige's bed is still made. It's almost nine, and in two hours, the eclipse will be over. Mr. Hart's theory will never be put to the test.

I want to try. I want to go to the eclipse. I want it to feel like enough, knowing that even if I were to get stripped, I could have companionship. I could be happy. But the risk is so great. Mr. Hart dedicated so much of himself to this, and in the end, it doesn't matter, because I can't bring myself to get out of bed and do what he has suggested.

You won't even fight for the things you care about.

I jump when the door to my room flies open and Paige comes rushing in.

"Have you seen this?" she asks, turning on the television to a local news channel.

I sit up and rub my eyes, try to focus on the screen. It shows an enormous dark cloud hovering over a riverbank.

"Cloudburst?" I ask.

"It's dumped twenty-one inches in the past hour," she says.

The image switches to the riverbank, where hundreds of people huddle under tarps or stand in the middle of it all, laughing.

"It's the second day of the Eclipse the Heat Music Festival," she says. "The witches have already evacuated, and that river is rising at a dangerous pace. We're about to see a massive flash flood."

"Have they started evacuating the festival?"

"No," Paige says. "There are thousands of people; the evacuation logistics are complicated. But when the river overflows, we're looking at feet of water, not inches. In a crowd that size, if anyone trips or gets knocked over, they'll likely drown. The force of it will be extreme. There's no way they'll all get out safely."

I'm standing now, staring at the screen.

"We have to do something," I say.

"Like what? The path of totality cuts across the riverbank at an angle—the entire festival is in its path. We can safely stand on the other side of the river a few hundred feet north, but we'll be too far away to be effective. The storm cell is on the other side."

I watch the screen. The band keeps playing, and hundreds of people dance in the rain to the beat of the music, drenched in water. It's close to ninety degrees out; nobody minds the rain.

"Look at the current," I say, pointing to the river. "It's going to wipe out anyone who's on the shore when it floods."

"Exactly," Paige says.

"They have to evacuate."

"Ms. Suntile is on the phone with officials, but it would take hours to get that many people out. And we don't have hours."

"So we're just going to sit here, glued to our screens, and watch them die?"

"What else can we do?"

"Can we get as close as possible, then rush in once the eclipse is over? Totality only lasts a couple of minutes."

"The flood will happen before then. And if we tried to go in before totality, there's no guarantee we could get out in time. We'd all be stripped."

I pace around the room, adrenaline and fear coursing through me. My heart races as my eyes land on Mr. Hart's logbook.

"Mr. Hart thought I'd be able to survive an eclipse," I say, so quietly I'm not sure Paige even hears me.

She pauses. "What?"

I repeat my words, louder this time.

"No witch has ever survived an eclipse. Every single one of them comes out a shader."

"I know," I say, handing Paige the logbook and pointing to where she should start reading. "I'd try and get out in time, but if I couldn't..." My sentence trails off, hanging in the space between us.

Her eyes fly over Mr. Hart's words, and she shakes her head as she goes.

"There's definitely something to it," she says, still reading. "But it's a huge risk."

"Is it too big?"

She sets the book down and looks at me. I can see her warring with herself, going back and forth about what to say.

I might stay for the eclipse.

I might try to stop you.

"I don't know. But if you can't get out in time and Mr. Hart is right, you'll remain an Ever whose magic is no longer a danger to the people you love."

"It feels like a huge risk to take when I can't even make my love last longer than a season," I finally say. Love is for the summer—that's how it has always been. And even though I started falling for Sang in the spring, it was summer that pushed me over the edge. Pushed me into love.

As soon as I say it, I know that's what's holding me back.

I love Sang now, but I have no reason to believe that love will survive the autumnal equinox.

Sang is different—the spring showed me that. But I've never been able to make a relationship last beyond summer, and if the ring of fire taught me anything, it's that hoping is a hollow sentiment.

"First of all, there are as many kinds of love as there are stars in the sky. You only think you can't love someone *romantically* for longer than a season. Fine—that still leaves you with all the other kinds of love." Paige grabs a bottle of water from the dresser and takes a long drink. "Second, that's completely absurd."

"How is that absurd?" I broke up with Paige before the equinox, but I still felt it—something changed. I didn't long for her in the same way anymore.

"I've been watching you with Sang since autumn. It's now summer."

"And?"

"And you've been in love with him since at least winter. Probably longer."

There's no way I've loved Sang since winter. Before him, romance outside of summer wasn't something I was capable of—romance in winter would be downright absurd. And while the spring was special, it was summer that intensified my feelings, drenching them in love.

Wasn't it?

"You're only saying that because we started dating in spring, which, granted, is new for me—"

"I'm saying it because when you started training with Sang, you stopped hating yourself. He was able to make you see yourself through his eyes and actually like what you saw." Paige pauses and looks at me dead-on. "Listen, do you believe Mr. Hart's theory?"

I look down. "I want to," I say. "I care about whether all those people die. I care that our atmosphere is devolving into chaos and our witches are dying from depletion. I care about Mr. Hart's belief in me. Maybe I should fight for all those things." I say the words slowly, not quite believing I'm saying them at all.

"That's not what I meant," Paige says, but when I look at her, I know she's considering my words. She pauses, and for several seconds we stand in silence, watching each other.

"If you're going to go, you have to go now," she finally says.

"I'll try to get out in time."

My hands shake as I pull some cash from my duffel, my heart pounding against my ribs. The dream elixir peeks out from inside my sweatshirt, and I carefully pick it up.

If there were ever a time to make a wish, this is it.

I take off the top, and the earthy, floral scent rises up to greet me. I breathe in deep, let it calm my racing heart and shaking hands and restless mind. I close my eyes and apply it to both sides of my neck, both wrists.

"Please let this work," I say over and over.

"You about done with your perfume?" Paige asks, making sure I know how ridiculous she thinks I'm being.

"It's a dream elixir." I put the top back on and carefully place it in my bag.

"Whatever," she says, handing me my phone. A timer is set for one hour. "By the time this goes off, you have to be hauling ass out of there if you want to make it out before totality. I'll wait to tell Ms. Suntile where you are so she won't have enough time to go after you."

"Okay," I say, sliding my phone in my pocket.

I walk to the door, pausing when my hand touches the cool metal handle. "I'm really doing this," I say, shaking my head.

"You're really doing this," Paige says behind me.

I turn to look at her. "I'm sorry I didn't fight for you," I say. "I should have."

Paige swallows but keeps her eyes on mine. "*Go.*"

I open the door, rush down the emergency staircase, and run out the back of the hotel.

I hop in a taxi and look out the rear window.

No one follows me.

thirty-eight

"This is your life, and you have to choose how you want to live it."

—*A Season for Everything*

I've never seen so much rain fall from the sky. I'm completely drenched, my clothes heavy and clinging to my skin. My hair is down, soaking wet, and I curse the hair tie I left sitting on the bathroom counter in the hotel. I'm about a quarter mile up the river from the Eclipse the Heat festival, and I can barely hear the music over the pouring rain. The stage is covered, but I can't believe bands are still playing.

There is so much rain I can barely see a few feet in front of me, let alone all the way to the festival. The river rushes past me, rising with each passing minute. I don't have much time.

I squint into the sky as water pours down my face. The cumulonimbus cloud is so dark, so ominous, that I can't see the sun. The partial eclipse is well under way, and I feel bad for all the people who came out for the festival and aren't able to see it.

But that's the least of their worries.

Lightning brightens the sky, and thunder claps soon after. I expect to hear screams from the festival, but instead, people cheer. They think it's a wild summer storm, an amazing story they'll be able to tell for years to come. They don't know the danger they're in.

I have to get to work.

I close my eyes, and magic surges inside me, big and eager in a way only summer magic can be. It jumps to greet me, aching to be released into the world, to touch the storm, to calm the river. It rolls around inside me until I have no choice but to set it free.

It rushes toward the clouds, diving in at once. If I can reduce the strength of the updrafts until they stop, the storm will dissipate. Magic wraps around the updraft and pushes down down down, but the force of it is unlike anything I've encountered before.

It doesn't respond to my magic, doesn't even falter.

The updraft keeps going, and my magic is helpless, rising with it.

I take a deep breath and try to calm my racing heart, still my shaking hands. I have not come here for nothing. I can do this.

I inhale, a long, deep breath that makes my chest and belly rise. When I exhale, a huge swell of summer magic jumps into the storm, an intense, bold rush that holds nothing back. No other season can absorb as much magic from the sun as summers, but even the colossal strength of the season isn't enough to dampen the updrafts in this storm.

My arms shake, and I'm gritting my teeth, already so exhausted. But the cloudburst keeps going as if I'm not even here, as if I haven't risked everything to stop it. Rain continues to fall, and the river continues to rise, and time continues to run out.

I pull out my phone and check the timer. Eleven minutes. I'm supposed to leave in eleven minutes, and I haven't even slowed the rain. I've done nothing.

Maybe I should leave now. Go back the way I came, get out of the path of totality, and know that I tried. At least I tried.

But something keeps me planted here, tells me to keep working.

So I do.

I take another deep breath and begin again. Summer magic is already at the surface, impatiently waiting, ready to be thrown back into action. But when I release it, it doesn't drive toward the updraft the way I expect. It doesn't fight against the rising air.

Instead, it darts across the river and feels...cold. Like ice.

I turn toward the river and narrow my eyes, try to see past the rain. I feel for my magic again, and it is undeniably tangled with winter.

The path of totality cuts across the river diagonally—the bank directly across from me is out of the path, completely safe for witches. I can't see past the rain, but I know they're on the other side. And while they're too far away to control the storm, they aren't too far away for me. I can reach them.

My magic can reach them.

I'm overwhelmed with understanding and laugh into the

rain. I don't know if it's Paige or someone else, but there is a witch across from me on the other side of the river, offering their magic.

Summer magic delights in other people, and it rushes across the river as if it's greeting an old friend. It wraps itself up in winter, and I pull it back, toss it to the storm.

The updraft falters. Not a lot, but it falters. It knows I'm here.

I pull more magic and keep working on the updraft, pushing down as hard as I can. A sudden blast of cold shoots through me, and the thread of winter gets stronger and stronger and stronger.

I have no idea why it's getting this strong, but I send more magic across the river and pull.

And as I do, I'm greeted with the transitional magic of autumn.

Then the aggressive magic of winter.

The patient magic of spring.

And the intense magic of summer.

I can't see a damn thing, but I can feel it, all four seasons rising up around me as if I'm the sun.

I don't understand what's happening, but I know in the deepest parts of myself that this is right. Something inside me is shifting into place, coming together instead of pushing apart, and my entire body responds as if this is the moment it's waited for my entire life.

It's so loud, the rain and the river and the music and the people, and it frays my attention, making it hard to focus. Hard to think.

I'm pelted with rain, and a sudden rush of cold over my feet makes me look down. The flood is starting.

No. I can stop this. We can stop this.

I don't need to think. I just need to act.

I raise my hands into the air, and all four seasons rise with me. I throw my magic into the storm, and all four seasons follow, tumbling into the cloudburst and taking hold. Winter magic dries out the air, lessening the humidity. Summer focuses on the updraft, pushing down as hard as it can. Spring lines the bank of the river, forcing the water to hold. And autumn cools the air so it can't rise.

My whole body shakes with power, with exhaustion, with the knowledge that something bigger than I could ever have imagined is taking place right here before me.

Screams start in the distance as the rising river fights against the magic holding it in. With everything I have left, I throw magic into the clouds. Not just summer, but all of it.

The cloud fights against me, thrashing from side to side. It's strong, but it isn't stronger than we are.

The merciless rain finally slows to a sprinkle, then to nothing at all.

The river runs over, but the strong current, the incredible mass of it, stays within its bed.

The screaming stops. People will be wet, but they won't be swept away. They won't drown.

The cumulonimbus cloud dissipates from bottom to top, revealing a perfectly clear sky and the partial eclipse. I stare at it in wonder, the new moon posing in front of the sun, blocking almost the entire star. I marvel at how little sun is needed to light the Earth. The sky is a bright, vibrant blue, as if it's oblivious to the show taking place on its stage.

There's a break in the music, and I think I hear cheering from the other side of the river.

I turn toward the sound, and there on the other side is…everyone. Clapping and cheering and hugging. A huge group of witches that must be the entire Eastern upper class. And in the very front, I see Sang, Paige, Ms. Suntile, and Mr. Burrows.

I want to run to them, dive into the raging river and fight my way to the other side.

They came for me. All of them.

My phone starts vibrating in my pocket, and I pull it out to see the timer Paige set for me going off.

It's time to run.

I know I should run.

But I stay where I am.

Ms. Suntile is waving her arms wildly, pointing up the river, north. I follow her finger but don't see anything.

Mr. Burrows is holding on to Sang, who's struggling to get away, pushing and throwing his elbows. Paige rushes to him, but I can't tell what she's saying.

I'm confused and tired. So tired from dissipating the storm.

Ms. Suntile turns toward the group, then back to me.

In one coordinated effort, a single word made up of dozens of voices reaches me across the water: "Run!"

You won't even fight for the things you care about.

I could run. I could get out in time.

But as Paige's words knock around in my mind, I know with absolute certainty that this is my fight.

I trust in Mr. Hart, I trust in my magic, and I trust in myself.

I'm staying. I'm staying because I deserve to love without fear, and if this is my chance to reset my magic, to help it find the balance it's always needed, I have to take it.

I put my phone in my pocket and slowly tilt my head back.

The moon's full shadow sweeps across the Earth's surface, barreling toward me at more than one thousand miles per hour.

I look up as the moon takes its place in front of the sun, blocking it from the Earth.

And blocking it from me.

thirty-nine

*"You have to believe you're worthy of the life you want.
If you don't believe that, who else will?"*

—*A Season for Everything*

The air turns cold, freezing. Goose bumps form all over my body. Bright-white light encircles the moon, the sun's corona streaming out into space and into a sea of total darkness.

My connection to the sun is lost for one second, two, three, four.

I gasp.

It's more excruciating than I could have imagined, as if all the blood in my arteries and veins and capillaries has turned to ice, as if the shards will poke through the thin walls at any moment. Magic drains from me in a sudden cascade, leaving my body with the force of a thousand landslides.

Everything hurts, aches, throbs.

Sharp pain invades my body, as if the darkness is a knife, slicing me open until there's nothing left.

I can't hear the festival. Everything is quiet, deferring to the show taking place above us.

The birds are silent. There are no squirrels running through the grass, no bees humming, no rabbits eating. A dusty-rose horizon encircles the inky-black sky.

The world around me falls asleep, and my heart falls right along with it.

Everything that holds me together is being shredded, muscle by muscle, bone by bone, and I cry out beside this rushing river to a sun that can longer see me.

And suddenly, I realize this was inevitable; I was always going to end up here. If I had never discovered my true magic, I would have stood in the path of totality to get stripped, the same path I'm standing in now to stop the cloudburst. The same path Mr. Hart thought would reset my magic, would correct whatever it is that drives it toward the people I love.

Maybe he was right. Maybe all my magic has ever wanted was to touch them, to feel that love and revel in it, if only for a moment.

Every road led here, to the eclipse I've been awaiting for so long. Every single one.

I'm not afraid. It was my choice to come here, to plant my feet on the ground and refuse to run. To love without fear. To put my faith in those who put their faith in me and believe I can survive this.

And I do. I believe I can survive this.

I think of my parents and Nikki and the future I want for

myself, and I know that right here, under the shadow of the moon, is where I'm meant to be. Alice never spoke of a magic like what I experienced today, never found a way to protect the people she cared about. So I'm standing here for her. For my parents and Nikki. For Mr. Hart. For myself.

I risked everything to come here, and standing in the dark, shivering and cold and soaking wet, I understand that my choice is what makes me powerful. It is my choice to be here, risks and all. No one else's. I trust that the Sun will take care of me.

My head aches from its absence, like a million hailstones have been dropped on me at once. I want to collapse, to bury my head in my hands and wait for the eclipse to pass, but something in the back of my mind pulls at me, begs me to consider it.

Encompassed in silence and drowning in darkness, I think of the magic that surfaced this year and changed my whole world, a magic I could only discover because of trust and respect and love. I think of what happened just moments ago, how I felt all four seasons at once, and while I don't understand it, I know it only happened because of the power that comes from being together.

I'm so cold. My teeth chatter, and I shiver.

My legs can't hold me up any longer, and I collapse on the ground. All of my organs have turned to ice, a cold so deep and fierce I can't remember the feeling of sunlight, can't remember what it's like to be anything but freezing.

Mr. Hart once told me that love carries risk for all of us, and I want to take that risk. I want to take that risk so badly I feel as though I could reach out and touch it.

Crumpled beneath the crown of the brightest star, *my* star, I realize I'm not okay with any of this. The sun is as much a part of me as my heart, and you can't survive without your heart.

For so long, that's all I have wanted—to be rid of the sun and rid of magic and rid of fear. But now I accept it all, want it all, choose it all.

My breaths are ragged and shallow, as if the ice is slowly freezing my lungs, as if I'll never breathe again.

But something inside me tells me to stay present, to experience this infinite darkness even though it hurts, even though it feels like I'm breaking.

Then, clarity. Perfect clarity.

I love that I change with the seasons. I've lived my whole life believing change is bad, that I'm supposed to be only one thing. But why would I ever want to fit into one tiny box? I want to thrive and experience new things and love in different ways and use the magic of all four seasons.

I want to live.

Change makes me powerful, and finally, *finally*, I'm ready to claim that power.

Here on the ground, under a black sky, my connection to the sun broken, all of my pieces fall into place. All of my insecurity and doubt fades into the darkness.

I want to be an Ever, and that's *my* choice. Not Mr. Burrows's or Ms. Suntile's or anyone else's. It is fully and completely my own.

Mosquitoes cluster in the air around me. Crickets chirp, and owls hoot in the distance, believing that night has fallen. Bats emerge from the trees and fly erratically overhead.

It's been two minutes and seventeen seconds without the sun, and my entire body is shaking, hurting, submerged in pain, as if I'm bathing in a tub of razors and needles and jagged edges.

But still I keep my eyes on the sky, forcing my head back. It feels so heavy, too heavy. But still I stare, begging the star to come back, begging it to fill me with its light.

The moon basks in its final moments between the Earth and the sun, and my heart aches. I shake from the cold and the darkness and the loss of myself, feeling the star's absence in every part of me.

Then the moon begins to move, beads of sunlight shining through its mountains and valleys, reaching out as if to touch me.

It's almost over.

I force myself to stand, keeping my eyes trained on the grand finale.

A thin ring of light appears, followed by a burst of brightness on top. It looks like a diamond ring in the dark sky, like the Sun is asking me a question.

Yes. My answer is yes.

This is who I am, who I am meant to be.

And I know now that if given a choice, I'd choose my life as an Ever above all else.

An inexplicable peace moves through me, like all my mismatched gears have finally slid into place.

Relief.

In one glorious burst of light, the Sun reclaims her place above me, and I am drenched in her warming rays. The sky brightens, and the most perfect shade of blue saturates the atmosphere. All the ice inside me melts away.

The sun hasn't reclaimed me, though, our connection still broken. I stand with my arms outstretched, my palms facing up, begging the sun to give me another chance, to choose me again.

I don't move my eyes from the star. Normally, it wouldn't burn me the way it would a shader, but without my magic, it stings. And still I stare. I stare and stare and stare, an unspoken promise that I will do better, that I will trust the Sun and trust myself. But above all else, it's a declaration of love. A pure, vibrant, all-consuming adoration for the Sun that's free of the resentment I've held for so long. A love so strong it warms me from the inside out, even though my magic is gone.

A love that is undeniably worth the risk. I will stand here forever if that's what it takes.

CHAPTER

forty

"The shaders insist that seeing an eclipse can be life-changing. It seems they are correct."

—*A Season for Everything*

I don't know how long I've been standing here. Long enough for my neck to hurt and my eyes to burn, long enough for the birds to start chirping and the squirrels to start running and the bees to start humming.

Long enough to reaffirm over and over and over again that this is the life I want.

Suddenly, a shock runs through me, powerful and familiar. It's a rush of gratitude, aggression, hopefulness, and passion— transition, ice, growth, and heat. Autumn, winter, spring, and summer.

My eyes stop burning, and my body fills with the magic of the sun.

Our connection is back.

I laugh, fall to my knees next to the river, and thank the

Sun for coming back to me. I put my palms in the grass, feel the individual blades and damp earth and tiny rocks from the riverbed.

It's so recognizable, the magic I've had my entire life. And yet there's something different about it now, about the way it settles inside me, perfectly nestled in my core as if the space was made precisely for it. It's comfortable and calm, the way Nox is when he's curled into the tightest of balls, wholly content.

And that's when I know Mr. Hart was right. The eclipse offered a kind of reset, and my magic came back to me, totally under my control. It's powerful and fierce, strong enough to help the atmosphere heal, and it's *mine*. It listens to me, and I listen to it.

I look across the river, desperate to see Sang, but he isn't there. Most of the witches are gone, but Paige still stands on the other side, watching me.

I wish we were close enough to talk, to hear each other's voices, but the river is too wide and too loud. She points upstream, and I turn to look.

Sang is running toward me, so far away I can barely make out his features, but I know it's him. I look back to Paige, and she motions for me to go.

So I do.

I run toward him, run toward the person who has seen me in every season and loved me all the same. Run toward the person who has helped me see myself. Run toward what I want.

I'm getting close, so close, and I force my legs to go as fast as they can.

He's finally here, and I don't stop when I reach him. I run into him, his arms wrapping around my waist as I cling to his neck, and he picks me up and squeezes me tight.

I wrap my legs around his waist, not caring that my clothes are drenched, that my hair is a total mess, that there's dirt all over my skin. We cling to each other, tears streaming down my face, and I don't care if he sees.

"I love you, witch or not," he whispers into my hair, and I cry harder, because I know he does, because he has never once given me a reason to doubt it, not in any season.

We turn slowly, holding each other beneath the partially eclipsed sun, and when I've clung to him as tightly as I can, let him know he's all I wanted to see, I slowly release my grip, and he sets me on the ground.

Then we look at each other for the first time.

He stares at me as if he's never seen me before, uncertainty and awe etched on his face.

"Clara?" he asks, his thumbs gently tracing the skin around my eyes. "Can you see me okay?"

"I see you perfectly," I say. "Why?"

"Your eyes. They're different." He grabs his phone and takes a picture, holding it out for me to see.

I look at the screen. My eyes are no longer the deep blue of the ocean. They're bright, a marbled gold that's almost illuminated, like a star has taken up residence in my irises.

I breathe out, unable to stop looking at the photo.

Sang tips my chin up and studies me, that same intense stare that's made me wild since we first met. "You feel okay? You aren't hurt?"

"I feel amazing," I whisper.

I close my eyes and summon a small bit of magic, just enough to form a breeze and send it dancing around him. He laughs, shaking his head in disbelief.

"You weren't stripped," he says, still searching my eyes, his hands on either side of my face.

"I wasn't stripped."

"How is that possible?" His voice is quiet and reverent, waking up every trace of longing I've tried to bury since summer began.

"If you kiss me right now," I say, keeping my eyes on his, "I promise I'll explain later."

His eyes move down to my mouth. "Deal," he says.

His lips meet mine, and I kiss him without hesitation or fear or worry. He weaves his hands through my hair, and his breaths are heavy, matching my own. I open my mouth and tangle my tongue with his, kiss him deeply, kiss him with greed and desire and longing.

He pulls me into him, closer still, wrapping his arms around my ribs, igniting every inch of me as if he is fire and I am wood.

We share breaths and kisses and touches next to the river our magic met across not thirty minutes ago. Music drifts toward us from the festival, the world continuing on as if something extraordinary didn't just happen.

I spot someone running toward us out of the corner of my eye and give Sang one more kiss before reluctantly pulling away.

"If Mr. Burrows weren't right over there, I'd be pulling you someplace a little more private."

Sang groans. "That man has been the cause of a lot of torment this year."

"Tell me about it," I say.

Mr. Burrows reaches us, and Ms. Suntile is right behind him. I'm shocked when I look up the riverbank and see the rest of my class in the distance.

"Are they all coming to see me?" I ask, my voice unsteady.

"Yes," Ms. Suntile answers. "What you did—" But she cuts herself off. "My Sun, what happened to your eyes?"

I had already forgotten about them, and I look down. "I don't know. It must have happened during the eclipse."

"Are you hurt?" she asks.

"More importantly, were you stripped?" Mr. Burrows interjects.

"No," I say. "I'm not hurt. And I wasn't stripped."

They let out sighs of relief in unison, and Mr. Burrows shakes his head as he looks at me. "You never should have taken that risk. It was irresponsible, reckless, and shows an utter lack of regard for what's happening in our world right now." His words are mean and stern, but I don't care anymore.

Then Ms. Suntile starts to speak, and they talk over each other until she gives him a warning look and he defers. "Mr. Burrows is right—that was not a risk you should have taken. Had you been stripped, the consequences..." She trails off, letting her unfinished sentence hang heavily in the air. "But it was also exceptional. Do you realize what you did?"

I look at her and shake my head.

"During the cloudburst, you weren't only pulling off-season magic. You were *amplifying* magic—everyone's. You made us all stronger. We were able to use our own magic to help." Her voice shakes, and her eyes tear up.

Mr. Burrows sighs. "It was phenomenal," he says. "The truth is that I could never have taken the risk you did, Clara. And what came out of it is beyond anything we could have imagined."

"I wish you could have seen it." Sang laces his fingers with mine. "Witches were crying and hugging, completely over-whelmed at being able to use their magic that way. It was an unprecedented moment for all of us."

"Clara, you have such a gift." Ms. Suntile looks at me with wonder and pride, and it makes me uncomfortable, in a way. I can hear the undertones of pressure and expectation, but it doesn't make me want to run. It makes me want to exceed them, soar right past them as I figure out the expectations I have for myself.

"I could feel it," I say, remembering the distinct magic of each season rising to greet me. "All four seasons." I look to the sun. "I don't know what to say." Amplifying everyone's magic all at once, every season, is something I never could have dreamed of doing a few months ago. I would have said it was impossible.

The rest of my classmates reach us, forming a circle around me, dozens of voices talking over each other. I laugh and answer questions and listen as people describe what it felt like to use their magic in the off-season. Some of them cry when they explain it, and my heart fills with their words, their facial expressions, their excitement and joy and awe.

I don't know that I've ever felt better about anything in my entire life than I do knowing that my magic enables the witches around me to use their own.

Ms. Suntile takes charge as if I'm a celebrity, telling everyone I've had a long day and that I probably want some rest. I'm thankful when we get back to the hotel and the only thing I'm supposed to do is nap.

Paige stays in the lobby with some of the other winters, and Sang walks me to my room, never letting go of my hand. When the door closes behind us, he pulls me into him and exhales, a strong, heavy sigh that rustles my hair. He pulls away and searches my face, but I remember my discolored eyes, and self-consciousness drives my gaze to the floor.

He tips my chin up so I have no choice but to look at him.

"Clara," he says, watching me, and I'm sure his next words will be as serious and genuine as the tone of his voice. Then he says, "They make you look pretty badass."

We watch each other for several seconds before bursting into laughter—wild, unrestrained laughter that feels so good after the events of the day.

I lie down on my bed, and he lies down beside me. We're both on our backs, quiet, and he runs his fingers up and down my arm.

"I want to write a book," I finally say.

"What kind of book?"

"More like a letter. A really long letter to the Everwitch who comes after me, so they don't have to figure all this out on their own. So they don't have to see their loved ones die or be confused about how to use their magic. So they can feel understood." Alice's memoir has been an enormous comfort to me, but I lived without it for seventeen years, and it doesn't detail the kind of magic she had. I had to figure it out for myself, and having a place to go for information would have been so helpful. But more than that, I thought I was alone for so long. I don't want that for the next Ever.

"I love that idea," Sang says, his fingers still moving up and down and up and down. We're both quiet for a few minutes, minds wandering to different places, or maybe the same one. We're so close, but it doesn't feel close enough. Maybe it never will.

Wind blows through the open window, carrying the best parts of summer, and I breathe in deep, holding the season in my lungs. It fills me with longing, a relentless squeeze in the pit of my stomach that I can no longer resist.

I roll onto my side and look down at him, his eyes moving to my lips, lingering.

I close my eyes, bend down, and kiss him.

He puts his hands on either side of my face and opens his mouth, and I get lost in him, lost in the way his fingers feel on my skin, the way his hair tickles my face, the way his lips are soft and taste like black tea and honey.

I get lost in the certainty of what I want, what I've wanted for so long, and when he pulls away just slightly, I look him in the eye and ask for more.

He rolls me to my back, one hand behind my head, the other following the lines of my jaw, my neck, my collarbone.

I reach for him, and his lips are back on mine before his smile fades.

forty-one

"Our Earth is tired—let her rest."
—A Season for Everything

Everything is burning, so many flames it looks as if we set the sky on fire. The sun looks hazy and distorted through all the heat that's rising, a shimmery mass that reminds me of the sunbar Mr. Burrows created in winter.

Once again, witches have come to Eastern from all over the world to take part in our wildfire training. The control field is packed with bodies, sweating and dirty from all the heat and ash. Ms. Suntile stands off to the side with the other teachers, as well as officials from the Solar Magic Association and shaders from the National Center for Atmospheric Research.

It's the first time shaders have come to one of our training sessions, a result of the conversations we're starting to have. They're listening to us, they're asking questions, and they're putting in the work to reverse some of the damage they've done.

We aren't in this alone and shouldn't act like we are; the atmosphere is hurting, and that's a problem for all of us, witches and shaders alike. The challenge is great, and we have a lot of work ahead of us. But we're in this together, and if there's anything I've learned this past year, it's that together is where the magic lies.

An enormous fire rises from the center of the field, smoke billowing high above us, reaching toward the sky. It's our final day of training, and the summers, springs, and autumns have already had their turns.

Now, it's time for winter.

I close my eyes and send my magic through the group, recognizing the bite of winter right away. It's cool and sharp, sending a chill throughout my body. It feels so good in the summer heat.

My power weaves through them, dancing around the winters, inviting their magic out to play. I slowly raise my hands, and a few of them gasp as their magic gets stronger inside them, growing to its full intensity in the middle of summer.

I will never tire of this, of magnifying a sleeping season, of waking it up and coaxing it back to life.

Wake up, winter. There is fun to be had.

Winters can't harness the sun or deal with the heat—that magic is reserved for summers. But they can sure as hell make it rain.

"Okay, winters, get to work," Mr. Donovan says over a loudspeaker.

I keep my magic wrapped around them, an invisible magnet that lures their power to the surface, getting stronger and stronger with each passing second. I remain steady behind the group. Even. Calm.

I'm giving Sang a run for his money.

Winter magic dives into the ground in search of moisture, darting every which way, aggressive and quick. The winters work together, pulling water from the earth and combining it until a large, dark cloud hangs in the air above them.

Mr. Donovan instructs them as they work to put out the fire, and I smile when a single raindrop hits my forehead. Here we go.

The sky opens up and drenches us in seconds. Cheers rise up from the crowd—from the winters participating and the witches watching, from the officials at the SMA and the shaders from NCAR.

No matter how many times we do this, the feel of rain on our hot skin will always be a victory. We're getting stronger, and each session is a reminder of that strength. We're still in the game.

I tilt my head back and let the rain run down my face, wash the ash away, soothe the burning in my eyes from all the smoke. I wish Mr. Hart were here. I wish he knew that all the time, encouragement, and love he poured into me wasn't a waste.

I think he did know. It was me who had to learn.

The last of the flames die out, the soot on the ground and the rising tendrils of smoke all that remains of the massive fire.

Mr. Donovan officially ends the training, and the control field empties as the witches disperse, going to the dining hall or to the dial to relax. Ms. Suntile calls me over and introduces me to the officials, and I shake hands and answer questions and explain my magic as best I can.

When they leave to continue their meeting in one of the conference rooms, I'm thankful to be excused. I turn around and see Sang waiting for me, and I rush over to him.

"Oh my Sun, feed me," I whine. I take his hand, and we head toward the dining hall, not even bothering to shower first.

"You looked great out there," he says, filling me with pride.

It's a hazy day on campus, low clouds hovering above Eastern, playing hide-and-seek with the sun. It's warm, and the flowers on campus brighten everything, a celebration of summer and all its colors.

I practically run toward the dining hall when it comes into view, the breakfast I had this morning long since forgotten. Paige walks out and hesitates when she sees us. We haven't spoken much since the day of the cloudburst, since our fight. But the way she looks at me from across the control field and during classes makes me think we're healing.

"I know you just finished, but would you like to join us?" I ask.

"No," she says flatly, and I almost laugh.

She turns to walk away, then pauses. "What you did was extraordinary, taking a risk like that. Don't let anyone tell you otherwise."

"I don't think I could have done it without you," I say, remembering her voice in our hotel room.

Go.

"Probably not," Paige agrees. "You've always been an overthinker." Her eyes move between Sang and me, and her expression changes, but I'm not sure what it means. She looks almost vulnerable. Then it passes, and she walks away.

"She's maybe the most *winter* winter I've ever met," Sang says when she's gone.

"I know. I like that about her."

"Me too."

We walk into the dining hall, and when I've piled my tray with as much food as I can manage, Jessica calls us over to the summer table.

"Sit," she says, motioning to two empty seats.

We talk about magic and the wildfire training for a few minutes, and then the conversation shifts to after-graduation plans and upcoming trips and inside jokes and the Summer Ball. We laugh and talk over each other and laugh some more.

This should have been my experience here all along, and it hurts, thinking about all the meals I ate in my cabin, all the ways I avoided people, all the time I spent alone. Mr. Hart and Nox were my best friends—my only friends—and I wish I could go back in time and hug my younger self, tell her it wouldn't always be that way.

I'm so happy to be here in this loud dining hall with clanking dishes and so many voices. Sang's hand brushes against mine while we eat, his pinkie wrapping around my own. It's such a casual thing, a small touch in the middle of this too-loud room, and yet it's everything.

When we're done eating and leave the dining hall, Sang walks me to my cabin before heading to his apartment.

"It's too bad you didn't get a chance to move back into one of the houses," he says as I open the door and walk inside.

"I would have liked that," I say. "Although, this secluded cabin beneath the cover of the trees has its benefits." I give Sang a mean-ingful look, keeping my eyes on his as I walk backward to my bed.

"It certainly does," he agrees, taking my hand when I reach for him. I pull him toward me, and we crash onto the bed. He lands on top of me and props himself up on his elbow, his fingers playing with my hair. His hand is smudged with paint, and I smile to myself.

"Did I tell you I used your dream elixir?"

His entire face lights up. He looks so happy, and it's this reac-tion I want to elicit over and over again, forever ever ever.

"I used it right before I left for the cloudburst. I put it on my wrists and neck and spoke my wish out loud," I say, committing to memory the way he looks right now.

"What did you wish for?"

"That it would work."

"And it did," he says, a huge smile spreading across his face, dimples and bright eyes and so much joy.

"It did." I pause then, heart hammering in my chest. I'm saving the words, can't say them yet, but I want him to know. "But I think it had a side effect."

"What do you mean?" he asks, fingers still tangled in my hair.

"Do you remember when I said my resolve was rather strong?"

"I do," he says, watching me.

I swallow hard. "I was wrong," I say simply.

If Sang's smile lit up my room before, it's now the Sun herself. He could light the whole world.

And I bask in it.

forty-two

"There are two things you should know up front. One: your magic is dangerous. Two: you can learn to control it."

—*A Season for Everything*

Today is the last day of summer, and the Sun hangs on to it as if she has something to prove. I'm an official graduate of the Eastern School of Solar Magic, and it feels better than I ever thought it would. As the autumnal equinox approaches, I'm not nervous or scared.

I'm content. Ready.

I'm standing on the control field, waiting for Sang. The Sun gives up her place in the sky, and dusk settles over the vast field with a heathered shade of blue that makes everything feel peaceful. So much has happened on this field, but it no longer holds only pain for me. It also holds my successes and progress and hope.

In a few hours, the field will be full of witches celebrating the equinox, welcoming autumn. The sweet scent of spiced cider will fill the air, and people will laugh and talk beneath the dark expanse of night.

But I have my own plans.

Sang walks onto the field, a picnic basket hanging from one arm and blankets draped over the other, and my heart falters at the sight of him. Maybe one day I'll be used to it, to the way his mouth pulls into a smile the instant he sees me, but not today.

"Hi," he says, setting the basket on the ground and wrapping his arms around me. I melt into him, into his broad chest and earthy smell and strong arms, and for just a moment, I forget that I'm leaving tomorrow.

I'm moving to London to work with the Solar Magic Association on developing a protocol for how and when to use my magic. Shaders from some of the most prestigious organizations in the world will be there, too, working on it with us.

Instead of witches dying from depletion, their magic will be amplified. They'll be able to help. They'll be safe. And even though our world is suffering, struggling to breathe, I'm hopeful that our magic, combined with the shaders' work, will make a difference.

Will make *the* difference.

Sang pulls away and delivers a small kiss to my lips, then picks up the basket.

"You're very prepared," I say.

"I just like my girl to be comfortable." The words fill my chest with a pressure I can't explain, as if my heart is expanding to hold everything I feel for him. "Shall we?" he asks.

I walk to the trail with Sang behind me, and we begin our climb. It's quiet under the canopy of the trees in this space between day and night when everything seems to still. We hike up in comfortable silence, our breaths mingling with the wind.

It's my first time going to the meadow with Sang. Not alone to leave a message for him, wishing I could talk to him, see him, touch him. We're going together.

My breaths come heavier as the trail inclines, and knowing he's one step behind me fills me up the way air fills my lungs.

His presence, his existence, means so much to me. He doesn't have to do anything or say anything—he just has to *be*. That's all I want.

We chase the light as we continue up, an infinite twilight that sees us through to the top.

When we get to the meadow, *our* meadow, I'm at a loss for words. Sang catches up to me, and we stand at the edge in silence. The full moon rises overhead, illuminating our flowers so they seem as if they're glowing, iridescent, reflecting the stars.

I can't believe this is the last time I'll see our meadow. Maybe other witches on campus will discover it, and it will become their secret place. Maybe they'll sit beneath our birch tree and find solace, peace, calm. Maybe they'll come here to laugh or cry or think or paint. Maybe they'll have conversations through flowers the way Sang and I did.

Sang takes my hand, and we walk to our birch tree. He throws a blanket over the dirt, and we sit down, looking at all the flowers that surround us.

"It really isn't an efficient form of communication," he says, and I lean my head into him and laugh.

"It really isn't."

He kisses my forehead and drapes the other blanket over our laps, then pulls out a thermos of hot tea. He sets a big piece of chocolate cake between us.

"You sure do know the way to my heart," I say, taking a sip of tea.

"That's the idea," he says.

Our eyes meet, and I can't look away. I want to memorize their depth, the way the center of gold, of sunlight, trails into rich brown, the way they crinkle at the edges when he laughs.

Sang pulls out a single candle and puts it in the piece of cake. He lights it, and against a backdrop of branches rustling and crickets chirping, sings me "Happy Birthday." Then he hands me a package wrapped in white paper, secured with dried herbs and twine.

"What's this?" I ask.

"Open it and see."

I tear open the wrapping paper, and inside is a hardbound journal. The words *A Season for Everything* are engraved on the cover in gold letters. When I flip through the pages, there are four section breaks, one for each season, each with a different flower that Sang painted himself.

"For your book," he says.

I'm speechless, and I run my fingers over the forest-green cover, trying to find the right words to say. I don't think I've ever seen anything more beautiful.

"Sang, this is amazing," I manage to get out around the lump that has formed in my throat. "Thank you." I lean in and kiss him, and he smiles against my lips.

"I'm glad you like it."

"I love it."

He kisses me again, then looks out over the meadow. "You know what I've been thinking about?" he asks, his voice quiet and deep in thought.

"What's that?"

"Lightning." He holds his hand out in front of him and pulls moisture from the ground until he's formed the smallest cumulonimbus cloud, hovering above his open palm, stirring in the space between us.

"It doesn't matter where you are when you see it," he says, the storm above his hand lighting up with a flash. "Thunder will always follow." And with that, the small cloud rumbles. He takes my hand and transfers his mini thunderstorm to me.

I laugh at it, so small and contained, and when I command another lightning strike, the electromagnetic charge moves through my body with ease. Totally natural.

Sang stands and walks to the far end of the meadow. He motions with his arm and pulls from my storm until he has a thundercloud in front of him as well.

Two parts of the same storm, separated by a field of wildflowers.

Summer magic flows through me, and I make another lightning strike. Seconds later, Sang's thundercloud claps in response. He takes one step closer to me.

My storm lights up again, Sang's cloud thunders in response, and he takes another step closer.

Lightning.

Thunder.

One more step.

With each cycle, Sang gets closer and closer until he's back on the blanket. He sits down next to me, and I command one last bolt of lightning. The storms are so close together now that his thunder rumbles immediately after.

"You're my lightning," he finally says, his voice low, still playing with the storms in front of us. "And thunder always follows lightning."

I look at him, my mouth dry and my heart slamming into my ribs as if it's trying to get out to hear him better.

"Always?" I ask.

He takes my free hand and weaves his fingers through mine.

"Always," he confirms, the word pouring over me, soothing me like one of his balms.

With lightning in our hands and stars above our heads, I pull Sang into me and kiss him, greedy, deep, long, and eager, soaking up every drop of him before I leave.

The storms dissipate in front of us, and I lie on my back, pulling Sang down with me.

He wraps his arms around me, and I do the same to him, clutching each other like we'll never let go, like I won't be moving thirty-five hundred miles away tomorrow. His lips are on my mouth, my neck, my chest, and I hold his face between my hands, run my fingers through his hair and down his back.

The autumnal equinox is in seven minutes.

I kiss him for all seven, touching him, memorizing the way his body feels against my own, the way my worries yield to him and my brain stops racing in his presence.

The way I feel as if I'm enough, as if I've always been enough.

Thirty seconds.

I roll onto my side and look at Sang. "Will you keep your eyes on mine when the season changes?"

"Of course."

I lace my fingers with his and hold on tight, but I'm not scared.

Three.

I won't let go.

Two.

I won't.

One.

iris

autumn

forty-three

*"It won't always be easy. In fact, there will be days
that are so miserable you'll wonder why you do this at
all. But I promise you one thing: it will be worth it."*
—*A Season for Everything*

I let go of Sang's hand. I let go because I don't need to anchor myself to him to know that I love him. I let go because I'm certain I'll want to reach out again.

I let go because letting go doesn't mean what it used to.

I keep my eyes on his as I tell him what I've never been able to tell anyone else on the first day of autumn. "I love you," I say, confident and sure.

He brushes a stray piece of hair behind my ear, his fingers lingering on my skin.

And he smiles because he already knows.

ACKNOWLEDGMENTS

This book is my wildest dream come true. Thank you so much for reading it.

I have dreamed of being an author since I was ten years old, and it is only because of the support and encouragement of so many people that this is now my reality. I doubt I will ever be able to convey the depths of my gratitude, but I'm sure going to try.

First, to Elana Roth Parker, my incredible agent who pulled me from the slush pile and saw the potential in this story. Thank you for fighting for my dreams and being such a fierce champion for my work.

Laura Dail Literary Agency, especially Samantha Fabien— thank you for your enthusiasm and support.

To my amazing editor, Annie Berger. You saw straight to the heart of this story and helped me turn it into something I'm immensely proud of. Thank you for your brilliant insight and being so wonderful to work with—your love for this story has made it so much stronger.

To the entire Sourcebooks Fire team, including Cassie Gutman, for turning my manuscript into a book that shines, Alison Cherry, Caitlin Lawler, and everyone else working behind the scenes to bring *The Nature of Witches* into the world. To Beth Oleniczak, thank you for your excitement and tireless work to get this book into the hands of readers. To Nicole Hower, for designing the cover of my dreams, Monica Lazar for the incredible photo, and Michelle Mayhall for the gorgeous interior—I blame all of you for the hours I've lost to staring at this book. And finally, thank you to my publisher, Dominique Raccah. I could not imagine a more perfect home for this story.

Rachel Lynn Solomon, I am forever grateful that you were my first writer friend. Thank you for being my sounding board, answering my most ridiculous publishing questions, and letting me introduce you to flatbreads. I love you.

Adrienne and Kristin, Annie Porter from the nineties classic *Speed* says that relationships that start under intense circumstances never last. But ours has, and I'm so thankful.

Adrienne, thank you for inviting me on that retreat and then never letting go. I can't wait for our next five-hour dinner. Kristin, your fierce loyalty and the way you support your people astounds me. I will never forget the way you scream-cried when I sold this book. Isabel, thank you for being so incredibly generous with your time and talents. You're my favorite late-summer / early autumn witch. Adalyn, you inspire me to dream big for myself and believe those things are possible. Thank you for never letting me forget my worth. Shelby, thank you for not leaving the group chat when you discovered what a crier I am. Your steady presence is everything, and I cannot wait to hug you in person. I love you all.

Thank you to this book's early readers, many of whom read it several times. Your feedback and encouragement mean so much: Christine Lynn Herman (whose brilliant suggestion to write epigraphs has stayed with this novel in every iteration), Jenny Howe, Miranda Santee, Tyler Griffin, Rachel Lynn Solomon, Heather Ezell, Tara Tsai, Courtney Kae, and finally, Rosiee Thor, whose unfailing belief in this book pulled me through my worst moments of doubt.

I am so fortunate to have found the Pitch Wars community early on in my journey. Thank you to Brenda Drake and the incredible class of 2016. And to my mentor and dear friend, Heather Ezell: you gave me my very first yes and taught me so much. Thank you for your endless support, wisdom, and love.

To Cristin Terrill, Beth Revis, and the Wordsmith Workshops community, especially the 2018 Port Aransas group—thank you for all the brainstorming, feedback, and delicious food.

To my fellow 21wonders, I am grateful to be debuting with such a talented and supportive group of writers. I can't wait to read all your books.

To everyone who read my earlier manuscripts, especially Peter Mountford—thank you for being so encouraging. Anthony and Sharlene—you believed in me before I believed in myself. Thank you.

To Julia Ember, Diya Mishra, Stephanie Brubaker, Nova McBee, #TeamElana, and my #mentorsonthemountain/sound friends. I am so thankful to be on the journey with you.

To my non—writer world friends who have cheered me on and supported me during this journey. From the bottom of my heart, thank you. Endless love to you all.

My pup Doppler has sat by my side as I've written every single book and never once tired of her spot, even through five manuscripts and eight years. Infinite snuggles to my best girl.

Chip, you completed our family and gave us the most perfect group of best friends there ever was. You and Mir are our people. Thank you.

To my family, grandmother, and especially my parents. Mom and Dad, thank you for raising me to love books. Our Red Robin and Barnes & Noble dates are some of my favorite memories, and I'm so lucky to have had your support and encouragement all these years. I hope this book makes you proud. I love you.

Mir. What can I say that would ever convey the depth of my love and gratitude for you? You were my first soulmate, first cheerleader, first fan, and biggest support. This book would not exist without your ride-or-die love for me. I can't believe how lucky we are. I love you.

To Tyler, my love. So much of this book was inspired by the way you love me. Thank you for calming my anxious mind, seeing me in every season, and making me so sure of being loved. From the first day we met, you believed I would get here. You gave me the space, time, and confidence to write this book, and I am forever thankful. I love you with everything.

And finally, to Jesus, for surrounding me in love and creating a world with so much magic.

Photo © Dawndra Budd

Rachel Griffin was born on the vernal equinox and is a proud spring witch. She has a deep love of nature, and when she isn't writing, you can find her wandering the Pacific Northwest, reading by the fire, or drinking copious amounts of coffee and tea. Rachel has mentored in Pitch Wars since 2017 and became a certified weather spotter for the National Weather Service while doing research for this book. She lives in the Seattle area with her husband, small dog named Doppler, and growing collection of houseplants. *The Nature of Witches* is her debut novel. Visit her on social media at @TimesNewRachel or online at rachelgriffinbooks.com.

FIREreads
S #getbooklit

Your hub for the hottest young adult books!

Visit us online and sign up for our
newsletter at FIREreads.com

 @sourcebooksfire

 sourcebooksfire

firereads.tumblr.com